ON ONE CONDITION

S.I.N. SERIES

book two

D1227477

K. BROMBERG

PRAISE FOR K. BROMBERG

"K. Bromberg always delivers intelligently written, emotionally intense, sensual romance . . ."

—*USA Today*

"K. Bromberg makes you believe in the power of true love."

—#1 *New York Times* bestselling author Audrey Carlan

"A poignant and hauntingly beautiful story of survival, second chances, and the healing power of love. An absolute must-read."

—*New York Times* bestselling author Helena Hunting

"An irresistibly hot romance that stays with you long after you finish the book."

—#1 *New York Times* bestselling author Jennifer L. Armentrout

"Bromberg is a master at turning up the heat!"

—*New York Times* bestselling author Katy Evans

"Supercharged heat and full of heart. Bromberg aces it from the first page to the last."

—*New York Times* bestselling author Kylie Scott

ALSO WRITTEN BY
K. BROMBERG

Driven Series
Driven
Fueled
Crashed
Raced
Aced

Driven Novels
Slow Burn
Sweet Ache
Hard Beat
Down Shift

The Player Duet
The Player
The Catch

Everyday Heroes
Cuffed
Combust
Cockpit
Control (Novella)

Wicked Ways
Resist
Reveal

Standalone

Faking It

Then You Happened

Flirting with 40

UnRaveled (Novella)

Sweet Cheeks

Sweet Rivalry (Novella)

The Play Hard Series

Hard to Handle

Hard to Hold

Hard to Score

Hard to Lose

Hard to Love

The S.I.N. Series

Last Resort

On One Condition

Final Proposal

Holiday Novellas

The Package

The Detour

Published by JKB Publishing, LLC

ISBN: 978-1-942832-45-4

Cover design by Indie Sage, LLC
Editing by Marion Making Manuscripts
Formatting by Champagne Book Design

Printed in the United States of America

This love left a permanent mark
This love is glowing in the dark
These hands had to let it go free, and
This love came back to me . . .
—Taylor Swift

ON ONE CONDITION

PROLOGUE

Asher

Fifteen Years Ago

L EDGER CUTS THE ENGINE JUST OUTSIDE THE GATE TO THE FARM. Lights are still on in the house, which means Gran is probably peeking out the window to make sure I'm home by my curfew.

I shift in my seat to look at him.

He has both of his hands propped on the steering wheel as the ticking of the cooling engine filters in through the open windows. He glances at me and gives me a lopsided smile before emitting a nervous chuckle.

It's like everything changed between us over the past few hours and yet nothing really has.

He's still him.

I'm still me.

And yet ... we're connected now in a special way that I don't think I expected to feel.

"Are you okay?" he asks softly, his eyes searching my face.

I nod, surprised at the sudden awkwardness after what we just did. "You?"

"Yeah." That crooked smile evens out as he laces his fingers with mine. "I promise I'll be better at it next time."

"How exactly do you plan on practicing?" I ask. He whips his eyes to mine and then his face softens when he realizes I'm just teasing him. "Ledge?"

"Yeah?"

"It was perfect," I whisper.

His Adam's apple bobs as he nods. "It was, wasn't it?"

I squeeze his hand and look toward the house just in time to see one of the curtains move.

"I have to get inside."

"I know. I wish you didn't have to, though." He stares at me for a beat before climbing out of the truck and rounding the hood to open my door for me. There's something about the way he looks at me that makes me wish we could just climb into his truck and keep driving.

Away from this town.

Away from its judgment.

Away from its dismissal of me.

Ledger must see it in my eyes because he wraps his arms around me and pulls me into him. His skin is warm from the summer night and smells like a mixture of sunscreen and sun.

"We'll only be apart for a few hours," he murmurs against the crown of my head. "My dad will be busy with Barbie or Bunny or whatever her name is, and your gran and pop will be asleep."

I nod, my bottom lip between my teeth, as I look up at him. "Meet back by the willow tree, right?"

"Yeah. In our spot."

"At eleven thirty?"

"Mm-hmm." He leans down and presses his lips to mine. His kisses always make me feel. Warm. Wanted. *Loved.* It's the best feeling in the world.

And truth be told, of the handful of boys I've kissed, Ledger is definitely the best at it.

The creaking of the screen door sounds seconds before I hear, "Asher, honey?"

"Coming, Gran," I call out with a roll of my eyes as I take a few steps toward the house, Ledger's and my linked hands outstretched between us for as long as possible until they break. I turn and face him. "Promise you'll be there? At the tree?"

"On one condition."

"What's that?"

He holds his hands out to his sides. "That you'll love me forever," he whisper-yells before flashing me a grin that could light up the darkened sky.

Laughing, and feeling like nothing in the world could ever ruin this feeling, I jog back to where he's standing and press a kiss to his lips. "I promise."

I turn and take off running through the fields toward the house, emitting a whoop as I go. When I hit the steps of the veranda, breathless but still giddy, I turn back to look at him one last time. He's standing in a strip of moonlight. His hands are shoved in his pockets, his back is against the bed of his truck, and he's looking straight at me with that smile still on his lips.

I blow a kiss in his direction and know that I'll always think of him like this. My moonlight boy who said he'd love me forever.

CHAPTER ONE

Ledger

Dear Sharpe International Network,

We, the members of Cedar Falls City Council, are writing to object to certain issues pertaining to your recent purchase and current renovations of The Retreat. While we value free enterprise, we also value the citizens of our town and their livelihoods. In your quest to resort-ize, commercialize, and bastardize our town, many small businesses that have been staples in our community for generations now worry about being wiped out by your big-business mentality.

In the original application for your conditional-use permit submitted to our City Council on February 13th, Sharpe International Network proposed that your resort would create new jobs and help stimulate our economy. As of the date of this letter, you have yet to keep your promises. All contracts issued by S.I.N. thus far have been awarded to firms from Billings and beyond. Not from Cedar Falls proper.

While we understand you are a business that needs to remain profitable, we are a town that needs to protect its citizens and their way of life. The City Council has decided that it will only grant a final certificate of occupancy after the following condition has been met. A founding board member from your firm must stay in Cedar Falls for two full months to oversee the project. We feel that with boots on the ground, you will see the importance of following through with your promises and ensure that the city council of Cedar Falls can communicate promptly with said founding member as needs arise.

Until that condition is met, neither a final inspection nor a certificate of occupancy will be granted.

Until then,

Cedar Falls City Council

"They're kidding, right?" I laugh the words out as I glance from the email on my laptop and at my brothers. "Bastardize their town? Such bullshit. When The Retreat is done, it will bring more tourism to Cedar Falls. More business. More everything to boost their economy."

I knew buying the property, in this specific location, was a bad decision.

But the past is the past, right? What happened years ago are things my brothers don't even know about. *And I plan to keep it that way.*

"Apparently they think differently," Ford says from his seat across the conference table. His feet are on the table, his hands clasped behind his head, and his eyes narrowed as he rereads the same email on his laptop. "And why aren't we contracting locally?"

"Because the local companies aren't big enough to handle it? Not of the caliber we need?" I take a guess. "Ask Hillary," I say of our on-site project manager. "She'll have the answers."

"We can ask her all we want," Ford says, "but it's not going to fix the problem."

"Or stop them from holding our permits hostage," Callahan adds.

I look at Ford and then at our brother, Callahan. He's standing at the wall of windows that line our conference room, staring at me with the same expression Ford has.

There are three of us, identical in appearance, and yet so very different in every other aspect.

"Why did we agree to purchase this place again?" I groan and pinch the bridge of my nose. Headaches upon headaches upon headaches. "I thought new projects were supposed to be thrilling and exciting."

"Nothing is thrilling and exciting when you're as uptight as you are, Ledge," Callahan says and smiles as only a little brother can.

I flip the fucker off.

"Dad. *Dad* is the reason," Ford says to bring back our focus, knowing damn well how easy it is for Callahan and me to get distracted by our squabbling. "We were trying to do something in his honor. Remember?"

And he's right. We bought the old hotel to upgrade it into a S.I.N. property in Dad's honor. A place we could all take our families someday and give them the same experience we had as kids. Nature. A different perspective. Time to unplug for a while. *Unplug? Jesus, the thought of going for more than an hour without my phone gives me the hives.* Somewhere my brothers and I could be a family instead of work partners and remember what it was like to be a kid.

But who knew the one town where we spent a few months each summer was going to make it so hard for us to do so?

"Can somebody tell them that we'll make good on our promises?" I ask. "Can't that be enough? Two months in that Podunk town is enough to drive a grown man crazy."

"Yes. We forgot. You were the only one not thrilled with the idea," Callahan says with a roll of his eyes. "Pretty-boy Ledger is too good for the country now."

"Not too good, but Jesus, couldn't we have picked a more contemporary location? One with more places than Main Street as the big attraction?"

"Montana is hot property right now," Ford says with a shrug.

"Yeah. Yeah." I wave a hand his way, knowing he's right. "But . . ." It's not New York? It's too far away from everything? My last time there was an experience I wish to forget?

"Dude, you loved that place when we were teenagers," Ford says.

He's right.

I did.

Right up until I didn't.

"Hell, it was the only place Dad let us be teenagers instead of his Sharpe protégées." Callahan crosses his arms over his chest and clears his throat. The pang is there for all of us. Our father's absence is still monumental.

I smile at my early memories of Cedar Falls. The long days outdoors and the late nights necking in the woods. How our father, Maxton Sharpe, would release his tight reins on the three of us because it was a small town, and he thought trouble wouldn't find us. *It still did.* The freedom we were given there was unparalleled to the rigors of prep schools and the pristine reputation necessary back home.

The reputation that had us rushing out of there fifteen years ago and never looking back.

Not that my brothers knew otherwise.

"There was fishing and hiking and beers—"

"Lots of beers," Ford says, and I know we're all thinking about how we bribed Dad's staff to buy them for us.

"And who could forget all those small-town country girls," Callahan adds with a cocky smirk. "They were desperate for boys from anywhere but there, thinking we were way more sophisticated than we really were."

"Ah, the good old days," I murmur.

"Maybe that one girl," Ford says. "What was her name? Ashlyn? Ashley?"

"Asher," I murmur and run a hand through my hair. *Asher Wells.* Another pang but for very different reasons. "God. That's a name I haven't heard in years."

But I lie.

Isn't that the first person I thought of when my brothers approached me with the idea of buying the hotel? Asher, the girl who handed me my first real heartbreak. The first real scare. And to this day, it's still one of the only secrets I've kept from my brothers.

A secret that's so old and buried that it does no good to bring it up now.

Jesus.

Asher. My lavender girl.

I can still see her sitting beneath the willow tree with leaves tangled in her hair and fire dancing in her eyes.

"Asher. That's it." Ford snaps his fingers. "The only female I can remember who gave you a taste of your own medicine by breaking your heart before you could break hers," Ford says. "Or maybe you learned it from her. The art of not getting too attached."

"Whatever." I roll my eyes. "Just because I choose to date and not get tied down like you," I say to Callahan, "doesn't make me an asshole."

"Not an asshole. Just . . . *perfectly Ledger.*" Callahan chuckles. "Why'd she break up with you again? Your dick too small?"

Both Ford and Callahan burst into laughter. I shake my head and cough out the words, "Fuck you."

Next topic, please.

"Do you think she's still in Cedar Falls?" Ford asks absently.

"Doubt it. She couldn't wait to get the hell out of that town." *I hope she did too.*

"Okay. Enough reminiscing about the whole two minutes it took to lose your virginity, and the poor girl who had to endure those short, fleeting moments," Callahan says, earning another flip of my middle finger. "How are we going to handle the situation with this bullshit request?"

"They have us over a barrel. We don't have any choice but to comply," Ford says.

"You checked with our lawyers? Can they add this stipulation?" I ask.

"They can do whatever they want to do," Callahan says. "We dealt with strict demands on the Santa Fe project and, after wasting money fighting the city in court, we still had to comply."

"Fuck," I mutter as I run over the construction schedule in my head and the plans for the grand opening. Two months before obtaining occupancy permits will delay us. "This is going to cost us. We'll have to push the grand opening back. Give it a cushion *just in case*."

"It's a bump in the road," Ford says, ever the pragmatist. "All projects have them."

"It's a ridiculous request, is what it is."

"So you've said. Ridiculous as it may be, we've already bought the place. With millions of dollars on the line, we don't have a choice, do we?" Callahan asks.

"We're too busy. None of us can afford to lose two months away right now." I run a hand through my hair. "That's what we hire project managers and directors of construction for. We need to find a workaround. That's all there is to it."

Callahan looks at me as if I'm being unreasonable. "And what exactly do you propose to do because throwing money at them—which is what you're going to suggest as a solution—will only make us look more corporate than we already look."

"Or guilty of what they're accusing us of being," Ford finishes for him.

"So, what is the solution then? Hire everybody in town? Fine. We'll do that," I say. "To not put the stores on Main Street out of business? It's not our fucking fault if that happens. We sell hospitality. How is that going to put the hardware store or bakery out of business? I mean, this letter is absolute bullshit."

"It is what it is," Ford mutters.

"What did Dad always tell us?" I ask. "To situate ourselves in a position of power. So how do we do that? What's going to give us the upper hand?"

"We go to Cedar Hills for two months," Ford states.

"Falls," I correct, glancing over the email again before shutting my laptop. "It's Cedar Falls. And since you're heading out there to live for the foreseeable future until this is fixed, it's probably best you get the town's name right."

"Me?" Ford barks out the word and puts his hands up in surrender. "No can do. This trip is squarely on you, Ledger."

"The fuck it is." I glance back and forth between my brothers as grins widen on their faces. "Not happening." I push up out of my chair and move toward the windows that Callahan just vacated, before turning to face them. "Absolutely not," I say as disbelief slowly trickles through me.

I know their schedules.

The projects they're tied to.

The obligations they can't leave mid-operation.

But I swore I'd never step foot in that town again.

Callahan barks out a laugh the minute he sees the realization hit my face. *This one is on me.* "What was that?" he teases.

"Look. I have an appreciation for all places. Urban. Tropical. Country. But wouldn't this better suit—"

"When have you ever liked the country?" Ford asks.

"I did. As a teenager."

"Ha. But now with your Rolex and designer shoes, you're too good for it?"

"Wouldn't this project be better suited to one of you who knows the . . . *less* urban areas better?" Christ. Please save me from this proposed misery. Sure, the past is the past, but it's not a place I want to revisit. Was it great as a teen? Yes. Is it even better for our clientele looking for this kind of retreat? Of course, it is. That's why we bought the property.

But it's definitely not what I like now.

The past is the last thing I want to dig up, regardless of whether Asher Wells is long gone or not.

"What's the problem?" Callahan asks as he pops a grape from the fruit platter in the middle of the table into his mouth. "Is spending two months in Montana not on the *Ledger-approved ten-year plan*?"

Ford stifles a snicker as he looks at Callahan and says, "I'm sure we could squeeze it right between the bullet points of 'I'm not getting married until I'm forty' and 'I want an article solely about me in *Forbes Magazine*.'"

"To think he doesn't want us in that article." Callahan sighs and shakes his head in mock sadness, clearly enjoying himself at my expense. "You still have a ten-year plan, don't you?"

"Of course, he does," Ford says.

"I was just checking. I wasn't sure if he'd moved on to making mood boards or whatever the in thing is called these days."

"Vision boards, Callahan. Keep up with the times." Ford chuckles.

"You guys are assholes," I mutter, but I'm secretly enjoying their banter. It was less than fifteen months ago that the three of us were in a different place, a different headspace, where Ford and I were at complete odds with Callahan. Disappointment. Anger. Resentment. Unresolved feelings that arose after our father's death threatened to tear us apart.

But look at us now. Now we can call each other assholes and fuckers, laughing while we do it, knowing our bond is stronger than ever.

"Yes. Right. We're assholes," Callahan scoffs as he turns to me, humor etching the lines of his face. "Have you progressed from your bullet-point planning to making vision boards now?"

"Fuck the both of you," I say while fighting a smile.

"He hasn't denied it," Ford says.

"Not once," Callahan continues.

"There is no vision board," I assert.

"But there is still a ten-year plan somewhere, right? Complete with goals and dreams laid out in spectacular fashion or some shit like that?" Ford asks. "Are there bullet points or is it a tiered outline? Or have you made posters of each item and have them plastered on the walls of your home office?"

"I'm voting the poster route. Laminated. Glossy and—"

"If that's the only thing you guys can razz me about, then so be it," I say while flipping them off again.

"It's not the only thing," Callahan says. "We're going to have even more fun watching you get used to the slow-paced country life of Montana."

"Sixty days." Ford draws out the two words. "That's a long time for you to be outside of the concrete jungle and off the structure-approved plan."

Sixty days.

Fuck.

That's forever in my world.

CHAPTER TWO

Asher

H₂ DRAWS MY ATTENTION THE MINUTE HE WALKS INTO HANK'S.
Draws?
Hell, more like he commands it.

Through the dim haze of the bar, I can make out a dark head of hair, broad shoulders, and expensive clothes. He has an unapologetic presence that says he doesn't give a fuck who's staring at him because he likes the attention.

And the locals in here *are* staring. Sizing him up. Wondering what the hell he's doing in a bar in Junction City when fancier ones—by small-town standards—are down the highway in Cedar Falls.

I study him from my spot behind the bar, expecting him to turn and walk out, and secretly wanting him to. There's something about him—an air of authority, a confidence, a *familiarity* I can't place—that completely owns my attention.

I've had enough trouble in my life with men like him.

He's just a customer, Ash. You're feeding his ego. An ego that most likely revels in the boost you're giving it. So, stop staring.

For once, I heed my own warning—it's not often it happens—and turn my back on him to dry glasses fresh out of the dishwasher.

But I know the minute he sits down at the bar. I can feel the weight of his stare and smell the faint yet expensive scent of his cologne.

And yes, I know it's expensive. After filling in for my best friend, Nita, from time to time, I can tell the difference between a drugstore cologne and a high-end one. Junction City is on the outskirts of Cedar Falls, the gateway to the wealthy person's recreational areas. Ski slopes on one side of town, rivers and lakes on the other, and a whole host of scenic "look at me" places for pictures to be taken and posted on social media in between. They stop into Hank's Bar for a quick drink and to experience that small-town atmosphere while bitching about its lack of Cristal or some other fancy shit.

So yes, the man at my back might be handsome and is more than likely charming as hell, but I've been there, done that. The flirting, the cell number left on a napkin, the promise of a good time while he's in town.

Sometimes I take up the offer because variety is few and far between when you've lived in one place your whole life. Other times I just smile and endure the flirting, knowing the whirlwind weekend of great (sometimes) sex and pretending I'm *one of them* isn't always worth the emptiness that comes when they leave.

Because despite the promises, they never call.

Ever.

"I think the town you're looking for is about twenty miles that way," I say, motioning in the direction of Cedar Falls without turning to face him.

"And how do you know what I'm looking for?" There's amusement in the tenor of his voice. There's also something else that has me pausing.

"Well, no one stops in Junction City unless you're a local or utterly desperate," I say as I dry another glass.

"Maybe I'm not like everybody else then."

"That remains to be seen," I murmur and wipe my hands on a towel.

"So, apparently, does my ability to get a drink in this place."

My laughter is sharp as I turn to face the smart-ass, impressed with his quick wit. But when I finally see him, my next words die on my lips.

I stand behind the bar, eyes blinking, head reeling, and look at the man who was once the boy who stole my heart.

And then broke it into a million pieces.

My moonlight boy who said he'd love me forever.

But the person in front of me isn't a teenage boy anymore. No. He's undeniably *all* man, who has only gotten more attractive with age. His dark hair has a wave to it that's been styled with product. His eyes are astute and aloof. And the smile he offers damn near knocks me off my feet before freezing me in place as a flash of recognition shoots through his amber eyes.

Ledger Sharpe.

A name I've never forgotten . . . even if I wish I could have.

"Asher?" His voice sounds as shocked as I feel before his eyes quickly dart to his right and left—as if he's expecting someone else to be there—before coming back to mine. "What . . . what in the hell are you doing here?"

"Ledger." His name is a breathless two syllables as I try to gain my bearings. "I—what—I mean . . ." *Why?*

Why are you here?

Why does seeing you bring back a million emotions—elation, anger, surprise, shame, longing—despite the passage of time?

Why are you even more handsome now?

Why did you leave without a word?

Why did I give you so much power to break my heart?

"Christ." He runs a hand through his hair, and it falls back perfectly into place as he stares at me, with his head shaking ever so slightly and his jaw lax. "Never in a million years did I think that you'd still . . ."

"What? That I'd still be here?" I ask. The chuckle that follows is self-deprecating. And just like that, I'm transported back to that night. To those life-altering events and the scars they left behind. To the shattering of my heart. My guard is up. "Yeah, you know us simple folk. *We never leave.*" My smile is strained despite my racing heart. Even after all these years, the humiliation exists, the embarrassment over what I felt is still real, as I try to process the fact that Ledger Sharpe is in front of me.

It's what I prayed for night after night—for him to come back. But that was fifteen years ago.

Life has changed.

I've changed.

"You know what? I'm going to go." He abruptly stands up from the seat he just sat in, the scrape of the stool drawing even more glances our way. *He's angry? What the hell?* And yet for some odd reason, panic I shouldn't feel sparks to life.

"Ledger. *Wait.* Don't go . . ." There's misplaced desperation in my voice that I hate the sound of.

I hate feeling it even more.

His brow furrows as if he's confused by my request—as am I—but with his eyes locked on mine, he slowly lowers himself back onto the stool. The low hum of chatter throughout the bar begins anew as customers go back to their own business, bored already with whatever is going on between us.

But I'm not.

I'm rapt with attention, struggling with seeing him again after all this time, while attempting to process the tumult of emotions storming through me. For a few unspoken moments, we study each other, and I can only assume he's remembering everything about our past too.

His expression begins to soften despite the tension remaining in his shoulders. "It's been a minute, hasn't it?" he finally says, but there's an edge to his tone, an uneasiness about him. It's almost as if he's uncertain how to act when I know he entered this bar moments ago, an extremely confident man.

"It sure has," I murmur.

Images flash through my mind. First kisses. First loves. First everything in that final summer that was filled with laughter and living, laden with promises and predictions for our future. A summer where I felt like I was someone's everything for the first time in my life.

There's unsettled silence between us. The kind that years apart and lives lived causes—when you know the person that *was*, but not the person in front of you *now*.

Those amber eyes of his always won me over. The same eyes staring at me now, asking questions I don't think I know the answer to even if he were able to put words to them.

I clear my throat. "What can I get you to drink?" I ask as if he were some random customer. I need to stop my thoughts from tumbling too far into a past we cannot change. A past that hurt for way too long.

"What craft beers do you have on draft?" he asks.

"We only have domestic. I'm sure that's not up to your standards—"

"Meaning?" His brows furrow.

"Meaning guys like you, ones with *pedigree*, prefer the expensive shit," I say with a bite to my tone. That one word will be forever burned into my memory.

"*Pedigree?*"

I grab a glass and dry it again, needing something—anything—to do with my trembling hands. The anger that riots through me burns its way into hurt. "Yep. Nothing average or run-of-the-mill will do for you."

His chuckle is low, but his eyes are curious as he leans back, head angled to the side, and crosses his arms over his chest. I can assume he's a smart man. Does he think time would fully erase the hurt after what happened? After what was said and the insecurities and humiliation it caused?

He may not have been the one to say it, but he went along with it.

Does that matter, though? It's been, what? Fifteen years? *What's done is done, Asher. Let it go.*

Our gazes hold for a beat until he gives the subtlest of nods that seems to indicate he's going to play along with whatever attitude I'm giving him.

"You imply that I think I'm too good for a Coors Light and in turn too good for this place in general." It's a statement. Not a question. And the look he gives me says he wants whatever fight is brewing here. "That wasn't the case before, was it? And it sure as hell isn't the case now."

Liar. It's my first thought.

Leave the past in the past. That's my second.

I draw in a deep breath, determined to heed the second one, but struggling with the task already. Scars may fade but they can still run deep. "I'm not implying anything. I've learned the hard way about men like you."

"Men like me?" He lifts a lone eyebrow, confusion etched in the lines of his handsome face. "I don't remember you being this judgmental before."

"Huh. And here I thought you didn't remember me at all."

He startles. "*Didn't remember you?*" He coughs the words out in disbelief, his eyes narrowing. "After everything we shared? After the hell I went through? How can you—"

"The hell *you* went through?" I all but screech. "What about—"

A ruckus breaks out in the rear of the bar, with shouts and the clatter of glass bottles falling. I move to calm the situation, but Hank is there already, breaking up the fight between two regulars we all know by name because this isn't the first time it's gotten heated between them.

I take advantage of the quick reprieve and short distance from Ledger to try and gain some clarity and gather my thoughts.

The hell I put him through?

The last time I saw Ledger Sharpe was the night I gave him my virginity. It was also the night that my naiveté in thinking all people are considered equal was shattered.

I squeeze my eyes shut and take a deep breath.

My anger, my snark to hide my hurt—hell, this whole direction of our conversation—won't get us anywhere. Not that I want it to. But in the same breath, I can't deny the emotions seeing him has dredged up.

Go. Be nice. Be polite. Make small talk. Then serve him his beer so he can get on his way back out of my life.

Again.

He tracks me as I make my way back to him. "Look. Everything is perfect. Obviously, we have a past. It's best if we leave it alone." I muster a strained smile I don't expect him to believe. "Sound good?"

His snort is unconvincing, the displeasure in his eyes even more so. "Sure. Fine." He shrugs nonchalantly. "Right after you explain to me what you mean by *men like me* . . . because last I knew you, you seemed to like *men like me.*"

Touché.

I did.

I still do.

I'd be lying to myself if I said otherwise, and yet, *men like him* are the reason I've lived my adult life trying to prove I'm more than enough. That I'm more than a motherless girl with no future. It was *men like him* who cast me aside because I didn't meet the Sharpe standards.

My thoughts become crazy as the memories renew my fury. *Don't be angry.* Ignore the hurt. It was years ago. But it's so much easier to hide behind the anger and use it as a defense than to admit seeing him has opened wounds I thought had healed and faded.

I clear my throat. "Men like you," I state and find my footing that his unwavering stare is constantly knocking askew. "Clearly one who thinks he's too good for this establishment, this town, the people in it . . . maybe even this state, but for some reason, shock of all shocks, he's sitting at this bar."

"Not by choice."

"Of course not. You just proved my point. On that note"—I lift my chin toward the direction of the door and lean my hips back against the counter behind me—"you know where the door is."

"Asher Wells speaks her mind now? That's new," he says with mock surprise and, for the first time, I see a hint of the personality that my teenage heart used to be madly in love with.

"I'm not the same person you used to know. A lot has changed, Ledger."

"Clearly." A ghost of a smile paints his lips. It's smug and arrogant and, Jesus, does it suit him perfectly. There's confidence to back it now, an acknowledgment that he is who he is without apology. "I like the change. It's becoming of you—"

"No, you don't." I snort and cross my arms over my chest, a defense in and of itself. "You think I'm being a bitch—which for the record, *I am*. I think I have a good cause too. Just as I'm sure you've followed in your father's footsteps, opting to be the asshole whenever you feel like it, simply because you can. Or do you still toe the line, always doing what you're told? Do you still need Daddy's praise? To be the best of the best or you're not considered good enough?"

My temper gets the best of me with this incoherent ramble that I can't help. It's hurt or be hurt. It gets everything you once wanted to say out since this might be your only chance.

But I'm so caught up in my feelings that I don't give his grimace a second thought.

"Hey, Ash. Can I get another, sweetheart?" a regular asks from across the bar.

"Coming right up, Larry." I move away to pour Larry's beer, thankful for the reprieve. Maybe Ledger will give up and go back to wherever he came from while I'm distracted.

"Why am I sensing that I missed part of this conversation somehow?" *Or maybe not.* There's a chill to his voice, a stiffness to his posture.

I've pissed him off.

Good.

That's only an iota of what he deserves.

I stare at him, my jaw clenched and hands fisted. Why am I letting the memory of what happened still affect me? It was a long time ago. It's done and over with. "You know what? You're right. You're not worthy of my anger," I finally say, hating that while I tell him that, I still want to ask a million questions.

Why did you leave and never come back?

Why didn't you call?

Was everything you told me a lie?

Why did you let him tear you apart like that?

That's enough, Ash. Enough wondering. Enough anger. Enough forgetting what you promised yourself minutes ago—that the past is the past.

This is the first impression you give him of who you are and what you've made of your life? All you're succeeding in doing is looking unstable.

Get your shit together, even if it kills you.

"You're right. I'm probably not worthy of your anger." He meets my eyes and something softens inside me at his comment. At him giving me an out to somehow justify the spiteful words I just slung at him. "But hey, if I had known asking for a Coors Light would make you this upset, then I easily could have picked something else. A Heineken. A Corona. Which beer is best paired with the side of animosity you're serving?"

"Quit making fun of me."

He offers his lopsided, mischievous smile that has one reluctantly tugging on the corners of my mouth. I'm transported back to ice cream cones on the docks and kisses that left me breathless.

There's something about you that until this very moment, until seeing you standing there, I didn't know would still pull on parts of me.

"Everything good here?" Hank asks as he steps behind the bar, eyeing me with curiosity before taking in Ledger. "Asher taking care of you all right?"

"Yes. She was just about to pour me a Coors Light, but she had to finish reading me the riot act about how much she dislikes me first."

Jesus. I'm filling in for Nita. The last thing I need is to cause paying customers to complain and get her in trouble with the boss.

"Don't take it personally," Hank says, followed by his baritone bark of a laugh and a wink my way. "For what it's worth, she doesn't exactly like anyone."

I narrow my eyes at Hank as he emits a big belly laugh before moving to the far end of the bar to chat with some regulars.

"Asher?" Ledger asks my name like a question, but when I look his way, there's a sudden change to his expression. It's almost as if he just had an epiphany or figured out an answer to the question he never asked. "A minute ago, you said something. About what I put you through—" He gives a quick shake to his head and as quickly as the expression appears, it's gone. "I think you're wrong. We *do* need to talk about what hap—"

"Telling me I'm wrong isn't the best way to make me like you again."

"I didn't realize you had to try to. You never had to before." The quiet confidence in his tone paired with the bittersweet look in his eyes has me struggling to think of a response.

How is it possible to go from anger to uncertainty in such a short span of time?

Confused and unsettled by the sudden feeling, I turn around to find a clean glass on the counter behind me, even though there's a stack of them right in front of me.

I'm a grown woman, for God's sake.

We were teenagers.

It was a lifetime ago.

I've moved on with my life and so has he.

I rearrange more glasses before grabbing one and moving toward the tap. "What are you in town for? A trip with your family again? Is it your first time back since . . . *before?*" I ramble, my concentration on the beer and its foam head instead of Ledger. "The town has changed. The old hotel was bought and is being built into a resort. The whole town is up in arms over it." I pour some foam out. "The ski resort is even fancier than before, if you can believe that. The rich ladies and their outfits even more outrageous than the ones we used to make fun of."

Ledger sits in silence as I rattle off comments, avoiding eye contact with him. But when I set the glass down in front of him, he closes his hand over my wrist.

His touch.

At one time it was everything my teenage heart yearned for.

My eyes flash to his, but I don't pull my hand away. I'm sure he can see it in the look I give him—a tinge of nostalgia, a bit of what could have been—but he doesn't say a word. Rather, he just nods ever so slightly as if he understands, and offers a soft smile.

"You look good, Asher. More than good," he murmurs. "I hope you've been happy."

The kindness in his words almost unravels me. Vulnerability I don't want to feel wells up as tears threaten, which I successfully fight back. It's been a tough few months. Moving Gran to an assisted living facility. Losing Pop so unexpectedly. Then learning to shoulder the responsibilities to keep The Fields afloat when Pop guarded everything. Combined, it's all but drowned me. So much in such a short span that his sympathy, his sincerity, get to me.

"Trudging along," I say as I pull my hand from his grip. "And you? You're good?"

He nods again as he studies me in that silent, disarming way of his. "Are you still sketching those insanely beautiful landscapes? I always figured I'd stumble upon one somewhere and know right away it was yours."

"No. Not anymore."

"I thought you were going to art school. To—"

"Plans changed."

"That was your dream though."

"Dreams change." I look at the door as another customer walks in and welcome the distraction. "You never answered my questions."

"Because I wanted to know about you more." He takes a sip of his beer, his eyes never leaving mine until he gives a roll of his eyes. "Fine. What are your questions, Ash?"

He says my nickname like no time has passed, and we're still familiar with each other. I can't bring myself to correct him.

Maybe I don't want to.

"Why are you here?"

"I was driving to Cedar Falls from the airport. After a day full of traveling delays, I thought a beer was in order. I saw the sign for Hank's, the busy parking lot in front of it, and . . . here I am."

I cross my arms and huff at his response. He smiles.

"I didn't mean in Hank's, and you know it. Stop mocking me and answer the question."

"You always were bossy," he murmurs, showing me he does remember me. The old me, anyway. "That big resort that the whole town is up in arms over?" He raises his hand. "That would be mine."

Realization slams into me. "You're S.I.N.?"

"Guilty as charged." He glances around as if he's waiting to encounter animosity if anyone overhears him. "Sharpe International Network, otherwise known as *S.I.N.*"

Talk about being blindsided. I knew his father was big in the hospitality industry and ridiculously wealthy. That was clear by where they stayed, by the outrageously expensive everything Ledger and his brothers had, and by the cars they drove while here. But I had no idea S.I.N. was *that* company.

"How did I not know this?"

He shrugs. "We rebranded a while back and since we've added on so many international properties in the past ten years, we became S.I.N."

"We?"

"Yes. We." The grief in his eyes is fleeting, but I catch it nonetheless. "My father died two years ago."

"I'm sorry to hear that." My words are a polite reflex for a man vilified in my memories.

He nods in acknowledgment. "My brothers and I run the company now."

"For the company's sake, let's hope you don't bicker as much as you used to."

"At times."

I laugh. It's the first time I have, and somehow it eases the heaviness between us. "So you're here in Cedar Falls to do what exactly with the hotel? Calm the mob over its mere existence?"

"Something like that. Mayor Grossman deems it necessary that I stay here for the next two months to be at his beck and call or else he'll withhold our occupancy permits and prevent us from opening."

"I could lie and say that surprises me . . . but sadly, it doesn't. He's a greedy man who thinks more of himself than should be legal, and with reelection coming up . . ."

"Great. Something to look forward to." He rolls his eyes.

"Are you sure you don't want to drive back to the airport and escape while you can?"

"It's that bad, huh?"

"Depends on what side you fall on."

"And what side do you fall on, Asher?" he asks, but for some reason, I feel like the question he's asking means so much more than whether I agree with the new resort in town or not.

And before I can answer his question, Nita shows up like a whirlwind of energy and chaos, as is her usual fashion.

"Oh my gosh," she says, hastily tying an apron behind her waist as she pushes her way behind the bar. "Thank you. Thank you, thank you, thank you." She leans in to kiss me on the cheek, giving me the disruption I unknowingly needed. "You're a lifesaver. A total freaking lifesaver, Ash."

It's in that moment she must sense the connection between Ledger and me because her motions falter as she looks from me to him and then back again.

"Well, hello there handsome," she purrs in a way that only Nita can get away with without coming off as forward or desperate. "I'd offer to get you something a tad sweeter to whet your palate, but it seems to me that Asher here was taking care of you just fine. I'll—uh, go clear some tables so you two can, you know, finish whatever needs finishing." She looks Ledger over, and the nudge she gives me is anything but subtle.

If she only knew . . .

"No need to leave and clear anything," I say as I untie my apron and scrunch it into a ball, needing something to do with my hands. It's as if the events of the last fifteen minutes have come crashing down on me, and I suddenly need a minute alone to think and process and . . . *breathe.* "You're all set here." Nita eyes me cautiously, wondering no doubt, why I'm acting so weird. "I really need to get going."

"You're leaving?" Ledger stands up abruptly, his barstool loud as it scrapes across the floor when he does.

"Yes. I was only helping Nita out while she went to a school function with her son." I offer a strained smile as my heart races in my chest. "This isn't my—I don't regularly work here."

How does this end?

Do I just walk away? Do I get anything else off my chest while I have the chance to? Do I even want to? Or is this enough for me? Will I finally have the closure I didn't realize I needed simply from talking to him?

"That means you can stay and talk then."

"I can't. I have . . . things to do," I say and give Nita an air kiss on the cheek before heading toward the back storage room to grab my things.

I have a sudden need to flee. To have some solitude and some quiet. Two things that are impossible to have when his presence is clouding my every thought like it is right now.

I've just about reached the end of the bar and the door to the back room when Ledger grabs my elbow.

"Asher. Wait. You're going to leave just like that? Without another word?"

It's a horrible feeling, isn't it?

But I don't put words to the thoughts. Can't. It's best to leave this as is. In a better place. More settled. *As is.*

"I have to go," I say to save face, but when I turn and meet his eyes, my feet refuse to move.

"You sure?" He dips his head to be on my level so his eyes can search mine.

"I'm sure."

He rocks on his heels, clearly not believing my lie but letting me think he does anyway. For that, I'm more than grateful.

"It was great to see you, Ash." There's that lopsided smile again. It's genuine and real, and I hate that despite our past, a part of me sags at the sight of it. "Actually, it's better than great."

"It was nice to catch up. Good luck with everything."

"No. *Not yet.*" He sighs and glances around the bar before he meets my eyes again. "Look . . . we were kids, starry-eyed and not prepared for anything life was going to throw at us. Things happened that . . . that happened. Things I still don't understand, and that I'm starting to think neither of us could control. We could talk about the past and dwell on the what-might-have-beens, but that would be pointless."

"Agreed." I nod when, in reality, I want to dissect every word he just said to me. "It was good seeing you, Ledger." I start to walk away, but his words stop me.

"I'm going to be in town for a couple of months. I'd like to get together sometime . . . have a drink. Catch up." He glances down for a beat before meeting my eyes. "Be friends."

Emotion is thick in my throat as I stumble for a response I'm not sure I know the answer to. "Maybe." I push on the door and look over my shoulder at him. "We'll see."

When I walk through the door and it shuts, I lean my back against it and blow out a long, drawn-out sigh.

I can't see him again.

I don't want to.

I do want to.

Shit.

There's something about Ledger Sharpe.

Yes, he owned my heart once upon a time, but he's right. I'm not a starry-eyed teenager anymore.

So much has changed from the girl he once knew.

I'm stronger.

I'm independent.

I've finally found my purpose.

And I'll be damned if I'll let his handsome face and a pocketful of nostalgic memories get close enough to me to change anything about me this time around.

CHAPTER THREE

Ledger

PUSHING MY CHAIR BACK FROM MY MAKESHIFT DESK—THE kitchen table of my rental house—I scrub a hand over my face and sigh in frustration.

Nothing is holding my attention. Fucking nothing. Not the emails I have waiting to be answered, not the talking heads blathering on the television across the room about the expectations of record travel this year, and sure as hell not the absolute silence inside and outside this modest house on the outskirts of Cedar Falls.

Because all I can think about is Asher Wells.

What happened before.

The heartbreak.

The fear.

The constant looking over my shoulder every time I received an email or text from her that I'd leave unanswered.

But to make things even more confusing, tonight I felt her anger and sensed the hurt beneath the surface. I watched her struggle with both, and it wasn't until almost halfway through our conversation that it hit me—*she doesn't know.* What I was accused of. Why the Sharpe family up and left out of nowhere.

Why I never spoke to her again.

That has to be why she was so angry. And for good measure. But I was angry too. Wasn't I the one who'd had the most to lose?

That's the only explanation as to why she was so upset seeing me again. *It has to be.*

Christ.

I give a shake of my head to clear it.

It doesn't work.

She's still there.

Still owning my every thought.

How goddamn arrogant is that of me to assume I still affect her? There could be a dozen reasons why she was rattled and not a single one of them had to do with me. *Right?*

Just like there should be a dozen reasons why I should be working and not obsessing over her misplaced anger and a past I thought was dead and buried.

Jesus, Ledger. Get over it.

With a sigh and renewed determination, I read the email in front of me again. But I don't get past the second sentence because it's fucking impossible to focus.

She's making it impossible.

Asher Wells is still here.

She's really fucking here.

Talk about being blindsided. I was certain she'd left town long ago. I figured that the only people who would be left from that summer would be her gran and pop. I stressed over it, and then felt guilty that the teenage boy inside of me was relieved when I looked up Pop only to find out of his passing. That sounds terrible considering Pop didn't present any threat to me now . . . but it still worried me that he'd be here. That he'd remember.

But I was wrong about Asher. She is here. And when she turned to face me from behind the bar and those storm cloud-colored eyes of hers met mine, I was instantly transported back to fifteen years ago. Back to that last night, that last kiss, where she stood in the moonlight by my truck, those same eyes staring into mine as she promised she'd come back and meet me later.

And the disbelief and utter heartache that came next.

"*You're not to see her again.*"

"*Dad . . . what are you talking about?*"

"*I don't like repeating myself. You heard me.*"

"*I love her,*" I blurt out.

"*You're thinking with your dick, Ledger. Every good man does at some point, but this is the wrong time and the wrong person to do it with.*"

I shove up out of my chair. "You can't tell me what to do," I shout.

His hands are fisted in my shirt in an instant, his face inches from mine. His voice is a cool, even tone when he speaks next. "You'll do as I say. I will not have you disobey me on this. Pretend she never existed. Pretend this summer never happened."

Nothing can dampen the memory or roller coaster of emotions I went through that night. The pain, the anger, the confusion, the . . . *agony*.

I did nothing wrong . . . I know that.

Now.

And yet, hell, I'm standing in this quiet house remembering when it's been forgotten for so long, aren't I?

It's fucking stupid really. Hell, it's been over a decade. I've had many lovers since then, many women who've occupied my bed and my time so that Asher's and my teenage puppy love was merely a blip on my radar . . . and yet seeing her tonight . . . fuck, seeing her tonight gave me pause.

Nostalgia. Isn't that what this is? An unexpected walk down memory lane?

It's more than that and that's what's fucking with my head.

It's created the desire to know her now. It's reawakened an attraction to her I can't deny. It feels so wrong for me and yet so goddamn right. I'm not a player by any means, but I'm also not one who pursues my exes once we've parted ways. The *been there, done that* mentality in full effect. And yet there's something about Asher that had me pursuing her tonight. That already has me wanting to see her again.

"It's utter fucking madness is what it is," I mutter to the empty house.

The teenage girl owned me way back when, and the woman she has become seemingly holds my interest now.

I take a sip of my beer and step out the door into the backyard. It's not like I'm getting any work done anyway. I contemplate the silhouette of the mountains against the night sky. The stars burning bright overhead that the city lights I normally live beneath drown out.

She was just as beautiful as I remembered. Even more so. The mane of auburn hair is longer now. Those big, gray eyes of hers still overly expressive. The curves of her body more pronounced, more feminine, than they used to be.

Clearly, the years have physically been kind to her, and yet, I sense they've hardened that wide-eyed wonder she used to have too. I guess they have for both of us. My naiveté was ripped away that last night together. I wonder what stripped her of hers?

But with age comes experience. Wisdom. Perhaps hardship. That shy, innocent teenager she once was, is no more. She speaks her mind and clearly doesn't care who she offends. The jut of her chin in defiance wasn't there before. I love the sight of it and at the same time, am curious about what made her change.

Plans change.

Dreams change.

Weren't those her words tonight?

She shouldn't still be in Cedar Falls. She had huge dreams of leaving this town and an even greater talent to get her there. A prestigious art school. An apartment in the big city. The chance to experience real life—the good and the bad—on her own. Wasn't that what she wanted? What she aspired to do?

I bring my beer to my lips. What the hell was so important that she gave up her dreams to stay here?

Plans change.

I know better than anyone. Plans do change.

CHAPTER FOUR

Ledger

Seventeen Years Ago

"Pace yourself, Callahan." I glance over to my brother who has just shot-gunned his third beer in less than twenty minutes. He glares at me, crushes the can in his hand before tossing it over his shoulder, and then flipping me off.

"Okay, *Dad*." He rolls his eyes and then points to one of the girls to his side. "Grab me another, will you?"

I grit my teeth. He's out of control as per usual. Dad's been chill with us doing our own thing here—more so than he's ever been in our lives. The last thing I want Callahan to do is fuck it up by getting so shit-faced that Dad will notice and tighten the reins on our freedom.

Then again, it's Callahan. Screwups are allowed when you're him.

But not when you're me.

I glance at the beer in my hand and wish like hell I could say fuck it and be more like him. The problem? I'm sure if I did, our punishments would still be different.

You're my first born, Ledger. The one most like me. I expect more from you than anyone else.

Fucking great. *Perfect.* I down the beer and try to forget who I am. Try to enjoy this newfound freedom here in Montana when every second at home is academics and sports and positioning myself for a future that's preordained.

When I toss my can to the side, it's then that I see *her* standing on the outskirts of the party. Long legs. Tan skin. A red tank top with lacy white bra straps just beneath the fabric. Reddish-brown hair down her back. And . . . there's something about her standing to the side, observing like she doesn't exactly belong, that owns my curiosity.

That and the fact she's a walking wet dream.

I can't help but stare.

"Ledger. Bro. Can I grab another?" the local kid we've been hanging around asks me. Hell, in reality, everyone's been hanging around us considering we have the beer, but he's actually one we've befriended in the two weeks since we arrived.

"Sure. Yeah. Uh—who's that, though?"

"Who?" he asks as he steps forward to look in the direction that I lifted my chin.

"Her."

"*Lavender Girl?*" He snorts.

"*Lavender Girl?* What are you talking about?" I ask, desperate to look again but afraid to seem too interested.

"That's what we call her around here."

"Why?" But he's headed toward the cooler before I get the word out.

I chance a glance toward her again. And this time when I do, I'm met with a pair of gray eyes that don't look away.

I walk over to her, my nerves dampened by the beer. Her eyes grow wide, almost fearful, as I approach. Skittish. For some reason I get the impression that she doesn't normally run with this crowd. *Doesn't quite fit.*

Maybe I feel the same in a different way.

She's even prettier up close. Way out of my league.

Her breath hitches when I stop in front of her.

"Lavender Girl, please tell me you're not going to run away? I just want to say hi." I hold my hands out to my sides, my confidence bolstered by my buzz. "I'm Ledger."

Her lashes flutter as her eyes lift to meet mine.

Thud.

"Hi."

Then she smiles . . . and I'm a goddamn goner.

CHAPTER FIVE

Asher

I SIT BEHIND THE WHEEL OF MY CAR WITH THE DOOR OPEN, ONE LEG firmly planted on the ground, the other on the floorboard, and simply take in everything.

The house before me. Its paint is faded, and its steps are worn, but there is a presence about it that has a soft smile ghosting my lips. The porch swing is where I spent hours upon hours lost in the pages of a book while my grandfather, Pop, helped work the fields beyond.

Memories hit me.

A shadow passing in front of the window as Gran would move about with her perpetual need to tidy and dust and be occupied. Anything to make her feel somewhat normal despite the partial paralysis and ailments her stroke caused. And how I'd go back over it when she was fast asleep because her attempts were futile at best.

The blue hue on the walls from the television lighting up the room. Its hum was not to be outdone by Pop's booming laughter, which echoed out the windows he liked to leave open to let the summer's warm night breeze in.

The light scent of sage or cinnamon floating through the air. The creak of the raised wood floors as I'd walk over them to give each of my grandparents a kiss on their cheeks. A wall full of framed photographs documenting every embarrassing stage of my life.

There were never reminders of the things I was missing. A father I never knew. A mother that wanted freedom more than she wanted me.

Just pure and unconditional love.

Grief still raw and real overwhelms me. It's amazing how so much can change in three months. How life moves on and yet you feel like you're standing still. How everyone else's life goes back to normal while some moments I struggle to simply breathe from the grief that consumes me without warning.

Grief, I thought I was familiar with given I never had a mother or father, but now realize that I never truly understood until I lost Pop. *My rock.*

That's why I welcomed the distraction by helping Nita tonight. A chance to get out and away from the quiet and somewhat deafening solace that most nights are a comfort here.

And suffocating at other times.

Insects trill to the left of me and draw my focus to the land that has been a part of my family for decades. Our hands in the dirt, our sweat mixed with it, as we turned the fields each year. The fertile soil of this valley where lavender is planted in perfect rows, side by side. Year after year they survive the harshest weathers to thrive in the mildest of summers.

It's where I spent my childhood learning the meaning of hard work, discipline, and sometimes defeat—all softened by Gran's gentle hugs or Pop's quiet love.

The stalks rustle in the breeze swooping down off the mountains.

Home.

The place I couldn't wait to get away from fast enough. The place that called me back out of desperation and duty. The place that is a part of everything I am—good and bad.

And a place that sheltered me from the cruelty of the world. Cruelty I hadn't been subjected to until Maxton Sharpe, Ledger's dad, showed up on this very porch that night.

Ledger.

That's a person I haven't thought about in years. And I say *person* because to me, he's been frozen in time—a teenage boy with floppy hair, most days a shirtless torso, and a smile that told me I was his whole world.

But he's no longer a memory to recall. He's here. In Cedar Falls. And according to him, he will be for a while.

And he wants to *catch up.*

Classic avoidance. Isn't that why I drove endlessly tonight? Down road after road to avoid coming home to the quiet of this farm and the endless thinking it often prompts?

Driving with the windows down and the music blasting is so much easier than trying to figure out how seeing him again has made me feel.

I shake my head as I climb out of the car. It's been a long damn day, and a glass of wine and some reality television might be the perfect way to unwind. To distract.

But as I round the car, the porch swing creaks and, for a second, despite being startled by its sound, I half expect to see Gran there waiting for me to come home.

"Jesus." I jump when I see Nita, a bottle of wine in hand and a soft smile on her lips. "What are you doing here? Why aren't you at Hank's? Is everything okay?" My words come out in a tumble.

"Calm down, worrywart," she says, holding out a red solo cup filled with wine as I climb the steps. "It's past two. That's how long you've been driving in circles and then sitting over there in that car of yours. You were so preoccupied you didn't even see my car." She points to where her car is on the side of the house.

"You're right." I have no problem admitting it to her. "Sorry." I take the cup she's offering and plop down on the swing beside her, the motion making it rock.

Crickets chirp around us, and I'm grateful for the silence Nita gives me as I let that first sip of wine settle in.

"You want to talk about it?" she finally asks. "*About him?*"

"Him?" I feign ignorance.

"Oh, come on." She slaps my thigh playfully. "You and I both know that fine piece of man at the bar tonight is who has you overthinking, probably driving around aimlessly, singing *Total Eclipse of the Heart* at the top of your lungs."

I shrug, hating that she's right, before holding up the red solo cup to avoid her question. "This is classy."

"You know how we do it." She laughs and taps the edge of hers to mine. "So . . . do you want to explain to me why Mr. Sexy Man left you this for a tip?"

Nita holds up a crisp one-hundred-dollar bill and written in Sharpie across its face is a telephone number.

"Huh." I wish I could say I feel indifference, but I feel anything but.

"*Huh?* Is that a good huh or a bad huh or simply a shut-up, Nita, huh?"

I take the bill from her and play with its corners until the ten numbers in bold black marring its face blur together. "It's the *it appears Ledger Sharpe likes trying to buy forgiveness from his ex-girlfriend type of huh.*"

"Wait. *What?*" she screeches. "You dated that man? That fine-looking specimen I was flirting innocently with?" Her eyes are wide and her expression is surprised.

"I did, but it was a long time ago though."

"Like how long?" She shifts so she can face me, her penchant for gossip rivaled by no one.

"Like from age fifteen to seventeen."

"Oh, girl." She waves a hand at me. "You were just babies." She takes a sip and makes an approving sound. "If you ask me, I think you need to see how much better the man is now."

"Jesus," I mutter and take another drink. "Thanks, but I didn't ask."

"That phone number," she says, pointing to the hundred in my hand, "says he wants to do the same."

My only response is a heavy sigh as I lean my head back to look at the stars and push the swing.

"What are you not telling me?" she asks.

"His family used to come here every summer. Him and his brothers. They're identical triplets—"

"Hold up. There are three men in this world who look just like him?" She holds a hand to her chest in a dramatic fashion. "There's hope for me yet."

"I hate to break it to you, but there is no hope." Especially if they all turned out like their father. Willing to play in this town so long as they could throw their cash around and leave it all behind. "They're one of *them*," I say, and she knows exactly who I mean by *them*. The wealthy. The people who look at townspeople as their servers, guides, or waitstaff, but definitely not their equal.

She pushes my shoulder. "Let a girl dream, now, will you? Fantasy has no boundaries." She closes her eyes and a *cat ate the canary* grin graces her lips as if she's imagining just how good it could be. A soft hum escapes as if she's satisfied. "Okay. Fantasy played out. Now you can carry on."

"There is so much wrong with that."

"I know, but I never claimed to be wholesome." She flashes me a grin. "You've been keeping secrets from me. Now tell me about them. *About him.*"

"His father and the three boys—Ledger, Callahan, and Ford—would come to Cedar Falls every summer for three months. The dad was always working in some capacity and so the boys had the run of this place without much supervision."

"In a small town like Cedar Falls?" She whistles. "The girls must have been salivating."

"Yep. We all were but . . . one night . . ." I remember the fireworks exploding over the lake and how their booms echoed around the valley. How after the display I stood on the outskirts of a party on the shore, wanting to join in with my classmates but feeling out of place, always on the outside. I was just about to leave, but then I saw him, *Ledger*, and my feet refused to move. He was tan and had the cutest lopsided grin and, when I looked back again, he was right in front of me.

Lavender Girl, please tell me you're not going to run away?

My smile is bittersweet as I remember. "One night we met and from there on we were inseparable."

"Three months inseparable?"

"It was more than that. It was three months for three summers. We talked during the rest of the year and then fell right back where we left off when he arrived in June. It was like we both knew there were other people we flirted and messed around with during the time we were apart, but when summer happened, we only had eyes for each other."

"For three years? What happened?"

I nod. So many good memories. "We made plans that last summer together. Big plans. Ones for our future. Ones for us." I smile wistfully. "Looking back at it now, I know they never would have worked. We came from two completely different worlds, but we thought they would and, at the time, that's all we saw. That's all that mattered."

"He was your first, wasn't he?" she asks softly.

"We were each other's . . . at least that's what he told me, and I believed him. We'd fooled around before then—a lot—but the night we finally went all the way ended up being the last night we ever saw each other. Until tonight that is."

"What do you mean it was the last night? How did I not know any of this? I've been your best friend for almost thirteen years. Apparently, you've been holding out on me."

My heart thumps in my chest as I stare at myself in the mirror. My cheeks are flushed and my smile is wide.

We did it.

We actually did it and . . . oh my God, it was . . . okay? I giggle, unable to take my eyes off my reflection.

Do I look older?

Changed?

Like a woman?

I mean, I know it's not supposed to be great the first time. Well, at least according to the girls at school it isn't, but the way he kept asking if I was okay. How gentle he was when I could tell he was trying so hard to go slow. How he held me afterward and whispered how much he loved me.

I wouldn't have wanted it any other way.

Tires crunch on the gravel driveway outside, but all I can think about is getting ready. Once Gran and Pop are asleep, I'm sneaking out to meet Ledger again.

There's a knock on the front door.

I don't want this night to ever end.

Muffled voices float down the hall and through my closed door.

Possibilities fill my head. Meeting up while we're in college. Becoming engaged. Getting married. Having the life away from here I've always dreamed of.

I hold my hand up and look at it as if I have a wedding ring on my finger. Asher Julia Sharpe.

"It has a nice ring to it." I smile again, unable to take my eyes off my reflection in the mirror. I'm so glad I saved myself for him. So glad that soon we'll go to college and be able to be with each other all the time.

He said we'll find a way to make it happen and I believe him. I've never believed anyone more in my life.

The voices raise in pitch. Pop is upset? That's a rarity.

It gives me pause and then, I hear the next words loud and clear.

"The last thing he needs is someone like her *to bring him down," a masculine voice says. But the voice definitely isn't Pop's. Nosy, I head down the hall without thought, curiosity and dread on equal footing. "He has a bright*

future ahead of him, an empire to run, and I won't have him sidetracked by a motherless girl with no pedigree and no future. This is non-negotiable. Do you understand?"

"You have no right to come in here and order us around. We're not your—"

"He's my son. I have every right to look out for his best interests. And she's not it."

I subconsciously reject the idea that they're talking about me. Why would someone ever say that? But as I turn the corner and the man standing before Pop comes into view, I know I'm wrong. Maxton Sharpe. Ledger's dad. His features are similar enough, but it's the way he carries himself, his mannerisms that are just like his son's, that confirm my assumptions.

"What do you mean I'm not in his best interest?" *I march into the room, tears already burning in my throat.* "You think I'm going to bring him down because I'm not rich or—"

"Asher, go back to your room. Right now," *Pop demands, his eyes steely, his voice hard. I can't remember a time when he's ever spoken to me like that before.*

"Pop—"

"Go!" *he shouts without looking my way.*

"No. Stay," *Maxton says to me before looking back to Pop.* "She needs to hear this." *Maxton's eyes soften as he takes a step toward me, but I'm not fooled by them.* "I'm sorry if you heard what I said. I was harsh." *He hangs his head as if he's apologetic, but it's all for show. Even I know that.* "I was merely trying to push you away to protect you from the truth."

"What do you mean *the truth?"* *I ask.*

"I'm ashamed to admit it, but my son used you. He got what he wanted from you, Asher," *Maxton says, his eyes boring into mine as shame washes over me.*

Gran and Pop now know what happened tonight.

He knows.

The room spins around me. Our private, meaningful moment, now public knowledge.

"What are you talking about? He didn't use me. He—"

"He's not meeting you later like you two planned either." *No, no, no.* "I had his phone. I read his texts. You're not the only one, if that helps." *I want to cover my ears and stop the noise.* "In fact, he's been seeing a couple other girls this summer and is out with one of them right now. He's—"

Liar.

"No, he hasn't," I whisper, my head shaking and my mind not believing.

"He has. He is. He's down by the willow tree right now." I wince. "Oh no, he didn't con you into thinking that was your special spot too, did he?" His sigh is heavy as he shakes his head, disappointment all over his face.

Tears blur my vision as I stare at a man I've never met but truly hate. "I don't believe you. I need to talk to him. There has to be an explanation."

"Does a teenage boy really need one other than hormones?"

I stare, blinking at this man who just turned my world upside down. All I can think of is Ledger's easygoing, flirty nature. The way he fit in with everyone here. All the girls wanted him. It was even a running joke between us. Am I the fool here? For believing him? I mean, it would be so easy for him to be with one of them during the hours I worked here at the farm.

Gran squeezes my hand, and it breaks the pieces of me I'm trying to hold together.

He's wrong.

He has to be.

Cedar Falls is a small town. Gossip is the norm here. Rumors are the currency teenagers trade. I would have known. I would have heard about it.

"We're leaving Cedar Falls tonight. I think it's the best course of action after . . . everything. I'm sorry. I never taught my son to treat girls this way."

"I think you need to leave now," Pop says, opening the door.

"I've blocked your number from his phone and erased your information from his contacts, so he can't hurt you again. I think it's best for everyone, all around. A clean break. I'd hate for this to get . . . messy, if you know what I mean." Maxton gives Pop a warning look that I don't understand.

"You're lying. You have to be," I shout as tears I didn't realize I was crying hit my lips.

"I'm sorry. Truly I am."

"No. This isn't—he wouldn't—"

"I thought he was better than that too." He bows his head briefly.

A sob lodges in my throat. "Gran." I look over at her, and she squeezes my hand. "He wouldn't . . ."

"Come on, Ash." When her arm goes around my shoulder, I sag into her. "Let's go to your room."

I struggle, wanting to hear the rest of what is being said, needing to, but Pop pushes Maxton out the front door and shuts it behind them.

More is said. More arguing. More . . . I don't know what.

All I know is that when I ran out the front door against Gran and Pop's wishes later that night and went to the willow tree as we'd planned, Ledger wasn't there.

"Whew. That's rough. When I'm wrong, I admit it and yes, I was wrong about the man. Shit. I'm usually good at reading people too. Clearly, he is a dick of epic proportions," Nita says as she pours more wine in our cups.

Her words make me smile. "Honestly, I don't know what to think." I shrug, thinking of the look Ledger gave me after Hank interrupted us. The unspoken epiphany it looked like he had. "For the longest time, I believed that Ledger had used me. That he took pride in taking my virginity before moving on. I was humiliated and heartbroken and hated Ledger as much as I loved him."

"I sense a but coming here."

I nod. "But I *knew* Ledger. Like, you don't spend three years getting to know somebody and be wrong like that."

"Do you think his dad was lying to you about it?"

"It all came down to pedigree. Something I didn't—*don't*—have. He looked at me as a girl from the wrong side of the tracks. Think about it. I have no parents who claim me. I live in this small town that's a blip on a map. There is no way I could ever be good enough for the golden son he was grooming to take over his empire." Even saying the words now cause a mixture of disbelief and disgust.

"I'd like to say it makes sense but only in the worst kind of way."

"I know what you mean—and I agree."

"What did Gran and Pop say about it?"

"Whatever Pop talked to him about that night outside is a mystery. Pop grumbled about assholes and avoided all talk of the Sharpes, while Gran babied me and my broken heart for months. She told me that's what the boys we don't want in our lives did and was glad he was gone." I take a sip of wine and savor its tartness on my tongue. "I think it was easier for them to let me be heartbroken than to believe I wasn't good enough."

"So his dad lied to you. He was fine being blunt and honest about his reasons until he came face-to-face with you. Then what? For some reason he took pity on you and decided to blame his son for breaking your heart rather than Ledger doing it himself?"

"That's my guess," I murmur.

"Did you ever try to call him? Ledger? Get in touch with him? Did he try to call you? I mean, it's the twenty-first century, there are so many ways to talk."

"I did try. My texts and calls didn't go through so I'm assuming his dad did block my number. Either that or Ledger got a new cell. I left messages on his social media. His email. Nothing. That's why at first, it was so easy to believe that Ledger did use me. If that weren't the case and he still loved me as I loved him, he would have tried to get ahold of me, right?"

"True, but his dad was a powerful man who—"

"Controlled him? I don't know, Nita. He was an adult going to college that next month. Surely, he could have reached out once he was living on campus. It just . . . it just never made sense to me." I push the swing. "And then I got to the point where I realized that even if we did reconnect, it wouldn't matter. It's not like his father would suddenly approve of me or think I was good enough for Ledger. I didn't want to open myself up to that kind of humiliation all over again."

"So, you let it go?"

"I did. I had to. Besides, a guy like Ledger was a catch. It was easier to think he'd already moved on to some girl with a prestigious last name and a fat bank account."

"What if you thought wrong?" she asks softly.

"I can't live my life in what-ifs."

"I can understand that."

"You know what stung the most though?" *What told me what we had wasn't real . . .*

"He never contacted you."

"Exactly." I give a definitive nod. "He knew where I lived and could have written me. He knew my phone number because it didn't change. If you truly love something, you fight for it."

"And he didn't fight for you," she murmurs.

And yes, it's ridiculous to expect that from a teenage boy about to start his life out from beneath his father's wings, and yet what we had was special. Unique. *Ours.*

"Pop would have fought for Gran." My smile is bittersweet thinking of their love. "That's the only real relationship I've known to compare it against."

Nita leans her head back, closes her eyes, and pushes the swing with her foot. "That was fifteen years ago. You've changed for the better in that time. I'm sure he has too. Maybe tonight was Fate's way of stepping in to try and fix past wrongs."

"That's absurd."

"I don't think so." She places her hand on mine. "If you think it was his dad's doing, then maybe there's more to the story. Maybe there's a reason he didn't reach out. Maybe this is your second chance."

"That's a lot of maybes."

"Maybe it is," she jokes.

I smile and remember the way Ledger looked at me tonight before I left. As if there was a story in his eyes he was ready to tell. A story I'm not certain it matters that I hear.

"When he stopped me at the end of the bar, it was to ask me if we could meet to catch up sometime."

"And?"

"I don't know."

"You don't have to. All you need to know is that seeing him tonight got to you enough that you went on a long drive home. You only do that when something affects you. *He affected you.*"

"Perhaps."

"Past aside, when I walked into Hank's and saw you, the look on your face . . . it's not one I see on you very often. You looked . . . I don't know. I can't put it into words, but now, I'm not exactly sure I like that he's the one who put it there."

Another owl hoots followed by the distinct flap of its wings. We both watch as one swoops out of the trees and down to the ground to grab something near the rows of lavender.

"Do you have any idea how his dad's words affected me? How many ridiculous scenarios I have played out in my head in the months, maybe even a year or two after he left? I used to imagine becoming some famous artist and that Maxton would be at one of my art shows, completely enamored with my work. He'd try to buy a piece of my collection, and I'd refuse his money. I'd tell him it wasn't for sale for men like him. That he wasn't good enough to buy them. And then I'd remind him of who I was, where I was from, and tell him how very wrong he was." I shake my head softly, staring into the night and remembering how I'd play the scene over and over in my head. "Guess that won't exactly be happening now, will it?"

"What's that supposed to mean?"

I snort. "Look at this place, Nita. I'm holding on by the skin of my teeth right now. Between Gran's medical debts that nearly crippled our savings, to the fire a few years back that wiped out basically everything but the house, I wouldn't exactly call Asher Wells a raging success. Not to mention how Pop took his expertise in running this place with him. I have no idea what I'm doing."

"I don't want to hear your bullshit. You're still fighting, still holding on. So many people in this world aspire to own their own business. Look at you. You *do* own one."

I appreciate her pep talk but see it just like that. A way to make me feel better. And although I know there is the Ledger scale and the Asher scale in terms of both esteem and liquid assets, I think the real issue is that seeing Ledger reminds me of a time when Gran and Pop were my whole world. Still in my world. When I had them to turn to—to wipe my tears away, pull me in for a quick hug, and promise me everything was going to be all right.

"I'm being ridiculous. Sorry. I just miss Pop so much and Gran's presence around me every day," I whisper on a sob.

"Oh honey, I know."

I scrunch my nose and groan. "Just ignore me. Better yet, ignore everything I said tonight. I sound like a Negative Nancy." I emit a self-deprecating laugh. "I'm just struggling is all. It's like I lost a part of myself when I lost Pop, and seeing Ledger unexpectedly tonight when I'm already emotionally vulnerable, kind of knocked me off my stride. I became this wishy-washy woman who didn't know if she should hate him or make peace with him, when I'm not a wishy-washy person at all."

"It's okay to be vulnerable. It's okay to be confused. Hell, it's perfectly okay to be wishy-washy every once in a while." She puts her hand on mine and squeezes. "You've been to hell and back these past few months, and wishy-washy is a lot better than I'd be in your shoes."

"Thank you. Truly." What would I do without her friendship?

"Any time. What did Gran always tell you?" *What didn't Gran tell me? She was always offering me tidbits of her wisdom.* "*Life will always throw you hard times, Asher Julia Wells, and having a pity party won't solve anything,*" she says, mimicking Gran's tone as she nudges my shoulder. "But I think tonight, in Pop's memory, Gran's absence, the unexpected appearance of an ex, and being wishy-washy, we throw one. But we'll definitely need a lot more wine if that's on the agenda for the night."

"Good thing my kitchen is stocked."

CHAPTER SIX

Ledger

"W HY?"

"Why what?" Mayor Grossman asks from his seat in the middle of the raised lectern amid six other city council members. There's a smarmy look on his ruddy face that tells me I've been invited to this Cedar Falls City Council meeting with a purpose in mind other than to welcome me to their *robust* city. Insert eye roll.

"Why the two months?"

"Because someone like *you* doesn't understand the Cedar Falls way of life," he says.

"Someone like *me*?" *Seriously?* Asher was definitely right. This man is on a power trip simply for the sake of show and poll numbers.

"Yes. You think you're better than we are. New York City and all that." He waves a hand of indifference as if that will explain his lack of reasoning.

"*And all that.* Gotcha." I chuckle and just as I'm about to speak, he carries on with his ridiculous show of authority.

"You don't get us, our town, or our desire to preserve our way of life. You see dollar signs and profit—not lives and their livelihoods."

"And so, my presence here for two months serves what purpose?" Requiring that I come to a town hall meeting to watch you pound your chest is bullshit. "With all due respect, Mayor Grossman, I know this town. I know its people. I spent summers here growing up as a kid, hence why my brothers and I wanted to buy this resort as an homage to our late father. He loved this town."

Murmurs ripple through the audience at my back. Too bad I can't tell if they are for or against me.

"That's a novel idea but you can't barge into this town and think your money will make you welcome. You may have known Cedar Falls ten, fifteen years ago, but that doesn't mean you still know it now."

Something catches in my periphery and I look up just in time to see Asher cross her arms over her chest and give a subtle head shake. I'm guessing she's saying the same goes for her. *That I knew her then and don't know her now.*

I lose my concentration and have to force myself to remember where we were. What I'm doing.

"Isn't this why you've insisted I be here? So I can get to know the town to your satisfaction?" I meet the eyes of the other six council members.

"We have a running history in which we do good for and by the people of Cedar Falls," the mayor continues without answering my question.

"As any city council should."

"And you have a reputation for coming in, gutting a town of its jobs and charm without any regard for the city."

"I beg to differ, Mayor Grossman." Jesus Christ. This is Ford's realm. The kissing the babies and shaking hands shit. Not mine. "Sharpe International intends to leave a positive footprint wherever we have a property."

"A positive footprint?"

"Yes, sir. As noted in the request sent to my office, we failed on our promise to hire locally. I'm here to satisfy that condition, among other things."

"Among other things?"

Why does he keep repeating what I'm saying?

"Yes, sir."

"But let's face it. You're only here because we threatened to hold your permits unless you came here to understand our way of life."

I stare at him and question where he's going with this. "We take a vested interest in all our properties. While I can't say that our schedules would have allowed one of my brothers or me to stay in town for a full two months during the renovation, we definitely would have been here on and off to check on its progress. And what we couldn't check on personally, we fully trust Hillary Deegan, our on-site project manager, to do just as good of a job as we do." I pause for dramatic effect. "We always strive to go above and beyond for the community. In turn, that helps make our resort profitable. And *that*, Mayor Grossman, puts dollars back into your community."

"Above and beyond. A vested interest." He lowers his glasses to the top of his nose and stares at me above their frame as I nod.

Can we speed this up? I have shit to do. Millions of dollars to spend and deals to make. Things way more important than kissing some pompous man's ass for a simple goddamn permit.

One that we can't live without no less.

This is below my pay grade. So fucking below it my back aches trying to stoop to its level.

Doesn't he have a cow to go tip somewhere? A defenseless animal to kill in the name of sport?

"Is something the matter, Mr. Sharpe?"

"Of course not." I offer a *go-fuck-yourself* smile. "What else could I possibly have to do than to stand here and listen to you repeat my own words back to me?"

"Like above and beyond and a vested interest," he repeats.

"Correct." *Check your temper, Ledge.* "Just like those."

"Strong words coming from a man who just last night was overheard at Hank's saying"—the mayor looks at a paper in front of him—"'the best part about this town is that I get to leave it when my two months of torture are up. It's a fucking fishbowl.' Now, correct me if I'm wrong, but those were your words, weren't they?"

Motherfucker. Someone heard my conversation with Ford while I was standing outside of Hank's.

Goddamn small town, everybody knows everybody, and everybody loves to know everybody's business.

I'm fucked.

Utterly and totally fucked.

Mayor Grossman waits for my response with expectant eyes as the citizens who chose to attend chatter behind me. They aren't exactly thrilled with my insult to their town and in turn, them.

"Mr. Sharpe?" he prompts.

Backpedal.

Fix your fuckup.

Evade.

"My intent wasn't to insult—"

"Of course, it wasn't." His smile matches his tone—sarcastic. "But since you find our town . . . *lacking* in all areas, then we, the town of Cedar Falls, have decided to put it on Sharpe International to make some improvements in the town being as *our success will be your success* and all."

"Improvements?" *What the actual fuck?* "Meaning?"

"Meaning we feel it's important that a venture as big as yours should have more of an investment in the overall well-being of our community. Should help make our citizens profit while you do."

Is he extorting us?

"There is nothing in our agreement with the city that states an investment is required in the town over and above the resort itself."

"Well"—he glances at the other council members on either side of him before looking back at me—"you know us *Podunk folk*, we don't exactly abide by rules. It'd be a shame to do all this construction and spend all this money, especially now that you're in the home stretch of it, and not be able to get your certificate of occupancy. What is it they say? Another day, another dime wasted?"

I emit a nervous, disbelieving chuckle as I scratch my temple.

Think. Fucking think, Ledger.

But there is nothing to think about. They've got me over a barrel and they know it. We have tens of millions already invested in this property and its renovations. We can't exactly abandon it, and no one's going to buy a half-constructed resort if we were to bow out.

"And what exactly do you expect from us?" It's all I can think to ask. I'm normally not thrown by curveballs. I am this time.

Without having lawyers at my back to consult like I normally would, I'm still ninety-nine percent sure Grossman has zero authority to do this. He's a dick. Plain and simple. What he doesn't know is I've dealt with much worse dickish behavior in New York City. I know how to play this game. How I need to appear that I'm at this *Podunk* town's mercy regardless of the legalities of it.

Kill them with kindness.

Jesus. It just might kill me in the process.

"You're a successful businessman, Ledger Sharpe." His smile doesn't reach his eyes. "I'm sure you can think of something to appease us."

CHAPTER SEVEN

Ledger

"HOLD THE FUCK ON. YOU'RE SERIOUS, AREN'T YOU?"

"As a heart attack," I say to Ford as I lean back in my chair and close my eyes. "The fucker is going to extort us. From what I gather, he's up for reelection soon, and it looks as if he's going to run on the I-made-big-business-my-bitch platform."

"Hence the letter with the required two months and now this bullshit request."

"Exactly. The problem is the ultimatum he gave us is subjective in nature. There is no do this and get this, like there was with his first command. What he's asking now is just . . ."

"He's beating his chest."

"Along with other things to get off," I mutter.

"Can we just pause for a moment in your misery so I can revel in the glory that always-perfect Ledger fucked up?" He emits an exaggerated laugh. "You didn't think to be cautious talking on the phone to me when you were standing in front of a locals-only bar?"

No. *I didn't.* All I could think about was Asher and how by the time I'd run out to the parking lot to chase after her, she was gone.

"You called me at a bad time." It's the only excuse I can give without having to explain more.

"Then you shouldn't have picked up. Easy enough."

"Enough gloating," I say as I open my eyes and lift a hand in farewell to Hillary who's heading out the door to meet with God knows who. *Let the Cedar Falls City Council ass-kissing commence.*

"Fine. But it's such a rarity, so I have to enjoy it while I can." He emits a satisfied sigh. "The question now is, what are we going to do about it?"

"Hillary and I brainstormed a bit. We think our best bet is to bring in local artisans. Paintings by locals. Items in the numerous gift shops devoted to the local talent."

"Won't that harm their sales in town? Undercut them somehow?"

"We haven't worked the details out, but I'm sure we can come up with something to appease everyone."

"So basically, use the resort to showcase the people of Cedar Falls?"

I nod even though he can't see it. "Maybe a few other things. Hillary mentioned at the last city council meeting that they were trying to scrape together tax revenue to give the elementary school a new library or the assisted living facility on the outskirts of town a new HVAC system since theirs has been on the fritz for years."

"So help the kids and the elderly. No one can bitch about that."

"My thoughts exactly." I blow out an exaggerated sigh. "But still . . ."

"But still . . ." Ford repeats. "Other than that shitshow today, what are your thoughts on Cedar Falls as a whole?"

Only Ford and Callahan visited the location before we purchased the old hotel here. I was tied up in another deal and couldn't get away.

I can't say I was exactly upset by that turn of events. *For many reasons.*

"You mean beyond the signs posted in every window saying shit like *Big business kills small business* and *Take your S.I.N.s elsewhere?*"

"It's that bad?"

"There are a few that say *A resort equals more jobs* and *Tourism means more money*, so at least we have a few people on our side."

"Where were they during the town meeting today?" he jokes.

"Exactly." I draw in a breath and contemplate his question. "Cedar Falls. Well, it's definitely not Manhattan, that's for sure."

"You mean it's not rife with the stench of the subway or the smell of urine on exhaust-stained concrete buildings that you're so used to?" He laughs.

"There's definitely none of that here." I stand up and lean my ass against my desk. "Nor are there street vendors shouting at you or crowded sidewalks to push your way through or subways to hop on or—"

"Things most people would abhor—"

"But that I love."

"You're going to fight this assignment kicking and screaming every step of the way, aren't you?"

"I prefer to call it more of a silent protest."

"Ha. Says the man who's never bitten his tongue in his life. Don't worry, you'll be back in your tower in the sky in no time."

"Fuck off." Nothing at all wrong with my tower in the sky with the endless views of the city I love. "But as for this town . . ."

"You mean this *Podunk* town," he ribs, but I don't take the bait.

"Objectively, it's a good location and the facility has good bones to work with." I move to look out the window of the temporary office Hillary set up for me on-site. From this vantage point, I can't see the resort's trademark lake or the reflection of the mountains around us, but the serene image is burned in my mind. The same image I plan on having our marketing team use to push the hell out of this soon-to-be overhauled resort. "The additions we're making will only make it more attractive to our preferred clientele. They'll have luxurious lodging with a top-of-the-line spa for those who aren't big into outdoors and all of the activities to do if they are."

"Agreed. But that's what we do best," Ford says. "I'm asking about the town. You're good at reading things, and I want your take."

"First impressions? The town is still small but definitely scenic. It has a homey, mom-and-pop feel that will entice families as a whole, and a cool artsy vibe the childless socialites will love. Outdoor adventure outfits are everywhere so that will add to the allure." I scrub a hand over my jaw. "It'll more than work."

"Glad we're on the same page. I felt similarly. As for construction, are we still on schedule? Have we hit any hiccups?"

"Ask Hillary. That's her domain."

"True, but you're walking in with fresh eyes. What are you seeing?"

"We'll make the schedule, give or take a few days." I pause. "I take that back. Hillary is currently working on getting local contractors on-site. That might push us back because we're going to have to hire them regardless of whether they meet our skills needed or standards required."

"Simply to appease Grossman."

"Yep. So that alone might throw a wrench in our pace, but we're being held up anyway with this two-month bullshit, so I'm sure it'll even itself out."

"Okay. I'll let Charles know," he says, mentioning our director of construction. "She's already hiring locals? I love how quickly she works. That should help bolster public opinion."

"Your guess is as good as mine. I'm sure Grossman will pull something else out of his ass, some other hoop we need to jump through. Maybe this time he'll require we light it on fire or something to get a final inspection."

"We're damned if we do and damned if we don't."

"Easy for you to say while sitting in our office in Manhattan."

"I'm in your office. My feet are up on your desk."

"Funny."

"Your chair is rather comfortable. I'm gonna have to get one of these for my office."

I grit my teeth. The fucker knows how particular I am about my desk and is pushing buttons simply because he can. "Asshole," I mutter.

His laugh floats through the line. "God, you are so easy to rile up. It's rather pathetic, Ledge. How's the place you rented? Is it okay?"

"If you're asking if it's a log cabin with an outhouse for a bathroom and trophy heads of deer lining the walls to make my time here even more authentic, I'm sorry to inform you it is not."

"And to think I wanted to come and visit for a walk down memory lane."

"Spare yourself. *And me*," I joke.

"Come on. It would be fun. We could go to our old stomping grounds and pretend we're kids again. No responsibilities. No rules."

I smile at the thought. I did exactly that yesterday. Drove around where we used to hang out. I told myself it was for a bit of nostalgia, to get a lay of the new land here that's developed over the years, but somehow, I found myself by an old willow tree. And from the willow tree, somehow my car drove itself to the side of the road, enabling me to stare at a huge sign that said The Fields.

The house looked the same as I remembered it. White clapboard, a wraparound veranda, the red front door. It looks like the Wells's had expanded over the years since the lavender went as far as I could see, but I didn't pay much attention to that part of it back then. All that mattered was getting lost somewhere in the rows where Asher and I could lay on our backs, stare at the stars, and then make out without getting caught.

I don't know what I was hoping for in going there. Asher to be on the front porch? To have another chance to talk to her? Hell if I know.

"Ledge? You there?"

"Yeah. Sorry. What did you ask?"

"Your rental?"

"It works. Small house in a quiet neighborhood. It doesn't really matter since I'll be here working most of the time. Is that it? Is your micromanaging over now?"

He snorts. "Someone has to do it since you're not here to."

"Funny." How the tables have turned. It wasn't long ago I was putting Callahan through the paces, much like Ford is doing to me now. Back then, there was no laughing though. Only resentment.

"Make sure you give us an update on what happens."

"There you go micromanaging again," I mutter. "Don't you have something else—another five projects or so—to give someone else the Spanish Inquisition over? I assure you I have this handled."

Needing to stretch my legs, I move out into what will be the main lobby of The Retreat. With the changes we've made, it's expansive and more on-brand for a S.I.N. property. I glance down the wide hallway toward the random sounds of construction where we've added three wings to the existing structure. Ahead of me, men are working on tiling a wall that will be the entrance to the new luxury spa we've brought in-house. Three pallets of marble tiles line the far wall to be used for new flooring.

"This place will shine, Ford. We'll get through this bullshit with the city council and this place will fucking shine. Whether it's used as a winter retreat for the ski enthusiasts or an outdoor haven for those who like the outdoors in summer, customers will get the luxury they expect from us."

"Which is exactly why we bought it."

"Mm-hmm," I murmur as I head back to my office.

"Everything else good? You seem a little distracted."

"I'm fine. Just . . . busy. I'm heading out the door to meet up with one of the outdoor adventure companies in town. I want to see if they'll work with us and put together some exclusive packages for the resort."

"You know we have people for that, right?" He chuckles. "Last I checked, being hands-on with the details wasn't exactly your forte."

"And last I checked, I was in my office in Manhattan."

"When in Rome, right?"

A smart-ass comeback is on my lips when heavy footsteps have me looking up and doing a double take. Asher is storming down the hallway toward me. "Ford? I have to go."

"Problem?" he asks.

"That remains to be seen." I end the call without an explanation because I'm too busy watching her.

Every furious, gorgeous inch of her.

Her eyes lock on mine as she crosses the room and comes to a stop in front of my desk.

"Well, this is a surprise," I say, fighting back a smile that she scowls at. I may have wondered the other night why or how I was still attracted to her after all these years, but right now, I don't care what the answer is.

All I know is I am.

All I can comprehend is that we're different people now than we were back then.

And seeing her here, full of fire, only serves to make me want her more.

Her jaw is clenched as she smacks her hand down on the desk between us in a dramatic fashion. "I don't want your pity."

"Pity?" I ask as she moves her hand to reveal the hundred-dollar bill I left her with my number on it.

"Yes. I don't need a ridiculous tip from you because you feel sorry for me."

My smile is slow and deliberate. "And here I thought you were pissed because I left my phone number on it. *Whew.*" I mock wipe my brow. "So that means you *did* want my phone number then? Good. At least I read that right."

Her glare is adorable. The flush to her cheeks. The defiance in her stance. "You're not cute."

"People tend to tell me I'm more sexy or brooding over cute so yes, I agree with you on that one. Definitely not cute." I cross my arms over my chest, look down at the bill on the desk, and then back up at her with a lift of my brows.

She mirrors my posture, arms crossed over her chest, and just glares at me. She doesn't know what else to say, does she? She waltzed in here, made her point, and now doesn't know what to do.

What's going on in that head of yours, Ash?

"I think we should probably talk about things. Us. What happened," I finally say. "That way we can move on. Forward. Start anew."

"I moved on years ago." She juts her chin out but fuck if her eyes don't say differently. *Good to know.* "I don't want to talk about anything."

"We need to." I take a step toward her and her back stiffens. Hmm. Her indecisiveness and lack of confidence I saw in her the other night is gone. *Interesting.*

"No, we don't."

She always was stubborn.

"Fine," I say and then take another step, hoping my next words will surprise her just as they did me when they popped into my head. "Then we'll talk about how all I've thought about since seeing you the other night is how much I want to kiss you."

Her head jostles, her eyes widen, and her lips fall lax.

Good. We're on the same page. She feels whatever this is too.

"If that doesn't make you want to talk, I'm not sure what will," I say. Her eyes flick up and down the length of my body as I take yet another step.

"No." A shake of her head. "There's nothing to talk about." A shift of her feet. "The past is the past and that's where it's going to stay."

"All right." I close the gap between us so that I'm close enough to see the rise of her shoulders, smell the mint on her breath, and feel the heat of her body. She takes in a sharp intake of a breath. "If that's the case"—I lean in so that her hair tickles my cheek as I whisper in her ear—"I'm Ledger Sharpe. Nice to meet you, Lavender Girl."

It takes everything I have not to act on the urge to kiss her. Fucking everything. She was in my dream last night, on my mind in the shower, and who I looked for in the crowd after the town hall meeting.

I step back and reach my hand out for her to shake as her eyes hold mine, our breathing the only sound accompanying the silence in the room.

Asher looks me up and down in a slow appraisal, her lips ghosting in a smile and her eyes lighting with humor. "Thanks, but . . . I'm not interested."

She hesitates—briefly—as her eyes flick to my lips and back up before she stalks from my office with the same determination she walked in here with.

But that hesitation gave me all I needed to know.

Shoving my hands in my pockets, I walk out toward the lobby of the hotel so I can watch Asher's hips sway as she strides toward the parking lot.

I don't want to talk about it.

Fine.

Then we won't.

But I'm here for two months, Asher Wells. And in that time, we will most definitely cross paths. *And hopefully, do a hell of a lot more.*

CHAPTER EIGHT

Asher

I HAVEN'T EVEN MADE A DENT IN THEM.

Not at all.

I scoot the chair back from behind Pop's desk, look at the stacks of papers that he'd piled on every surface of his desk, and pinch the bridge of my nose.

I'm sure this whole process would go much faster if I stopped being distracted every couple minutes by thoughts of Ledger.

But I'll allow myself the thoughts of him after I walked into his office and successfully did what I set out to do. *Make a second* first *impression.* Show him that the scattered, emotionally indecisive woman he met the other night was an anomaly.

And fortunately, I was able to do just that before I took notice of the way he stood behind his desk, arms crossed and cocky as hell. Yes, his arrogance irritated the shit out of me, but I'd be lying if I didn't admit to myself that it turned me on too.

His firm thighs pressed against his slacks. The way his biceps strained the sleeves of his dress shirt. The purse of his lips as he challenged me. The timbre of his voice and the heat of his breath when he leaned in to whisper in my ear.

How is this possible? How can I want a man who walked away without a word? That goes against all reason and rationale and yet . . . here I am thinking about it, *about him*, when I have way more important things to deal with.

"Like these equally enthralling stacks of paper," I mutter to myself before taking a deep breath, determined to tackle another of them.

They have no rhyme or reason. I'm sure their composition made sense to Pop, but I've yet to figure it out.

Medical bills and assisted living bills for Gran. A letter from a supplier. Payables stamped past due for equipment. A credit card bill from two months ago. What do all these things have in common that he'd categorize them together? What is the method to his madness?

Was. What was the method to his madness? I'm still having a hard time thinking of him in past tense. Gran had been on the decline for so long that while putting her in an assisted living facility was the right thing to do for her medical needs, her absence here at the house was deafening. But Pop . . . despite his obvious grief, was joking with me on the front porch one day and then never woke from his nap on his rocker on the porch the next. I swear he died from a broken heart over being apart from Gran.

If only that kind of love existed for everyone.

The stacks, Asher. Focus on that. On your goal to at least tackle one stack a day until you clean this mess up.

Then what? When you can see the top of this desk, will it be real to you that he's gone?

I pinch the bridge of my nose and sigh loudly as I fight the tears that threaten. I refuse to cry. Refuse to break down—again. His presence looms so largely over everything and yet this house, this farm, everywhere he touched, feels so empty without him.

Especially as I sit here, surrounded by everything that represented him, and feel woefully underprepared.

Sure, I've been running The Fields since Pop passed, but if I'm honest with myself, I've been doing the bare minimum. This office, his haven, was too hard for me to face.

But the world moves on even though those of us left behind feel frozen in place.

I look around me. Little trinkets he'd kept over time clutter the shelf across from me. Some of my old landscape sketches are mounted on the wall to the side of me. A picture of Gran is framed on the desk next to the monitor.

This office was *his* haven. His place to hide when he said he needed a break from the estrogen in the house so he'd have an excuse to research whatever was his latest interest on the Internet. Or tiptoe out back and sneak a sip of whiskey that he thought Gran didn't know about. *She did.*

The space is a room toward the back of the main house, a large porch Pop closed in years ago, that has an exterior door facing the fields beyond. It served as the business center for The Fields as well as his solace.

"Next up, emails," I say to myself in mock enthusiasm and punch a fist in the air. I've been going alphabetically through the folders in his inbox. One by one, I've been opening each folder, reading through its contents and, if it's still relevant, I keep it. If not, I delete it.

Pop clearly was a pack rat when it came to emails too.

"Fuckers." I laugh when I see the inbox name and love how even now, he can make me laugh. I'm not sure what I expect to see in a folder labeled as such, but it's definitely not marketing emails from S.I.N. about buying the old hotel in town or updates on its status from the Cedar Falls City Council.

Pop knew who S.I.N. was, didn't he? Who owned it?

He was keeping track of their progress, of the company, but why?

Because once a father, always a father.

Wasn't that what he always said to me? That no matter how old I was, he'd always be my father, he'd always tell me the truth even when I didn't want to hear it, and he'd always try to protect me from it.

Is that what he was doing?

Making sure the man who damaged me couldn't hurt me again?

I scroll through the emails. They're all blanket newsletters, nothing personally addressed to him, and yet he kept them.

Sure, he'd grumbled about the resort coming to town, but when I pressed him on why, it was the same reasoning everyone else in town had, so I thought nothing of his displeasure. I simply figured he was old school and feared what the soon-to-be-completed resort would do to the other mom-and-pop businesses like ours.

It was a logical conclusion to make, but now that I'm staring at this cache of emails, I can't help but think there were other reasons for his dislike of it.

Reasons that date back to that night fifteen years ago.

It's all conjecture, really. Silly, imaginative conjecture, and yet once again, I'm led right back to Ledger.

It seems Fate keeps pushing me to interact with him.

The knock on the exterior door of the office makes me jump.

"Miss Wells?"

"George." I hold a hand to my chest. "You scared the crap out of me."

"My apologies, ma'am."

"It's fixed?" I ask about the irrigation line that sprung a leak overnight. We woke up to the south field being flooded, which is never a good thing with a crop like lavender that likes well-drained soil and a dry root base.

"We're still working on it. Danny went to the hardware store to grab some couplings and pipe, but . . ."

"But what?"

He looks at his ball cap that he's holding in his hands and then back up. "The card on file was declined."

"Crap. Sorry." I suck in a quick breath. "It's . . . I'm behind on everything. Pop's filing system is a little hard to figure out." I stammer out the excuse, pointing to the stacks I'm going through because I don't even know if I had the credit card bill that I'd be able to pay it. "I'll get you some cash." Within seconds, I've rifled through my purse and handed him fifty dollars. "That should cover it."

"Thanks," George says, but he's still standing there staring at me after I return to my seat.

"Is there something else?" I ask.

He twists his lips and shifts on his feet. "There are rumors you're going to sell The Fields."

"Sell?" I ask and he nods. "Who exactly would I sell it to?"

He shrugs and I can tell he's more than uncomfortable. "It's been a rough couple of years. Some of the guys figured with Pop gone that you'd sell off what you could. That way you might break even from . . . everything. Move on."

The fire that wiped out our crops and shed full of equipment and tools a few years back. The added land we had to purchase to cultivate to add quantity while the new crops came to fruition. Gran's care expenses kept adding to it. The barn Pop had built, the one he'd planned to use as a workshop, which now sits empty. The ridiculous expense of his funeral that added to it.

"This place, *this land*, has been in my family for generations. It will be passed to me when Gran is no longer here. As much as this life wasn't *my* dream for myself, George, it was theirs. I have every intention of keeping it going."

He nods. "But it's yours now and technically that means you can do whatever you want with it, right? I mean, there's nothing preventing you from selling it. That's what everyone's saying, at least."

What the actual fuck? That's the rumor going around? This town thinks so little of me they assume I'd sell out?

Then again, I shouldn't be surprised considering this is the same town that has always judged me for my mom's lack of discretion before I was born.

"My word is what's preventing me. I made a promise to my grandparents. To the people who have given me everything. What kind of person am I if I go back on that?" I say the words but wonder how I'm going to manage this. A farm to run. An office to manage. A life I'm not living. And bills that are inches thick.

The easy way out would be to sell.

He knows that. I know that. And as tempting as it is, *I promised.*

"And what about the resort people? Is it true they wanted to buy it?"

"What?" I cough the word out.

"Pop mentioned something about them trying to buy up everything and screw everyone over like usual." He shakes his head. "It had been a long time since I'd seen him that hot under the collar."

"When was this?"

"It was after he found out who bought the old hotel." He pushes his hair off his forehead. "He just kept going on about no matter how good their resort might be for this town, he'd never give them business after what they did."

I'm right. I know I am.

Pop still held a grudge over the man who looked down on the Wells family.

I nod absently because it makes sense. Pop knew who owned S.I.N. and he never forgot the man who insulted him, his pride, and most importantly, me.

"I'm sure he had his reasons," I say softly. "But I assure you, I have no intention of selling."

"Okay." Our eyes hold. "I'll tell the guys. It's just that we all have families and if we need to look for other jobs, then . . ."

"I get it." I nod, hating that my throat feels like it's closing up. "No one needs to worry. I know Pop considered you guys family, as do I. I don't want you worrying." I offer a strained smile and hope it reaches my eyes. Our gazes meet, and I can see he still has doubts. "What else is there? What other rumors are floating out there that I can squash?"

He looks at me with trepidation, almost as if even if I did disprove them, he wouldn't quite believe me.

And it kills me, because they trusted Pop without question. That just means I'll have to prove my words and my ability to run the business even harder.

His smile is quick. The dart of his eyes over his shoulder and back even quicker. "Nothing. There's nothing else." He takes a step back. "I need to take this to Danny so we can get the irrigation fixed."

"Okay. Let me know if you need anything else."

"Yes, ma'am."

"Hey, George," I call as he takes a few steps down the stairs, and I rise to move to the open door.

He turns back to look at me. "Yeah?"

"It's been a rough few months. I know the guys probably don't have much faith in me—*understandably*—but please know I'll do right by you, by them . . . by Gran and Pop."

"Yes, ma'am," he repeats. "I'll let you know when it's fixed."

I watch him walk away, his words repeating in my head. *Nothing. There's nothing else.*

I lean against the doorframe and stare out at rows of bright purple. Folgate lavender to the left is closing in on time to harvest. Royal Velvet lavender variant lining the slopes near the back of the property is coming along and will be ready in the next few months. And then there is our workhorse variant, the one that blankets most of our fields, Grosso lavender. That's where the irrigation line burst overnight and luckily George caught it on his early morning rounds.

We could have lost some healthy crops.

And that's something we definitely can't afford.

These are the rows I ran between as a child, losing myself in an imaginary fairy world where my mother existed and the men of Cedar Falls didn't wonder which one of them was my father.

This is where I wandered with tears streaming down my face after giving up my dream to go to art school so that I could stay here and take care of my grandmother after her stroke. Her medical bills were so overwhelming they ate all that had been saved for my education.

This is where I sat and stared at the purple until it blurred when my heart was shattered into a million pieces that late summer night.

"The last thing he needs is someone like her to bring him down. He has a bright future ahead of him, an empire to run, and I won't have him sidetracked by a motherless girl with no pedigree and no future."

And now, this is where I'm going to pull up my bootstraps and make something of the promises I made, even when I have no idea how I'm going to.

But I will because there's no way in hell I'm going to give Maxton Sharpe the satisfaction of being right.

CHAPTER NINE

Asher

"IT'S EVERYTHING I'VE EVER DREAMED OF, NITA." I SPIN AROUND my dorm room with an outfit held up to my body before looking at myself in the mirror. My smile is wide and my eyes are wild with excitement. These first two months at the Pratt Institute have been incredible. Everything I ever dreamed of.

I'm finally chasing my dream.

"Tell me all about it," she murmurs in her sleepy voice.

"It's the city. It's like it's alive with all its lights and high-rises and big classrooms with floor-to-ceiling windows. There's culture and refinement right beside the gritty and raw reality of life." Even I'm not immune to the dreamlike quality of my own voice. "I feel like it's a mixture of every place I've never been—"

"I think anywhere would feel like that compared to Cedar Falls."

"It's more than that." I sit down on the edge of my bed. I recall what felt like the endless undergrad classes I took at the community college to try and cut down on costs. The promises from Pop that he'd do whatever it took to make my dreams come true and give me the opportunities to be whomever I wanted to be. *My chance to be* the someone *others thought I couldn't be.* All the blood, sweat, and tears, and it's finally happened. "It's like I'm meant to be here."

"Of course, you are. It's all you've ever wanted. And with your crazy, mad talent, you deserve to be there."

I smile. "I'm sorry. I shouldn't be going on and on. Especially when I'm here and you're—"

"Still in Cedar Falls?" She chuckles. "Don't you dare hold out on me. I want to hear everything. Let me live vicariously through you. What about the men? Tell me all about them."

"You'd die. Finely tailored suits and dress shirts rolled up to the elbows."

"Forearm porn. Yummy."

"Definitely forearm porn. But it's so much more than that. They're educated and refined with a little bit of street thrown in. Ugh. Each one I meet is better than the next."

"These are the guys in the program? Because if so, you need to pull some all-night study sessions."

"No." I laugh because the guys in the program are eccentric and quirky along with talented. Even though I'm artsy, it has never been the vibe I'm attracted to. "I'm talking about the men in the city. The ones who walk fast on the sidewalk as if they are off to a very important meeting. The kind that makes you want to stop and stare because they exude an air of authority. They look . . ." *exactly how I imagined Ledger would look in his element.*

The thought comes out of nowhere. A flashback to a past I've learned to stop giving a second thought to.

I shake the thought away. How weird that it crept in, right now in this moment, after I'd permanently scrubbed him from my mind.

Or at least tried to.

But truth be told, I have looked for him in the crowd every once in a while before coming to my senses.

"Right?" Nita asks, bringing me out of my thoughts and to the present.

"I'm sorry. Your phone cut out," I lie.

"I said, so they're basically the polar opposite of every man here in Cedar Falls."

"Exactly."

"So older men, then. Classy. Worldly. They *are* right up your alley, then. You've always had a thing for that type."

"Maybe." I giggle. "You'll still come visit me, right?"

"Yeah." Her voice is soft, and I hate that she doesn't have this opportunity. Hell, I can't even believe that I am getting the chance. "I will."

"And everything back home is—"

"The same. Boring. Lonely without you here to be my partner in crime." She sniffs, and I hope I haven't made her sad. We've been inseparable since we met during our first semester of junior college. She had just moved to Cedar Falls with her mother and needed help finding her way on campus. I offered to show her to class since we were in the same general education math class. We've been thick as thieves ever since. She's the sister I never had. And doing this here without her feels like I'm gloating.

My heart constricts but my happiness overshadows it. And she'd want that for me. I know it, but it doesn't make it any easier.

It's like I'm starting over. No one knows me, knows my name or my history, and since I arrived months ago, I feel like I can be whoever I want to be. I can reinvent myself so I'm not Asher Wells the small-town girl and product of a promiscuous mother who isn't going to amount to anything, but rather Asher Wells, the aspiring artist and cultured city girl.

It's the most liberated I've ever felt.

My cell beeps, and I look at the screen to see that it's Pop. "Hey, I've gotta go," I tell Nita. "Pop's on the other line."

"Sure. Dump me for Pop," she teases, but she knows my love for my grandparents. "Call me later. Love you."

"Love you too." I end the call with her and pick up Pop's call. My cheeks hurt from smiling so much. "Pop! Hi. Oh my God. I have so much to tell you. I've—"

"Asher." His voice is a whisper with grief-laced despair in its threads.

"Pop? What's wrong?" My heart sinks to my feet.

"It's Gran. She collapsed. They're saying that—" His voice breaks into a sob. "I can't lose her, Ash."

My hands shake. The dress I'm holding falls to the ground as the world drops out from under me.

"I'm . . . I'm on my way."

"No. It's okay . . ."

But it's not.

I have to go.

I have to be there for the only people who have ever been there for me.

What I didn't know when I walked away from that world of opportunity—*of utter happiness*—was that I'd never get it back.

CHAPTER TEN

Asher

"Gran," I warn playfully.

"What?" she asks innocently, her speech slurred, while hiding my checker piece she just palmed from the board.

She gives me that soft, crooked smile that I've been on the receiving end of my whole life. It's full of love and warmth, even though I know she's struggling to simply endure most days. And yet, like the selfless soul she's always been, she's still trying to make me smile and feel her love.

I cling to the sight of it. Today's a good day. She's lucid and seems at peace.

Her first stroke paralyzed her left side completely, and it took over eighteen months to recover from. Five years later, her second affected her memory and added some nerve damage more than anything. And her third one, four months ago, left her struggling to make decisions and bound her to a wheelchair.

The decision to move her to the assisted living facility was agonizing. She and Pop hadn't been apart for almost sixty years, and there I was telling him I could no longer provide her medical needs. That I'd failed him. And that it was finally time to get her the help she needed.

His heart broke more than mine that first day we left her here, but he put on a brave face for me. I heard his soft crying through the bedroom door every night for the next few weeks.

I made the decision. I told him it was time. And then he died of a broken heart, alone, and without the love of his life by his side.

The guilt I feel over it steals my breath most days.

And the times I visit Gran when the staff tells me she's struggling more and more each day, that her mental capacity is declining faster, I wonder if it's her broken heart that is winning the battle or her worn-down body. Those days? Those are the ones when I pull out of the parking lot, park a mile down the road, and sob till I can't cry anymore because I feel like my decision was the catalyst for all of this.

It's a rarity that she feels good enough to get out of her bed and be wheeled to the rec room. The staff knows on those days to call me regardless of the time because I'll be there as soon as possible. That I wouldn't miss it for the world.

That call came today.

Her smile and mischief are the only things I need.

"You're going to beat me handily enough. I assure you, you don't have to cheat," I say, moving my black checker from one square to another for my turn. "Your turn."

But when I look up, Gran is looking across the room, fixated on something. Expression blank, eyes astute. For the briefest of seconds, I panic, worrying that something is wrong with her.

I follow her gaze and freeze.

What is he doing here?

Ledger is standing on the far side of the recreation room. He's huddled in a conversation with another woman in a sharp business suit and the director of the facility. They are discussing something in hushed voices, I assume to avoid disturbing the residents.

I watch for a few moments, as does Gran, until hands are shaken between the trio as if the meeting is over. Ledger's laugh carries over to where we sit and just before he walks out, he turns to scan the room again.

The surprise when he sees me is exactly how I felt when I saw him standing there.

He gives me a strange look—surprise, confusion, I don't know—before he says something to the people he's standing with and makes his way across the room.

"Well, look at this handsome thing walking our way," Gran murmurs as she attempts to sit up straighter when physically she can't. "Tall. Handsome. Those shoulders. I do believe he is just your type."

I cough to cover my laugh. Jesus. It seems Gran is friends with Fate. And who knew a handsome man could make her the most lucid she's been in weeks?

"He's not my type," I mutter, hating that it's hard to pull my eyes away from him.

I try.

I really do.

Liar.

"Ladies," he says with a subtle nod in greeting as he approaches our table.

Will Gran recognize him?

"It's all her fault," Gran says, pointing my way with her good hand, a sly smile on her half-frozen mouth and a twinkle in her eyes that I haven't seen in forever.

"What's my fault?" I ask thoroughly confused.

"Whatever it is we're in trouble for, dear. He's in a suit—and looking good in one I might add—so whatever he came over here for, it's your fault."

Gran just hung me out to dry.

I stare at her, slack-jawed. It's then I realize that I'm so used to Gran's slurred speech I know what she said. I'm just about to rephrase it for Ledger, but he beats me to the punch.

"No one's in trouble," Ledger says clearly making sense of her enunciation while unbuttoning his jacket as he comes to a stop. "I saw two beautiful women sitting over here, and I couldn't resist coming over and saying hi."

Smooth. Real smooth, Sharpe.

"Well, *hello* there," Gran says with a fingertip wave and a pathetic bat of her eyelashes. "Please. Join us."

Ledger glances my way, almost as if to ask if it's okay. Every part of me wants to tell him to leave me be with Gran and not cloud this time I have with her by adding the confusing mess of "us" to it. At the same time, I haven't seen Gran this spry in so long. A small, irrational part of me is afraid it'll leave if he does.

I give a slight nod in consent, prompting him to pull out the spare chair at our table and take a seat.

"Thank you," Ledger says, smiling warmly at Gran. I can tell he's looking for any sign of recognition, but she shows none and for that I'm grateful.

"Adele," Gran says and holds out her hand to him. Ledger's gaze flickers my way and before he can answer with his unique name that I fear Gran will most definitely remember, Gran's spitfire kicks back in. "And yours must be *Handsome*."

I have to give him credit because his expression of *what the hell* vanishes as quickly as it appears. "Okay. Sure." He chuckles as he shakes her hand, his cheeks flushing.

"It's always better to keep a little mystery when courting." She winks.

"Good to know," he murmurs.

"This is my granddaughter, Asher. She's single, you know. Ready to be courted."

"Gran," I warn.

"It's always important to know your options," Ledger says, his smile genuine.

"Exactly." Gran pats his arm and then squeezes there. "*Oh my.* Look how fit you are."

Did she seriously just say that?

Yes. Yes, she did, and she hasn't moved her hand away yet.

"Does your girlfriend enjoy that? Your strong physique?" she continues, adding to this deliberate show of flirting she has going on.

"No girlfriend," Ledger says, his eyes holding mine briefly.

Her grin is wide, and the finger she points at him when she slowly lifts her hand is gnarled from arthritis. "Get you a girl who likes to argue." She waggles her eyebrows. "That means the bedroom will never be boring."

"Jesus, Gran," I spit out as Ledger just looks at me with the lift of an eyebrow and a ghost of a smile.

"I'm old, dear. I have a lot of advice to give and like to say what's on my mind." She glances my way for a beat, her expression falling blank again, and I fear I've lost her. But just as quickly as it appears her mind fires blanks, she gives the subtlest shake of her head before focusing back on Ledger. "That's the freeing part of getting older. Not caring what anyone thinks of you."

"If that's the case, Adele, might I trouble you for some advice?"

Gran seems thrilled to have a purpose that's something other than sitting in her wheelchair. "Of course. Is it love advice? I'm really good at that. I was with my Richard for over sixty years." She holds a hand to her heart and gets a wistful smile on her face. "I argued a lot if you catch my drift." She winks.

Ledger coughs through his laugh, and I want to pretend I didn't hear my gran just say she was good in bed. Clearly, she's having more than just a good day today.

"Sure. I guess my question can be classified as about love in a sense."

"Goody." If she could rub her two hands together in anticipation, I'm sure she would be.

"There's this girl," he says. I immediately shake my head in response to Ledger Sharpe asking my grandmother for love advice about me. Because that's what he's about to do, isn't he? The glance he gives me partnered with the sly smile is all I need to see to know I'm right.

"What about her?" Gran asks.

"We haven't seen each other in a long time."

"Did you do something wrong to her? To hurt her?"

Ledger hangs his head for a beat to look at where he's playing with a checker piece. "The more time that passes, the less I know the answer to that question," he murmurs before looking up and directly at me. My breath hitches and my pulse starts to race. "Everything I thought was certain didn't feel so certain anymore once I saw her again."

"So you have seen her again then?" Gran asks, and Ledger finally breaks his gaze from mine to look at her as he nods. "Force her to talk to you. Tell her your side." Gran pats his hand in sympathy. "Easy."

"Not so easy. She refuses to talk to me about the past."

Gran smiles wistfully, almost as if she's remembering something from her own memory, before looking back at him. "Pin the girl down and kiss her. That'll remind her exactly of who you are and what you had. Then I'm certain she'll stop and listen."

A smile slowly crawls onto Ledger's lips. "You think that will work?" he asks Gran but holds my gaze, arching one brow.

"I do," she murmurs.

"I disagree," I say, trying to break up this little tête-à-tête. "If she's angry at you, she's angry at you and you don't have any right to invalidate that anger."

Ledger chews the inside of his cheek as he leans back in his chair. "No one's invalidating anything."

I snort and roll my eyes as Gran does her best to narrow hers at me. "Did you ever try to get in touch with her over the years? To talk to her?"

Ledger nods, and I immediately reject his response. *I lived it. I was there*, I want to shout at him. "There are two sides to every story, Asher."

His gaze pins me in place. The teenager I used to know wasn't as in control of his emotions as the man is before me.

But his jaw tics and his eyes swim with challenge.

"Okay, everyone," the activity director says to the room. There's shuffling and murmuring as heads turn to look her way. "We're going to move into the sunroom for a bit now and watch a movie."

Gran rolls her eyes before looking at Ledger. "Thank you for spending time with me." She pats his arm. "Maybe one day Asher here will find a nice man like you. We used to say to keep her honest, but I'd rather he kept her on her toes."

"The pleasure is all mine," Ledger says, reaching out and patting the top of her hand.

Gran blinks several times as she looks at him before turning to me. "I'm really tired." Her face falls a little and I can sense her starting to fade, as she often does. This is when the cognitive decline becomes apparent and for her own dignity's sake, I rise immediately so she's not embarrassed by it.

"Perfect time to rest then while everyone else watches the movie."

She nods slightly, her lack of words telling me her downward spiral is coming fast. Within moments, I have her favorite nurse helping her to her room for some privacy with a promise to put the game away and come kiss her goodbye after she's settled.

The minute she is out of earshot, I turn to find Ledger studying me. I'm annoyed with him, and I'm honestly not sure why.

Is it because he stole some of my time with Gran? No. That can't be it, because look how lively he made her.

Is it because I'm jealous that he was able to do for her what I wasn't able to?

Yes. No. Maybe.

All I know is, he has been nowhere for fifteen years and now, all of a sudden, he's freaking everywhere—in my town, in my thoughts, in an assisted living facility for God's sake.

I square my shoulders and head back to the table where he still sits.

"Thanks for amusing Gran. That was nice of you, but you can go now. She won't be coming back out for some time." The smile I offer him is strained. I then pick up the checker pieces and board.

"That's all you've got for me, Ash? Shame, I don't think Gran would be very receptive to such hostility." Why does he say things like that with a smile? One that says I'm being ridiculous, and he's not annoyed or fazed or anything in the least?

"And I don't think she'd be receptive if she knew who you really were," I grit out as I close the box on the checkers and head to the game closet down the hallway without looking back at him.

I don't realize my mistake until I'm at the far end of the long, narrow walk-in type closet, and his footsteps sound behind me. I put the game on the shelf in its place and turn to find Ledger standing there, his broad shoulders eating up the small space.

"What are you doing here, Ledge?"

"Talking to you." There's that disarming, *I'm not doing anything wrong but annoying you* grin again.

I blow out an exasperated sigh. "No. I mean *here*. At the facility. In this closet. *Here*."

"Talking to you," he repeats.

"Well, I only talked to you because of Gran. Now she's gone, so I don't have to be polite anymore."

"So that means you don't want to talk about what happened?" He takes a step closer to me.

"No. I told you I didn't. Let it go."

"Only if you will."

He's trapped me in my own words. If I let the past go, then I have no reason to be angry with him and every right to want that kiss he almost gave me—and that I've thought about *way too much*.

"Go away," I mutter. He steps closer to me and reaches out to play with a strand of hair that's fallen over my shoulder.

"*Pin the girl down and kiss her*. Weren't those Gran's words?" he murmurs.

The space closes in all around us. I shift to get out of the confined space and his undeniable presence that eats it up.

He's close.

Too close.

I can see the flecks of gold in his eyes. Feel the warmth of his breath whispering over my lips. Feel his fingertips as they release my lock of hair and trail ever so softly down my bare arm.

My nipples harden.

He's the one who walked away and didn't look back.

My fingers itch to touch.

He's the one who broke your heart.

My mind wants to forget.

Walk away, Ash.

He leans forward. The hitch of my breath fills the room. "This isn't over, Asher. Not by a long shot. I'm not a patient man, but I've waited fifteen years to kiss you again . . . what's a few more days?"

A lifetime.

He cups the side of my face and runs his thumb over my bottom lip. It's a simple act and yet his touch alone ignites every nerve ending in my body. His eyes are on mine, asking, wanting, pleading.

"Ash," he whispers, and my heart leaps. *My name on his lips.* Is it possible to miss a sound? If so, I didn't realize how much I did until right now.

He leans in as time suspends and—

"In the game closet." We jump apart seconds before the orderly, who I presume made that statement, clears the doorway and walks into said closet. Ledger coughs into his hand to hide his smile.

"Mr. Sharpe?"

"Yes," he says, turning to face her as I continue fussing with the box of checkers as if the lid of the box isn't on properly. My heart's hammering rapidly, and I'm not sure if it's because of him or my fear that one of Gran's caretakers might think I'm fooling around in here.

"Helen wanted to ask you a few more questions since she saw you were still here," the orderly says, referring to the facility director.

"Great." He smiles. "I'll be happy to answer them." He takes a few steps toward the door before looking back at me. Mischief sparks in his eyes. "Community outreach."

"What?"

"What I'm doing here. Community outreach." His eyes run up and down the entire length of my body, and I swear I can almost *feel* his gaze as he does.

And without another word, he walks out of the closet leaving me staring after him.

My fingers automatically go to my lips wishing he'd kissed me. Wishing I knew what he tasted like. Wanting to be reminded what it felt like again.

Ledger Sharpe was a caring lover the first and only time we were together.

Was that just because it was the first time? Is he still like that with the added finesse of years of practice?

I lean against the wall and bury my head in my hands.

When have I ever thought shit like this?

Go away, Ledger.

Go away and leave me to my boring life and unpredictable, sometimes fulfilling sex life.

I'm supposed to be angry at you.

I'm supposed to stick to my guns.

But, Jesus.

You're better than the memory of you ever was.

CHAPTER ELEVEN

Ledger

With a sigh, I pull into the driveway of my rental. It's simple, with its basic gray clapboard siding and flowers lining the path to the front door, but like I told Ford, it could be way worse.

But there's a reason I'm sitting in my car staring at the house. And it happens to be the same reason I drove back and forth down Main Street twice on the way home.

Asher.

The woman has eluded me. I went to the farm the other day, but when I knocked on the door, there was no answer. Then on the way home just now, I thought I saw her walking on the sidewalk and talking to someone in front of the hardware store. I figured I'd make a convenient stop and "accidentally" run into her, since I can't get her out of my head. But on the second pass by, I was clearly seeing things that weren't there.

You're losing it, Ledge.

"Clearly small-town life is making you crazy," I mutter as I climb out and around to my passenger door to grab my laptop and files.

"Hi."

I jump at the sound of the high-pitched voice behind me. When I turn, I'm met with a little girl about seven or eight—fuck if I know since kids aren't exactly in my wheelhouse. She has a pair of uneven, blond pigtails, black-framed glasses over a freckled nose, a box in her hands, and jeans with holes in the knees.

She stands and stares expectantly at me as if she's waiting for me to speak.

"Uh, hi." I look around to see if her mom or dad are around. "Can I help you?"

She twists her lips and narrows her eyes for a beat. I'm being sized up by a kid. Fucking perfect.

"I brought you cookies," she finally says, pushing the box toward me. "But I'm not sure if you like cookies because they are made with flour, chocolate, sugar, and real butter. You know, non-organic, gluten-filled crap."

Stifling a chuckle, I take the box from her and lift the lid to look inside. *Not bad.* "I'm from New York. Not California. I like all that *crap.* Thanks." I tip the box at her in a thank-you gesture, but she doesn't get the hint and move out of the way.

"New York, huh?" Her hands go to her hips. "Exciting stuff. Is it true there are rats in the sewers the size of alligators there?"

"Probably. It's the people you have to watch out for more than anything. They're the real rats who will eat you alive." *Come on, kid. Move along.*

"My mom told me you might be brusque and rude."

I do a double take. "She did? Why's that?"

"She said you wear a suit, are from the city, and probably don't have a personality worth talking to as a result of having the life sucked out of you from sitting behind the glass walls of a skyscraper all day."

I cough over my laugh. "But you're talking to me, right?"

"I am . . . but I haven't decided if I like you yet."

"Good to know." This kid is pretty spectacular. She'd fit in perfectly in Manhattan.

"Apparently the clean air we have here, plus getting a little dirt on your shoes, will make you nicer. Maybe." We both glance down at my shoes. "No dirt."

"I guess I'm still rude, then."

"I won't tell if you don't," she whispers and offers me a grin with a missing front tooth.

"What's your name?" I ask.

"I'm Tootie."

"Tootie?"

"Yep. It's short for Trudy because who names a kid Trudy these days? So I made up my own version of it that suits me better."

I feel like I'm talking to a thirty-year-old with her matter-of-fact statements, but that little giggle she gives reaffirms I'm not. "I think Tootie fits you perfectly." I smile at her. "Now if you'll excuse me, I need to get some work done."

"Do you have a girlfriend?" she asks as I step past her.

"Excuse me?"

"You know, a woman that comes over and then sneaks out about the time that school starts, and Mom tells me not to stare at her or ask why she's not wearing any shoes."

"Jesus Christ."

"If I can't say fuck, then you can't say Jesus Christ."

I open my mouth to speak but am at a loss for words as I glance around again for any parent concerned where their child is. "Um, Tootie? Does your mom know where you are? Shouldn't you be doing homework or something?"

"First, homework is a thing of the past. Some brilliant person declared it to be busy work and decided to free us kids from its shackles." She flashes a grin. "And second, Mom is inside on the phone telling all of her friends about you."

"Yay for no homework." It's all I can manage to say before Tootie continues.

"She said you have a nice butt, but you seem a little uptight. That she wouldn't mind kicking your tires—whatever that means." But her ghost of a smile tells me she thinks she knows exactly what it means. And regardless of how much I want to laugh, I'm a little uncomfortable having this conversation with a kid. "Oh, and she gives you two weeks before you run back to the city because you can't handle things here."

"Two weeks? That's all? Good to know." I glance at the house next door where Tootie pointed and see a woman standing in the window with a cell phone to her ear suddenly move out of sight. "It's probably best if you don't tell her that you told me that part about kicking my tires."

"Okay. Then I guess I should also leave out the part where I tell you that we didn't really bake these cookies ourselves. Mom bought them from Cedar's Bakery so she had an excuse to come over here and talk to you herself. Guess I ruined that plan."

"I'm glad that you did."

"Is it true you're here to fuck up our town?"

Christ. I cough over my laugh. "Who told you that?"

"Everybody who means nothing." She shrugs and, somehow, I completely understand what she means. "It's like adults can't ever make up their minds. They want more jobs in town but complain when someone like you tries to make them. They want more people to visit but then complain when there's traffic, or they have to wait too long for a table to eat at Bessie's Diner. You adults are *super* confusing."

"We are, aren't we?"

"For sure." She gives a definitive nod that has her pigtails bouncing. "So, are you?"

"Am I what? Messing up the town?"

"No. I don't care. It's not like it matters to me. I meant are you going to Connor's too?"

"Who's Connor?" My head spins with her constant change in topics. And also, why is everything in this town named after somebody?

"The man who owns Connor's," she says as if I'm an idiot.

My patience for talking to little people is about done. My sigh says as much and she just puts her hands on her hips to say the same. "What is Connor's?"

"It's where all the adults go to act funny and dance and . . . kiss." She shudders. "Sometimes when Mom has to pick up friends from there, I get to go inside for a second. I can't wait to be a grown-up."

"Huh."

"Yep. Huh," she repeats. "Time to go cause more trouble."

She skips down the sidewalk toward her house. "Hey, Tootie?" I ask so that she stops and turns to look at me. "Do you know an Asher Wells?"

Brilliant, Ledger. Ask an eight-year-old about her.

"Why?" She narrows her eyes at me.

"It's a long story." I give her a half-smile while feeling like an idiot. "I was just wondering if you did."

Tootie angles her head to the side as she thinks. "The purple lady?"

"Lavender?"

"Same thing." She rolls her eyes. "Yep. I know her."

The kid runs at the mouth and the minute I want her to talk, she clams up. Fucking par for the course for me today.

"That's all you're going to give me?"

She squints at me as if she's figuring out if she wants to tell me more or not. Almost as if she's protective of the people who live here from out-siders like me.

I can respect that.

"She's nice if that's what you want to know. And super pretty. My momma is jealous of her legs but not jealous about what people say about her."

"What do people say about her?"

She shrugs as if she doesn't know, but I do. *Christ.* Even after all these years it still seems Asher Wells is still being judged for her mother's pro-miscuity and reputation.

"We had a field trip to her pop's farm last year to learn about growing and stuff. Peter Doocey didn't listen and got in trouble for trying to pants Dylan Abernathy. There was a big to-do over it. Pop was nice. He even gave us ice cream and didn't care if it dripped when we ate it."

"Ice cream is always good."

"He's dead, you know. Died around C.J.'s birthday. That made me sad so I can't imagine how it made Asher feel. Probably way more sadder than me. Momma sent flowers to her but was angry over what she paid for on the Internet versus what was actually sent. It was a whole thing that I don't care to get into." She rolls her eyes and gives a shake of her head. "I wonder if we have another field trip there if Asher would be the one to give us the tour?"

"Maybe."

"Mom said hi to her in town the other day, but don't worry, they're not close enough for her to call her on the phone and talk about how fine your butt is. She only does that to Lacey."

"Good to know." I give a quick shake of my head. "Thanks."

"Connor's."

"What about it?"

"Are you going? She'll probably be there tomorrow night. It's the place to be on music night."

"Thanks for the info."

"Yep. No problemo." She flashes a mischievous grin and a wave before skipping away.

Really, Ledger?

You just asked a kid you barely know about a woman you want to know more.

You do seriously need help.

CHAPTER TWELVE

Asher

I NO LONGER STUDY THE FACE OF EVERY MAN IN CEDAR FALLS.

It took me a long time to get to that point, where I stopped comparing my nose with theirs, the shape or color of my eyes, or the curve of my mouth.

And I've learned to live with the silence and cold shoulders from the older women in town. The ones who wonder if I'm the bastard child their husband had when he cheated on them or had a torrid affair with the town floozy before they were married. The ones who fear my mom will someday come back, fill in the "father" portion of my birth certificate, and ruin their happily ever after.

Then there's the notion of siblings. Do I have a half-sister or half-brother? Do I have more than one? Am I friends with them? Do I dislike them?

I learned to stop obsessing over it a long time ago.

And yes, the odd stares and quiet murmurs have dissipated over the years, only to be stirred up when someone new moves into town and the Cedar Falls Stepford Wives step in to fill them in on everyone's business. But it doesn't make living life in this small town any easier. Reputations stick to last names even if you were simply born into it without a choice.

The upside to it all? It's freeing in a sense. People already have their opinions about me, so why not live my life and enjoy myself while I'm at it?

If I flirt openly with a man, then looks are exchanged suggesting I'm just like my mom. If I hide from the world and keep to The Fields, then it appears I'm ashamed of who I am.

I'm neither.

I'm simply me. The me that Gran and Pop loved and cherished and tried to be parents, grandparents, and friends to so I wouldn't do without.

And fuck the assholes of this town for judging and ostracizing me for something I had no control over. It's been thirty-two years, people, so get over it.

Just like Judy Jensen needs to right now from her seat on the other side of the bar in Connor's Tavern. It's not my fault her boyfriend pursued me last year. I told him no, time and time again. But the trouble he caused gave me the stigma that I'm a homewrecker against all rational logic.

Like mother, like daughter in their eyes.

The music is low and the chatter is loud, so I just smile and wave cattily to Judy to let her know I see her shooting daggers my way.

"She's such a bitch," Nita says as she slides onto the barstool across from me.

"She is. Her problem, not mine."

"You want to know what else is a problem?" Nita asks, but the mischief in her eyes tells me something is going on.

"What?"

"You sitting here, checking the door every few seconds to see if a certain someone is going to walk through it."

"You're so full of shit."

"You didn't deny it," she says with a knowing smile.

She's right. I didn't, because I have been checking the door every time it opens, both wanting and not wanting Ledger to walk through it.

Our almost-kiss from the other day is etched in my mind, replaying on a loop.

"It's not a crime to want to see him."

"Clearly," I say.

"And it's okay to wonder if the chemistry is still there, which . . . for the record, it is."

"Thank you for the observation." I take another sip of my wine and stare at Judy until she looks away again. "I have chemistry with a lot of people. Besides, isn't it normal to still have it with someone you've been attracted to in the past?"

"Not so sure on that one. Nice try, though. In my personal experience, I'd rather stab my exes with a fork in their eyes when I'm done with them, not stand in a game closet and lie when you tell him you don't want to be kissed."

"It was not a lie."

"Whatever you say," she says, clearly not believing me.

And she shouldn't. Because no matter how many times I tell myself I don't want him, I'm still pulled right back into that connection with Ledger we had years ago when I see him.

"Look, it's completely okay to forgive him for whatever his father did that night. We don't blame kids for their parents' actions, right?" She lifts her eyebrows, unknowingly tapping into the thoughts I was just having.

All I can do is shake my head. "Touché."

"And if you believe the flip side of the coin and that Ledger did, in fact, cheat on you, play you, what have you, you can always chalk it up to the past and forgive him." She smiles wide and waves to someone over my shoulder before turning her attention back on me. "You guys were young. Naïve. I don't know. People change with experience. They mature and become more considerate."

"Are you sure we live in the same town because a lot of these people here haven't gotten any better—in any respect—with age."

"True." She laughs and holds her hands up in acknowledgment. "I stand corrected."

"At least you admit it," I say.

"I do, so long as you understand that it's completely okay to want to take Ledger up on his offer to catch up. To talk. The two of you can be Cedar Falls outcasts together."

"Funny."

"I try to be." She flashes me a dazzling smile.

"Why are we having this conversation again?" I groan. "Haven't we talked about this ad nauseum?"

"Then stop mind-fucking *it* and fuck *him* instead."

I choke on my sip of wine. "Way to be blunt."

"Is there any other way to be?" She dazzles me with a smile. "How about I be even more blunt?"

"I have a feeling it doesn't matter if I say yes or no because you're going to say it anyway."

"Glad we're on the same page." She gives a definitive nod and then chuckles. Oh, she's definitely starting to feel her wine as much as I am. "So here's the thing. If you want to continue to hate him as you have every right and are so desperately trying to do . . . then girl, let's just admit that there is nothing wrong with a good, angry, hate fuck."

"Jesus." I try not to spit out my wine. I was not expecting her to go there. But then again, it is Nita. She holds nothing back.

"What? Are you telling me that a bout of hate fucking isn't good for the soul? The back-scratching, shoulder-nipping, skin-bruising variety of sex?" She mock shudders in pleasure. "It's invigorating. Primal. *Incredible.* Maybe that's exactly what you need to get over this hump and . . . I don't know. Forgive him. Write him off. Use him as he used you."

I absolutely hate myself for picturing what she's saying. For imagining his lips on mine and that deep tenor of his voice groaning my name. For being turned on by it. For wondering what Ledger's like in bed. Because with age comes practice and . . . yes, now I'm definitely wondering.

"You're delusional," I say despite my body's visceral reaction.

"Perhaps, but you know I'm right."

"Well . . ." I say and give her a look saying I can't argue with her, which prompts us both to burst into laughter.

"There is another option too."

"What? The option that this conversation is ludicrous and you're out of your mind?"

"You have deflection down to an art form. It's really rather admirable."

I know she means well, but Ledger has already taken up too much free rent in my head since that night at Hank's. I've run every scenario through my mind. I've rationalized and justified and tried to understand how I can still desire a man who hurt me so deeply. It has to simply be physical attraction, right? Because we're nowhere near the same people we were years ago.

Stop saying the past is the past, Ash, if you keep dredging it up.

My only conclusion has been that it's probably best to keep him at arm's length. Self-preservation at its finest.

At least, that's my current theory.

And at the end of the day, the decision to sleep or not to sleep with someone is mine regardless of how hot Nita's description of it might be. Sure, Ledger is incredibly attractive. Yes, there is no question about our chemistry. But he lives in New York City, and I still live in Cedar Falls.

That one fact hasn't changed over time.

Then there's the fact that if we were to . . . act on this tension vibrating between us, it would merely be a fling. That's all it could be. Call it self-preservation or learning from past mistakes, but I simply don't have time for a fling. Not one I already know will hurt me in the end.

Plus, I prefer to not give the Judy Jensens of this town more fodder for their gossip. The rich city guy choosing me and not one of them just might push them over their pretentious edges.

"Yoo-hoo. You still with me?" Nita asks as she passes her hand back and forth in front of my face.

"Yes. Sorry. Just thinking about something I forgot to do today," I lie.

"*Like Ledger?*" She laughs at her own joke while I roll my eyes. "I still think you should call him."

"Maybe," I say for the sake of ending this discussion.

"Now's as good of a time as any." Nita looks at my cell phone on the table and lifts her eyebrows.

"Tomorrow's an even better one."

We both burst out laughing. "You're being ridiculous."

"I know I am, Nita," I say, rising from the table and enveloping her in a hug from behind. "But is it so wrong that I want to sit here with my best friend, drink till I'm tipsy, and dance with some random man who'll probably step on my toes more times than not? Uncomplicated is my goal for tonight. I've had a shitty week, and I want to stop dwelling on the fact that the one and only man I've ever let break my heart is somewhere in this town tonight. Maybe I'll call him. Maybe I won't. But the one thing I know for sure is I want another glass of wine, and then we'll go from there."

"Whoa, girl. Take a breath." Nita laughs. "Anything else you need to get off your impressively cleavage-ridden chest tonight?"

"Nope." I sit back down beside her and emit an audible exhale. "But it felt good to get it all out."

"To manifest it?"

"Something like that," I say and take another sip of wine. My buzz is just within reach, and it's something I welcome wholeheartedly.

"There is one problem with your line of thinking though," Nita says, giving a nod to Connor as the fresh drinks are delivered to our table.

"What's that?"

"You know there are no *random* men in Cedar, right? We know every single one of them."

"That's true. Then I'll rephrase and say dance with a harmless man. Does that work?"

"It does. Harmless is good. I just might look for one to occupy my—ahem—*time* tonight as well."

"Oh really? Is that so?"

"Yep." Her grin widens. "Miller is spending the night at my mom's tonight, and I do not have to work either job tomorrow. So I'm childless with no one to take care of and have nowhere I need to be by a certain time tomorrow. It's glorious."

"And a rarity." My smile softens as I meet her eyes. Being a single mother isn't easy, but I've never heard her complain once. She loves her son and their life despite doing it all on her own. "You most definitely deserve some of that back-scratching sex more than I do."

"Amen, sister." She gives me a high five and then startles. "Uh-oh. I think you're going to win the race to being horizontal."

"What are you talking about?"

"There's a man standing at the end of the bar right now giving you the eye."

Ledger.

Why is he my first thought? And even worse, why, when I turn to look where Nita is motioning, am I disappointed that the man looking my way isn't him? Instead, it's Carson Allen.

Of course, it is.

"Carson's always giving me the eye." I roll my eyes at her before looking back at him and waving.

"That man has loved you ever since you backed into his car six years ago," she murmurs as he starts to make his way through the crowd.

"I think he should take that as a reason why he shouldn't like me."

"But he's funny and harmless. You could do worse."

"*I have done worse.*"

Nita belts out a laugh as Carson approaches our table, his smile wide and laughter already on his lips.

CHAPTER THIRTEEN

Ledger

"THE DEAL IS ON THE TABLE, HIRO. THREE HUNDRED MIL," I say, moving about my office. My inability to stand still while being on the phone drives my brothers crazy.

"I understand, Ledger, but Takashi isn't going to budge."

Fucking Takashi trying to play hardball when he doesn't know that's my favorite way to play.

"He's not going to budge? That's a mistake and you know it." My chuckle is low and taunting as I run a hand through my hair and stare out the darkened window. "Three hundred is a more than fair evaluation. Your property is aging, your traffic is down, and Takashi has undermined it by using its equity to leverage his Tokyo project."

"How did—"

"Yes. I know about that. I assure you I'm more than thorough in my research before jumping into negotiations." I pause for effect. "No stone is left unturned. It's important to know what I'm jumping into before I make the first phone call to express interest."

Yes, Hiro, I know everything about everything. Like his affair with his assistant. Like how he's using some of the equity in the property we want to pay off his gambling debts.

Yes, I know he has no other choice than to sell.

His silence tells me my message was heard.

"I'm not in the business of lowballing people. This is a more than fair evaluation that he won't get from anyone else."

"Understood." His voice is a little less steady now. It's also more than bullshit that Takashi isn't speaking to me himself. No doubt he's standing beside him, listening to this whole conversation, too chickenshit to deal with me himself. Hiro clears his throat. "He'll have a decision for you by the end of the week."

"No. He'll have a decision for me by the end of the hour or the deal is off the table. Talk soon." I hang up without letting him respond.

Always negotiate from a place of power.

My father's words come back to me. My smile is bittersweet, the pang in my chest still raw.

He was a hard man. Demanding. Unmalleable. He loved his sons with all his heart, but he definitely expected perfection. And for reasons I had no control over, he expected it the most from me. I was his firstborn. I was the most like him.

I don't know the reason, but some days I loathed it, others I understood it. Regardless, it made me the man I am today, so I have to respect it.

And I'm not going to lie, the high I get from negotiating a purchase like this new project in Tokyo is pretty damn spectacular.

Even if it means my plans for the night to go to Connor's and see if Asher is there were thwarted.

It's not like you don't know where she lives, Ledge.

I have an hour to kill waiting for Takashi to respond—and he'll respond with a minute or two to go simply to let me know he's in charge—and a bottle of whiskey in my desk drawer that was a welcome gift from the owner of Cedar Falls Outdoor Adventures to drink while I wait.

At least someone in this town is glad we're here.

I stare at the bottle and then out the window toward the direction of Connor's where I'd prefer to be, and then back to the bottle.

I'm two glasses in when my cell rings. Like I thought, Takashi pushed it till the last minute. I have half a mind to let it go to voicemail and make him sweat it out, but I want this deal done so S.I.N. can move forward.

And so I can cross another item off my list of things I wanted to accomplish: expand the S.I.N. brand into Asia.

"Takashi."

"Sharpe." He doesn't sound happy. Not my problem. When you're the golden boy of one of Japan's biggest tycoons and are about to find yourself in a fire sale to cover your ass, you wouldn't be either.

"I'm assuming you have an answer for me."

His sigh is heavy, his distaste for me palpable. "Yes."

"*Yes?*" Say it, fucker. Say, *we have a deal.*

Another sigh of reluctance. Or distaste. Either one is fine with me. "I accept your offer."

I fist-pump into the empty room, but when I speak, my voice is controlled. "Congratulations, Takashi. I'll have my counsel reach out to yours and get the details situated."

"You gave me no choice," he says.

"No. You gave yourself no choice. I'm just being a smart businessman. I'll be in touch."

I end the call, sit my ass on the edge of my desk, and just take a minute for the acquisition of Miyako-Jima Resort to sink in. *Six months of negotiations. Three visits to Japan.* It will all be worth it though. I fire off a text to Callahan and Ford to let them know the deal is done, but it's late in New York, and I don't expect an answer.

High from the adrenaline rush of clinching a deal that will potentially open the Asian market for S.I.N. investments, I swallow the rest of what's left in my glass. Antsy and with too much energy, I grab my keys and head out the door of the resort.

Fresh air.

That's what I need. Fresh air and yet, my feet don't stop once I'm outside and have found it.

"Done for the night?" Bernie, our site security guard, asks.

"I am."

"It was a late one for you."

"Always is."

"Any plans? The night's still young, you know."

"I do. Thanks." I stop to look at him as if he just made me realize where I already knew I was going. "Have a good night."

It takes me a good fifteen minutes to walk to Connor's. By then, the whiskey's worked its way through my system, keeping me warm and simultaneously spurring me on.

The parking lot is crowded with cars, and the patrons have spilled outside onto the outdoor patio at its rear. It's a large place, and the live music and loud chatter floats out the open windows and hits me from the far side of the parking lot.

The front door has a crowd around it, so I veer around toward the back to avoid it. I'm just about to walk through the small gate that encloses a mixture of low and high tables when I hear a voice.

Asher's voice.

"Knock it off, Carson." I turn to see Asher pushing against the chest of a guy who has a good hundred pounds on her. "*Stop.*"

"C'mon. You've been cock-teasing me all night—hell, *for years,*" he slurs. "Just admit you want me—" The fucker smashes his lips to hers as she tries to struggle out of his grip.

Four strides. That's all it takes for me to cross the distance and get to them.

"Get off her," I shout as I push him away. He shoves me back, but I have my fist cocked and let it fly into the fucker's face before he can say a word.

"Ledger. *No.*" Asher's shout of my name mixes with the *ooof* made by the prick as he stumbles backward and hits the railing behind him.

"Are you okay?" I turn to look at Asher, my one hand out to keep her away and my other toward the guy.

"What are you doing?" she shouts at me as she runs to the man's side. Confusion blankets me. "Carson? *Car?*" Her hands are on his face, her voice full of concern. "Are you okay?"

She wanted him?

Wanted the kiss?

Carson mumbles something, his words garbled as he's clearly shit-faced, before chuckling and bringing a hand to rub over his cheek where my punch landed.

"What were you thinking?" Asher screams as she takes two steps to-ward me.

"He was all over you. He wouldn't—"

"He's harmless. *Fucking harmless.*" She looks from me and then back to Carson, who's clearly unaffected much to my dismay, and then back to me. "He's just . . . *Carson,*" she says in exasperation as if I'm supposed to know what that means.

And as if on cue, Carson's laughter rings out as he looks my way. "S'all good, man. S'all good. I'd fight for her too." He stands and wobbles a bit before stumbling a few feet toward the back entrance of the bar. His words repeat in my head. *I'd fight for her too.* "I need another drink after that." He turns to look at Asher again, smiles sheepishly, and then almost falls off the barstool he's trying to sit down on.

"*You*," Asher says, pointing at me as she stalks toward me, closing the distance between us. Her face is a mask of fury, and it's the most beautiful thing I've ever seen. "How dare you punch him. He's just Carson. Harmless. Friendly." She pushes hard against my chest, and I take a few steps back, more than surprised by her reaction. "Just *him*."

"I was helping you. Saving you."

"Saving me?" she screeches.

Her lips.

"Yes."

Are right there.

"You lost the right to save me, to have anything to do with me, after the night you humiliated me. The night you let me be humil—"

"The night I what?"

"Nothing." She grits the word out. "I don't want to talk about it."

I throw my hands out to my sides as she stands before me, a foot shorter and a ball of ire. The people on the patio are unabashedly paying attention to our fight, but I don't give a fuck. I've thought about this woman all goddamn week, and I'm not walking away this time.

But humiliated her? What in the hell is she talking about?

There is a look in her eyes—a look years ago I would have been able to decipher but that I can't right now. We're strangers. *Strangers.* The thought is fucking killing me when all I want to do is . . .

"Why did you come here tonight, Ledger?" she mutters.

I have a million smart-ass comebacks on my tongue. Every single one will fuel that temper of hers, but for some reason, as I stare at her standing with the moonlight in her hair, I'm reminded of another time, another place, when she looked similar.

My lavender girl.

And I opt for honesty.

"Because when it comes to you, Asher, I can't seem to stay away. I want you. Christ, I want you so fucking bad, and seeing that jerk kissing you just about did me—"

Suddenly her fists are in my shirt and her mouth is slanted over mine. *Thank. Fuck.*

My hands are on her face, my lips are against hers, my tongue seeks hers, without any thought other than *finally*.

Her anger is bitter.

Her desire is sweet.

Both riot against my tongue as my head swims with the taste of Asher Wells.

She kisses me with a hunger and fire that match mine. There's urgency and hesitancy. Desperation and confusion.

There's just her.

Only. Her.

Fucking hell.

She pushes me away with as much determination as I want to keep kissing her. Her chest heaving. Her cheeks flushed. Her eyes wide. "How dare you?" she grits out from lips swollen from mine.

"Dare me?" *What the hell? She initiated the kiss.* "What are you talking about?" *I need more.* "I didn't do a goddamn thing wrong." My chuckle holds no amusement, just utter disbelief.

And the second the words are said, the moment my laugh falls flat, Asher grips my shirt tighter and yanks me down so that her mouth is on mine again.

There are no thoughts but her.

No questions except for how quickly can we be alone?

And time is of the fucking essence.

CHAPTER FOURTEEN

Ledger

I CAN'T SAY THAT I SAW MUCH OF THE INSIDE OF CONNOR'S AS WE pushed our way toward the first open door and empty space we came to, but I'll thank who the fuck ever Connor is for having clean bathrooms and plenty of sturdy counter spaces.

Because the place doesn't matter right now.

Only the moment does.

We're on each other the minute the door slams at our backs, and I reach with one hand to lock it.

Our lips and our hands are in a battle to prove which one of us can claim more.

I've never felt like this before. The need. The want. The goddamn all-consuming desire. It owns me. It fuels me. It drowns me in everything that is Asher Wells.

The faint trace of salt on her neck as I lick my tongue up its line. The sound of her mewls as I grab her ass and grind against her. The taste of her kiss—it's wine and hunger and . . . everything I craved but never knew I needed.

I pull her tank top up and one cup of her bra down, eager to feel her skin. Impatient to suck on the pink of her nipple and make her moan.

And fuck does she taste good when I dip my head and do just that.

"Ledger," she begs between kisses.

My cock aches in that painfully pleasureful way where the anticipation owns my every action and reaction.

Her.

I just need her.

To be in her.

To have her.

To fucking claim her.

And when I shove my pants down my hips and she wraps her hands around my cock, my eyes roll back in my head and a groan falls from my lips.

Jesus.

If her hand on my cock renders me momentarily incapacitated, what is the feel of her pussy wrapped around me going to do?

"Asher." A nip on her lips. Another step backward to the counter. "God, yes." She strokes her hand up and over the crest of my dick, smearing the drop on the tip.

I've never wanted somebody so goddamn bad in my life and, as much as my mind tells me to slow down—to revel in the softness of her body, the curve of her hips, the high everything about her gives me—my libido says *fuck that.*

It focuses on the heat of her pussy as I slide my fingers under her skirt and between her thighs. Christ, she's soaking.

It fixates on her heavy-lidded eyes locked on mine as she takes a step back with her skirt hiked up around her hips and one breast still exposed and shoves those panties down and off one ankle.

It obsesses over the scent of her—her flowery perfume mixed with her undeniable arousal—and I know from here on out, every time I smell roses, I'll also smell her.

It concentrates on the way she scoots her ass back on the ledge of the counter, braces her hands behind her, spreads her thighs, and gives me the most beautiful goddamn sight I've ever seen. Asher Wells, open, wet, and waiting for me.

I slip the condom on without breaking stride, my gaze never leaving her—from her eyes firing with desire, to her lips bruised from my kisses, to the glistening pink of her pussy.

She's fucking perfection.

And when she reaches out to grab my cock and guide it into her, I know I'm a lost goddamn cause.

Because one push in, the first sensation of her squeezing around me, and I won't be able to stop until I'm panting and emptied.

"Now. Right now." She writhes her hips against me so that my tip just enters her. "*Please.*"

Done.

With one hand on my cock and the other on the back of her neck, I hold her in place as I push my way into every glorious inch of her.

Jesus. Fucking. Christ.

"*Ash.*" It's all I can manage before I brand my lips to hers in a piss-poor attempt to distract me momentarily.

It doesn't work.

The taste of her.

The feel of her.

Simply put, *her.*

I begin to move.

Slowly at first.

The sweet push in. *God, yes.* The pleasurable pull out. *Don't ever stop.* A thrust back in. *Harder.* A grind against her. *Ledger.*

Her mouth meets mine again. The frenzy of our kiss before has nothing on the violent desire this time. Her teeth nip and her nails scrape.

And I'm lost.

To the moment.

To her.

I dig my fingers into her hips to hold her still while I lose all control.

The pace I set is punishing and yet her murmurs, her moans, her tightening of her muscles around me, egg me on in a way I've never known.

My mind goes blank. My balls draw tight. My cock swells and hardens.

And for a few seconds, I'm in that tumbling freefall of pleasure that hurts so good it edges on painful as I thrust into her over and over and empty every last ounce of myself into her.

I'm exhausted. I'm exhilarated. I already want to do it all over again.

She's like that first hit of cocaine. One taste, and you're addicted.

That's the only thing I can compare it to. *Her to.*

My forehead is on her shoulder. Her legs are wrapped around my waist. Our hearts beat a violent staccato against one another's.

The rasp of our labored breathing fills the space, only second to the sounds of the bar filtering in through the locked door.

Fucking Christ. I try and shake the fog of climax—*the haze of*

Asher—from my head, but I have a feeling she's always been there somehow, in some way.

This wasn't exactly how I wanted this to happen, a quick fuck in a bar bathroom. But I saw that asshole with his hands on her and then her anger toward me and . . . *and then she kissed me.*

I lean back, brace my hands on the counter on either side of her thighs, and look up to find her staring at me, expression hidden by the dimness of the room. It's as if the sexual tension has been temporarily sated, and now we're left in that awkward space where the past may be the past, but it sure as hell can't continue to be ignored.

"Asher . . ." I don't even know where to start. How to start.

Her smile is soft, but her body language reads differently. Almost as if she's uncertain. Almost as if she regrets what just happened.

How do I move us forward?

"I promise I'll be better at it next time."

The flash of recognition in her eyes tells me she remembers. That line. That night. Standing by my truck under the moonlight.

Her lips curl up in a bittersweet smile. There is a depth to the emotion in her eyes and, sure as hell, as I stare at her, I can see her guard go back up and lock into place.

It's in the quick avoidance of her eyes and the lowering of her legs so she can hop off the counter and put some physical distance between us. I study her as she moves about the small space, confused.

She kissed me first.

She initiated the events that led to this.

"You take all the girls to bathrooms on the first date?" She tries to the sell the joke with a forced laugh as she shoves her panties in her purse and smooths down her skirt with her hands.

"I apologize. This"—I point to the space around us—"isn't exactly how I imagined this happening."

"Don't apologize. We got it out of the way, right? Now we can move on." Asher pulls her purse strap over her shoulder and heads toward the door.

The high I'm on crashes.

"What? Asher. Wait." I have my hand on her arm and spin her so she's forced to look at me. "What are you doing?"

"Leaving without saying goodbye." She lifts a brow and tries to shrug out of my grasp. "Isn't that what we do best when it comes to each other?"

I do a double take, her words cutting deep.

"We need to talk about what happened. *That night.*"

"I told you I don't want to."

"And I don't give a flying fuck," I shout at her, done with the cat and mouse game between us. "We need to talk."

"Why?" she asks, her voice low and even, her emotions so much more controlled than mine. "Do you really want to hear about it? Do you really want to know I cried for weeks and weeks after you left without saying a word? Do you want to know what it was like giving a person what I gave you and then to be treated like I never existed?"

"Asher." Her name is a plea. An apology. An . . . I don't know, but every ounce of hurt woven in the thread of her voice is because of me. *It's my fault.*

I'd fight for her too.

But I didn't. Isn't that the crux of this whole thing? I was scared and worried about myself. I was fearful of my father and the consequences of Pop's threats. Sure, I worried about her and the pain I felt over losing her—our friendship, our plans—but my hands were tied.

But she had to have known that.

Had to have understood why I didn't respond to her direct messages on social media.

"What? Is that too hard to hear for you? To know how much leaving me devastated seventeen-year-old me?" Her shoulders shudder as she draws in a breath. "How about how your father crushed my self-esteem, shredded it to pieces along with everything I wanted to be in order to keep me away from you? Or what about how I was deemed the town's slutty gold digger who was trying to get pregnant by you simply for a payday?" I stand before her staggered. Dumbfounded. And she must read my expression as something else because she gives a quick shake of her head as if she's done with me. "You know what? Never mind. It's not fucking worth it." She tries to jerk her arm from my grip, but I only squeeze it tighter.

The night you let me be humiliated.

"My father?" I ask. I fear the answer will rock my world for the second time in a matter of seconds but in a completely different way than Asher just did.

"He came to the farm that night out of the blue. Confronted Pop. They argued. I heard, and when I went out there to see what was going on, he told me . . ."

"He told you what?" I demand, wanting to pull the words out of her. But I don't because I fear what she's going to say.

"He said you got what you wanted from me and were already out with the next girl." Her voice is barely a whisper as fury simmers inside of me in a way I've never felt before.

"What else? What else did he say?" I yell, hating her flinch when my voice raises.

"He must have seen our texts. He knew everything that had happened that night. *About us.* Knew what we had planned after . . ."

Our blanket under the stars. How terrified I was, fearing I'd hurt her with it being her first time. The tears swimming in her eyes afterward as she told me she loved me. How we swore we'd find a way to be together soon.

That moment with her is crystal clear, but everything that happened later that night, which has been a blur for so long, slowly comes into focus.

"Wait a minute." My head spins, and I walk away from her as I try to rationalize the exact opposite of everything I've been told. Of the things I thought to be true. Of the truths I've believed for years. My stomach turns and my heart races. "He told you I cheated on you and you believed it?"

"I was seventeen and my world had just crashed down around me. I didn't know what to believe," she screeches, voice escalating and hands clenching. "What was I to do when an imposing figure like your father shows up and tells my Pop I better stay away from you. That I wasn't good enough for you, nor would I ever be. That he wouldn't stand for a girl like me to ruin the bright future he had planned for his perfectly *pedigreed* son. And then when I stood up to him, when I told him he was crazy, he dropped the second bomb. That you got what you wanted from me and had already moved on with someone else. That's where you were at that moment."

"That's not true, Ash. You have to believe—"

"It doesn't matter now. It might have back then . . . but it still wouldn't have lessened the sting of me being a *motherless, penniless girl* who better stay away from you, *or else.*" A single tear slides down her cheek and effectively cuts through me too.

Pedigree.

That's what she was referring to that night at Hank's.

That's what has haunted her and what she's harbored for years—and for good reason.

I hate myself for the tears that spring in her eyes. For the hurt that fills them. For things I don't even think I can begin to understand yet.

There's nothing I can do.

There's nothing I can say.

The man I loved and respected more than anything in the world lied to me. *Lied to her.*

I stare at Asher and see pieces of the girl I used to love. I also see the hurt my father caused reflected in the eyes of the woman she is now.

Needing to touch her, to soothe her, simply for my own selfish reasons, I step into her, frame her face, and use my thumb to brush the tear away. Her eyelashes flutter at my touch, her breath hitches in response.

"They were lies, Asher. All lies." My chest hurts and emotion burns in my throat as I pull her against me and wrap my arms around her. "I don't even know what to say."

A Sharpe man's words hurt her before. *Humiliated her.* I only hope she'll let another's words comfort her now.

She doesn't move at first. She stands frozen as if she's afraid to touch, afraid to believe me.

Asher was always like that. Physical connection was easy for her. It was the emotional side of her that she held on to. The side she locked away from the world, too afraid to be hurt again, given her mother's abandonment.

Even I understood that at age eighteen, and I understand it even more now.

At the same time, I hurt for her. I hurt for me. Have I believed a lie from the same man who manipulated her?

I don't want to believe it to be true.

I don't want to think my father purposely hurt me like that.

Sometimes people do crazy things to protect the ones they love, son.

Weren't those his words that night? His explanation for what Pop threatened? Or was it his sick justification for what he was doing?

Nothing makes sense right now.

Fucking nothing.

And just as I acknowledge that thought, Asher finally wraps her arms around me and simply holds on. She fits there perfectly, just like she used to. Just like I remember.

I breathe in everything about her. The warmth of her breath against my chest. The subtle shudder of her shoulders. The coconut scent of her shampoo.

We're standing here together, yet I feel a world apart from her.

Helpless.

That's how I feel in regards to the lies my father told Asher.

Furious and confused.

How I feel concerning the ones I'm pretty certain he told me too. Because after what Asher just said, I know there's no way Pop threatened to press charges.

None.

She would have mentioned it. She would have said that Pop pushed back with that accusation.

The part of me that needs an answer on this, pushes it down. She needs to feel validated, not overshadowed. She needs to be heard, not drowned out.

Christ.

What kind of man am I that I just went along with it? That I never questioned what my dad told me? That I walked away from Asher out of fear because of the blind trust I had in my father?

The party goes on beyond the door. People shouting and laughing. But I feel lost.

Like my footing, the foundation that I've built everything on—my father and our relationship—just shifted. And I haven't even begun to process what her peers said about her after we rushed out of Cedar Falls.

Asher's spine slowly stiffens, her muscles tense, and she pushes back from me. Her jaw is set, her eyes guarded. "They may have been lies, Ledger, but you never got in touch with me. No texts. No emails. No letters. You knew exactly where I was, where I lived, and not once did you ever reach out. You can blame your father for the first part, but the second part is on you . . . and that's almost worse."

"There's more to it. There's my side. There's—"

Bang.

We both jump as a fist pounds on the door. "Come on, man. I've got to take a piss."

"Asher. Let's get out of here. I need to explain why. Somewhere that's . . . not a bathroom."

She shakes her head and wipes more tears from her cheeks with the back of her hand, hurt and sorrow etched in the lines of her face.

Another pound. "Open the fucking door."

I take a step toward her and she holds her hand up to stop me. "Don't. *Please.*" Her voice breaks, and I swear the sound echoes through me.

She's shutting down.

She's putting walls up.

"It was a long time ago. It doesn't have to define this, us, seeing each other again. Right now—"

"It defined *me* though." She takes another step back and puts her hands up for me to stop. "Just . . . I need time, Ledger."

"Time for what?"

"Seeing you again. Like this . . . I need to figure out how I feel about it all."

I nod. "So, is this about the past? About the present? About the future? I'm confused."

"Jesus, dude," the voice on the other side of the door says. "I want whatever you took if you're lasting this long."

"Give me a goddamn second, will you?" I turn back to Asher. There's a sadness in her eyes that nearly undoes me.

"This is about me sticking to a promise I made myself, Ledger. To never put myself in a situation to be hurt again. I've had a shitty couple of months. They've almost broken me. I need to figure out how this—you being here, *this* happening tonight—all fits in. How you fit into it. I won't let you be the straw that breaks me again."

"Let me help you then. Let me be there for you. Let me . . . I don't fucking know, but let me do something." Exasperated and feeling desperate to what I feel is slowly slipping through my fingers, I run a hand through my hair and pace the small space, as uncertain about what to do as I am about how I feel.

What is it that you do want here, Ledger? More sex? To resolve the past? To get to know her again? Because you sure as shit don't know a thing about relationships.

But this isn't a relationship. It was sex in a bathroom. It's old feelings and a walk down memory lane. It's a connection between us that feels like it was never broken despite the lies told.

But when I meet her gaze, I know the answer is all of the above and something more that I can't express.

Maybe I want to wipe the sorrow from her eyes.

Maybe I want to hear her laugh more.

Maybe I want to know the woman she's become better.

That much I know is true.

"I don't need your help, Ledger. I can manage on my own. I *have* managed on my own."

"So that's it, then? Some bathroom counter sex and a *thanks for the good time?* There's more to this than that. I know you see it. *I know you feel it.*"

She nods, her voice a whisper when she speaks. "You're right. I do. But you're here for now. You'll be gone in two months. And I know for a fact that you're not an easy man to get over."

This time when she takes a step back to open the door and walk away, I let her go.

She's heard enough lies from a Sharpe man. The last thing she needs to hear is another one telling her she's wrong.

CHAPTER FIFTEEN

Ledger

Fifteen Years Ago

A QUIET MAXTON SHARPE IS NEVER A GOOD THING.
Never.

Anyone who works closely with him or lives with him knows this to be fact.

So when I walk into the office in the estate we rented for the summer, perched above the town of Cedar Falls, and see him sitting behind his desk with his hands steepled in front of him, I know I'm fucked.

I run the day through my head. The joyride to Billings with my brothers. Raising hell at the Farmers Market with some of the locals we've made friends with. Hanging down by the creek with Asher.

Having sex with Asher.

Asher.

Does he know I was going to sneak out later and meet up with her? But how?

Earlier.

I got out of the shower and he handed me my phone. Said I'd left it downstairs on the kitchen counter. I didn't remember doing that but didn't have a reason to question it or him.

Is that how he knows? Did he read our texts? Did he fucking snoop on us?

Oh, Jesus. I know what this is about.

He's going to have *the sex talk* with me, isn't he?

Whew. Just a little overdue birds and the bees, man-to-man chat that he's clearly uncomfortable with.

A little fucking late if you ask me, but it's better than whatever else I thought was going to be handed to me tonight.

Sex.

Asher.

Jesus.

Just the thought of her gets me hard. Her soft sighs. How tight she was. How incredible it felt.

And right or wrong, I'm having these thoughts standing in front of my father.

"Son." He motions to the chair for me to take a seat. I'd rather have this uncomfortable discussion standing, but no one disagrees with Maxton. No one but Callahan, but that's a different story.

"It's late. I thought you were going out with Bunny—"

"Barbara," my dad corrects regarding a "friend" he has made during our stay here. Everyone wants to be your "friend" when you're a multi-millionaire. Most will take whatever scraps you throw their way in the hopes of elevating their status as a result. "And my plans have changed."

"Okay . . ."

"We need to have a little talk."

"I assumed," I say sarcastically, but the sharp look he gives me tells me my snark probably isn't a good idea.

"That girl you've been seeing—"

"Asher."

He nods. "It's over between you two."

"What?" I laugh. Not the *"you're a grown man now and you can make your own decisions, but you need to make sure to use protection"* spiel like I expected. "Good one."

"I said it's over. You're not to see her again."

What in the hell is he talking about?

I look over my shoulder as if this is a joke and Ford and Callahan are hiding somewhere, ready to laugh. *They're not.* "Dad . . . what are you talking about?"

"I don't like repeating myself. You heard me."

"I love her," I blurt out. Clearly, by his reaction, that was the wrong thing to say.

He rises from his chair and rounds his desk so that he's standing in front of me. "You're thinking with your dick, Ledger. Every good man does at some point, but this is the wrong time and the wrong person to do it with."

I shove up out of my chair. "You can't tell me what to do," I shout.

His hands are fisted in my shirt in an instant, his face inches from mine. His voice is a cool, even tone when he speaks next. "You'll do as I say. I will not have you disobey me on this."

"Fuck that."

"*Fuck that?*" he says, releasing my shirt and taking a step back, head shaking and a soft chuckle I don't think I'll ever forget the sound of rumbling in the silence. "That's exactly what you did. You fucked *that*. And now because you chose to do so with someone . . . not of our status, her grandfather wants to press charges against you."

"Charges?" I spit the word. *He's so full of shit.* "For what?"

"Statutory rape."

All the air is sucked out of the room.

"*What?*" I fumble over the single syllable. Blood drains from my face as I stand in utter confusion and horror. "What do you mean *statutory rape?*"

"You're eighteen, Ledge. She's not. Pretty cut-and-dried."

My mind is too overwhelmed to think straight, to process that while he might have known Asher and I had sex tonight from my texts, how would Pop know? All I can hear is the word *rape*. All I can think about is how everything earlier with Asher that I thought was fucking perfect, is now a goddamn nightmare. "I don't . . . I don't understand."

"You're a smart boy. Surely you do."

"But it wasn't rape. She wanted it. She—"

"Do you hear yourself? Do you know how horrible that single phrase—*she wanted it*—would sound to a judge? To a jury? Would look splashed across the front page of a newspaper?"

"That's not what I meant." I pull my hands down on the back of my neck and try to think straight, but it's not exactly easy. *Rape?* What happened tonight was not rape. It was far fucking from it, but truth be told, I'm scared out of my mind right now.

Fucking terrified.

"Dad. I swear. You have to believe me. That's not what happened."

"It doesn't matter if it is or if it isn't. What matters is that Mr. Wells is threatening it."

My shuddered breath is the only sound in the room save for the whoosh of my pulse in my ears. "I'll go talk to them. I'll—"

"What? You'll make it right? That's not how the world works, Ledger. Far fucking from it."

"This doesn't make any sense." My voice rises in pitch with each and every word. "Talk to Asher. She'll tell you we made this decision together. That I didn't force her into anything."

There's no way she'd go along with this. Not a chance in hell she'd let this happen if she knew.

"Don't you get it? It doesn't matter what Asher says or feels or if it was mutual. All that matters is what her grandfather says. What he wants. What he threatened. The law is the law, son, and even a Sharpe and our money can't get around it. Especially when we're outsiders like we are here."

"*But Pop knows me. He knows I'd never hurt Ash.*"

My dad walks in front of me and meets my eyes. "Sometimes people do crazy things to protect the ones they love, son."

I stare at him, my whole body vibrating with disbelief and fear. "Fuck it. I'm going over there right now." I head for the door, but my father grabs my shoulder and yanks me back.

"Don't be a fucking idiot. That's the last thing you should do."

"It's the only thing I *can* do," I shout at him.

"Do you think I'm thrilled with this fucking situation?" he thunders in an unusual show of temper. One that only serves to reinforce how fucked I am. How fucked this situation is. "Do you think I want my son's name thrown around in the same sentence as the words sex offender? Because that's what you'd be. *A sex offender*. You'd have to register in every neighborhood you move to for the rest of your life. You have a kid someday who goes to school? Guess what? You won't be allowed near the school to pick him up because, you guessed it, you're a registered sex offender. This isn't a fucking joke."

I shake my head back and forth to reject his words, but I can't speak. I can't do anything other than hear what he's saying and be scared shitless. "I don't understand," I finally manage.

"*Exactly*. You don't understand. Not at all, because clearly you were thinking with your dick."

"Dad . . ."

"We're not nobodies, Ledger." He throws his hands up, his strides eating up the room as he paces. "We're a family with a flashy name and a pristine reputation, and I guarantee this would be picked up by the media in a heartbeat. Rich prep school kid. Penniless, vulnerable small-town girl. Throw the word 'rape' in there and the Internet will light itself on fire. Scandal sells papers, and you bet your ass this would be a scandal."

I sink into a chair, my face in my hands and my chest constricting more and more with each breath.

Asher. What does she think about this? What is she saying right now?

Oh. My. God.

"This can't be happening."

"Oh, it's happening all right. This is what happens when you mix with people who aren't like us. Who don't live our life or understand—"

"I have to talk to her. I have to—"

"Like hell you will." He picks up a paperweight off the desk, and I swear for a second, I think he's going to throw it. But he just stands there, gripping it in his hand. "Do you have any clue where I've been for the last hour? I've been at their farm. Negotiating. Begging. Trying to prevent that grandfather of hers from pressing charges against you. Trying to fix what you fucked up."

I'm too overwhelmed to ask the questions I should ask. Why was he at the farm in the first place? Why was he even talking to Pop?

Nothing makes sense other than the fear and confusion rioting inside of me.

Pop knows me. Asher and I have been friends . . . *more than friends,* for three years. He knows I'd never do anything to hurt or disrespect her. *I love her.* He has to know that.

And Asher. There's no way Ash said that I rap—

"We are leaving Cedar Falls tonight."

"No—I—"

"You don't get to have a say in this. Is that understood?" His voice is calmer now, but it's cold as ice as I stare at him like a deer caught in the headlights. "We are leaving Cedar Falls tonight. You must never contact her again—in any way, shape, or form. Not a goodbye. Not an explanation. Not a fucking peep to her or anyone else about this—*including your brothers.*" My eyes flash up to his. The man who always preaches my brothers need to be my everything is now telling me to hide this from them? To lie to them? "If we do all of those things, Mr. Wells has agreed not to press charges."

I choke over a sob I don't want to let out. My hands tremble, but I nod in agreement. What else can I do?

"If at any point you break this agreement—your silence—in any way, he will move forward and contact the police." He takes a long pull on the glass of Scotch in his hand before looking back at me. "And I mean *ever.* There is a ten-year statute of limitations so remember that. Pretend she never existed. Pretend this summer never happened."

My entire body trembles. All I can think about are *the what-ifs.* The *how did this happen.* The *I can't go to jail.*

Tears spring in my eyes as my whole body rejects everything he's telling me.

This can't be happening.

This. Can't. Be. Happening.

"Ledger. Son." His voice gentles as he puts a hand on my shoulder and squeezes. I'm not sure if it's the sudden affection when I'm so goddamn scared, or just all the emotion in the moment, but the first tear slides down my cheek.

Sharpe men don't cry.

"Dad. I'm sorry." The tear turns into a sob. I'm terrified. I'm overwhelmed. "I didn't mean for this to happen. I didn't . . ."

He squeezes my shoulder again, his face somber, his eyes laden with a disappointment I've never seen or felt before from him. "I fixed this, Ledger. I fixed this and, so long as you do everything I just told you to do, it's over."

But it's not.

Asher.

I love her.

He picks up my cell phone I threw on the couch when I walked in and starts messing with something. I'm so distracted in my own thoughts, in my own disbelief, that I don't think anything of it until he hands it back to me. "There. She's been erased. Her texts. Her phone number has been blocked. Her emails erased."

"Dad?" I ask it like a question because there are so many things I want to ask—do you still love me? Is this really going to go away? But I didn't do anything wrong.

He puts a hand up to stop me from saying anything else before moving toward the door.

"Get yourself together before you walk out of this room. You're a man. A Sharpe. Stop crying and act like one. Get packed. The jet is fueled and ready on the tarmac. A car will be here for us in thirty minutes. I've had an emergency call regarding some business dealings and have to get back to the city." He looks at me and nods to make sure I understand the story. The lie. The cover. "The matter is closed. The girl is dead to you and never to be brought up again."

When he walks out, I just stare after him in a daze.

How is this happening?

How will I ever make it right?

CHAPTER SIXTEEN

Asher

I KNOW LEDGER'S HERE.

In fact, he's been wandering through the lavender fields, the moonlight as his guide, with a bottle of whatever in his hand as his solace.

If it weren't for the headlights of his SUV cutting through the farmhouse windows over an hour ago, I never would have known he was out there.

But I stay where I am in the house, watching his shadow move through the night as I try to process the last few hours.

Try to forget the way his kiss tasted and how incredible his body made mine feel.

Try to figure out why I freaked out and walked away afterward.

Was Nita right about the hate fuck being a good way to get someone out of your system?

I thought it would be. The intensity and hunger in the act were welcome. What wasn't was the onslaught of emotions that came after.

I was overwhelmed by them. I thought the carnality of sex wouldn't open old wounds. I was wrong. But what scared me the most about being with him was how it made me . . . *feel*, when I haven't felt in forever. It made me *want* when typically I'm fine with shutting down. It made me acknowledge that Ledger is like my own personal double-edged sword. He has the ability to devastate me and put me back together without even knowing it.

Asking for space was my knee-jerk reaction to the fear. It was my way of questioning if I could do this. If I could invite him back into my life at a time when my emotions have been stripped bare.

Vulnerability is something I hate to feel, hate to be, and yet, that's all I've been left with lately with Gran's move and Pop's passing. I've been holding on by a thread, trying to find my place in this new life, with these new responsibilities.

So why would I willingly open myself up to more hurt? Why would I put myself in a position to become attached to someone who's going to be gone in a few months?

Time. Space. Solitude. I thought those were things I wanted, what I needed, to make sense of all of this, but now that he's outside wandering about, I realize how incredibly lonely I am.

This house, one that used to be filled with love, laughter, and warmth, is so silent . . . and empty. Every day without Pop gets harder. I yearn for the day when the pain will go away. I look forward to a time when the overwhelming feeling that I've yet to get a handle on The Fields dissipates. I pray for the day that the numbness will be gone.

Let me help you then. Let me be there for you. Let me . . . I don't fucking know, but let me do something.

I'm too stubborn, too proud to take him up on that offer, but maybe it's time to look at this situation from a different perspective.

I only have Ledger for two months. Maybe that's exactly what I need. An end date before we have a beginning one. Parameters and controls that I can't control but that I know going into this.

The question is, can I enjoy the time with him and shut off my emotions at the same time? Separate the two? Is it possible to revel in the pleasure instead of remembering or bracing for the pain?

I'm pretty sure that's my only option.

Just as I'm topping off my glass of wine, the steps leading up to the veranda creak.

I'm at the door and opening it before he gets a chance to knock. We take each other in, the screen door the only thing between us.

He looks tired. Emotionally exhausted. And the bottle I thought he was drowning his sorrows in is almost completely full.

He holds said bottle up. "I thought I needed liquid courage to face you, but I realized I needed a clear head more. I hate not being in control. The feeling of it. The chaos of it. The inability to fix and guide as needed. And that's how I feel right now." He looks down and nods for a beat before looking back at me. "It would be so much easier to process my father's lies if I had drunk myself into oblivion, but the things I need to say to you are far too important for me to fuck up."

"Ledger." I smile softly, hating the conflicting emotions owning his face. "I was wrong about what I said tonight. Earlier. I shouldn't have dredged it all up—I was caught up in the emotion of the moment." I realized things I had missed out on. *You*. "I don't blame you. I just . . . I just think we should leave the events of that night be and focus our efforts on getting to know one another again, much like you suggested at Hank's."

He angles his head and holds my gaze. Can he see I'm trying to meet him in the middle? That I'm still confused, but like him, understand there is some invisible string binding us together still? That I'm willing to risk the pain of losing him again just so I can be with him now?

"Okay." He nods, but his voice doesn't sound very convincing. "But to do that, I need you to hear what happened that night on my end. I need you to understand how I was manipulated."

I know what his father did to me. I sure hope he was gentler on his flesh and blood. "Please. Come in."

He nods, follows me into the house, and before he even takes a seat, he starts talking. "I was wasting time before it was time to meet up with you. Made my presence known so that when he left for his date, he would think everything was normal. Later, I was summoned to his office, certain he'd found out about what we'd done. That we'd had sex. I was waiting for a gruff request to use protection and be sent on my way." He looks down at his hands folded in his lap before meeting my eyes with a clarity that disarms me. "Instead, I was told Pop was threatening to press charges against me for statutory rape."

My gasp is audible. "*What?*"

He looks like a man with the weight of the world on his shoulders as he nods solemnly. "My father told me that Pop would press charges unless I left town and never saw or spoke to you again. If I broke any of the conditions he laid out, he'd act."

"That never happened. Pop never said an ill word about you. I . . . oh my God." My thoughts spiral as I picture an eighteen-year-old Ledger and the fear those words must have evoked. The panic. The shock. My voice is soft when I speak, when I realize the betrayal he must be feeling right now. "*He lied to you.*"

"Apparently he was so good at it that he lied to both of us." He chuckles but all I hear is the heartache woven in its chords.

"So you lived in fear," I finally say after I take a minute to let everything sink in.

He nods, and his voice is hushed. "Every time you'd message me or text me . . . it fucking killed me to not respond. I knew the heartache you were going through because I was experiencing it too, but the fear outweighed everything. For the first couple of years, each time my phone would ring with a weird area code or I'd hear an unexpected knock on the door—I worried that Pop had gotten angry and filed charges anyway."

"I'm so sorry, Ledger."

"You see these trust-fund kids all over the news when they screw up. Kids like I was with privilege and wealth. They're either made an example of or are an exception to the rule and then vilified on social media. I was too terrified to take that risk. It was a constant battle between self-preservation and the hurt I caused you in simply falling off the face of the earth."

"I would have done the same thing if I were in your shoes. Reacted the same way." I move to sit beside him. To lace my fingers through his and squeeze them in reassurance. "We did nothing wrong that night, Ledger. You did nothing wrong."

"I know that now . . . but back then the world was smaller and my freedom no longer felt like it was a given." He shrugs.

"We were young and were supposed to trust the adults."

"That's just it though. I did trust the adult. I trusted the one person that I've lived my whole life looking up to and idolizing, *my father.* And after what you told me at Connor's, after realizing everything he said to me was a lie too . . . I'm struggling with who I am as a man. With how I never questioned him. With how I followed so blindly."

"Anyone would have in that situation. Look at me. I basically did the same thing."

He hangs his head and nods, but I can tell my pacification doesn't make him feel any better. He leans forward, resting his elbows on his knees, and twists his hands together. There's more on his mind. I can sense it in the soft sigh he emits and the tension straining his shoulders.

"I owe you an apology," he says so quietly, I can barely hear him. "I've avoided the subject of Pop in general with you because of . . . *all this,* and how it made me feel. I was wrong to do that. He was your world. *Your rock.* I know what it feels like to lose that one person in your life who is that to you." He looks over at me and offers a slight smile. "I, at least, had brothers to help with the grief. You don't have that. I should have asked how you were doing with it earlier. I should have been a bigger man and offered condolences. I wasn't."

"Thank you." I press a kiss to his shoulder and squeeze my eyes shut to fight the tears that threaten. I had no idea how badly I needed to hear that. To have someone else who understands. To know someone has walked in similar shoes and can commiserate. To feel someone's compassion.

As heavy as the moment is, somehow Ledger's comments make me feel lighter.

"I'm not going to lie to you, Ash. I've spent the better part of the last few hours nostalgic and wondering *what could have been.* We were kids. We could have fizzled out when we went to college. We could have made it work and made memories together. I don't know, and it pisses me off that he stole those opportunities from us. What I do know is that I'm a different person than I was then. Just as you are. But it should have been our choice. Our decision. Not someone else's."

"I know," I murmur and rest my hand on his arm. *This is the man I thought he'd become.* Not the flashy elitist he was when he first entered town. But this man sitting beside me with a heart of gold. "You were the first boy, the first person, really, who looked at me without the shadow of my mother's reputation staining me. You showed me that it didn't matter who she was, it only mattered who *I* was. I think that's why it hurt so bad. You knew me for me. He judged me for her."

"This is where I ask that you do the same for me. I'm not my father, Asher." His voice breaks on the word father, and I can only imagine how deceived he feels right now.

"I know you're not." I press a kiss to his shoulder and murmur, "I'm sorry about what your dad did. If I weren't involved in the situation, maybe I could justify his actions by saying that someday when either of us has kids, maybe we'll understand why he did what he did. But I'd be lying if I told you I didn't hate him for taking those *what-ifs* from us."

"I know."

We sit in the comfortable silence, in a house that feels a little less lonely right now, both coming to terms with these new truths, each in our own way.

"Well, hell. That was a lot more than either of us bargained for on a Friday night, don't you think?" I say, desperate to lighten the mood and the profound sense of loss that this heart-to-heart has left me with.

I don't know for sure, but from what I see, all of the wealth and power hasn't changed the Ledger Sharpe I once knew.

"You can say that again." Ledger presses a kiss to the top of my head that kind of melts me a little. "But at least it's all on the table."

"It is," I murmur and, when I turn to face him, a startled breath falls from my lips at the proximity of his. "Would you like some wine? Some of whatever you have there in your bottle? I can go get some glasses."

I scoot off the couch in a flurry of motion. The urge to kiss him is real, but so is my sudden bout of nerves, which is absolutely ridiculous considering hours ago we screwed in a bar bathroom.

"Yes. Sure." His footsteps sound behind me and then stop, the weight of his stare heavy. "A glass would be great."

I open and close my cupboards like a madwoman who doesn't know where her own glasses are in her kitchen.

I open the wrong drawer for a corkscrew. Slam it shut only to have the wooden spoon flip up and prevent it from closing.

This is ridiculous.

I shouldn't be nervous.

I shouldn't look like a fumbling idiot.

I shouldn't—

"Asher. Stop," Ledger says as he takes my hands in his. My heart is racing, my pulse pounding in my ears. He stoops down so that we're at the same eye level. "I don't know the answer to what this is here. I don't know what happens in two months or even tomorrow, but I know seeing you again brought me right back to those summer nights I spent with you. Right back to wanting to see you again the minute I walk away from you."

"It's scary, isn't it?" I whisper.

His lips meet mine. Where earlier it was fire and heat, this time our first kiss starts with a slow build. Soft kisses. Quiet sighs. Murmured words.

His hand on my chin. My fingers threaded through the hair at the nape of his neck. The length of his body pressed against mine. His thigh positioned between the V of my legs.

Kissing him is a mixture of familiarity and newness, comfort and excitement, and longing and satisfaction.

Chills chase the featherlight touch of his fingertips down my arms. His stubble is coarse beneath my palm.

"Ledger." His name is a breathless whisper he kisses over.

"Hmm?"

A soft tug on my bottom lip from him.

"What are we doing?"

"Kissing." His tongue delves between my lips.

"But what are we—" I shudder as his hands find their way beneath my tank top and slide up the bare skin of my back.

Our mouths part and he stares at me with a cocky grin, desire darkening his eyes. "I'm proving to you I'll be better at it next time."

I laugh. It feels so good to hear it. "In that case," I say before stepping in and tasting him again.

Our pace this go-round is slow. Leisurely. It's a masterclass in taking one's time. In enjoying each second for what it's worth rather than rushing to the next one.

He laces open-mouthed kisses down the line of my neck, only lifting from my skin when he pulls my tank top over my head.

His shirt ends up on the floor by the kitchen table. My skirt is shimmied out of somewhere near the foyer. His shoes get kicked off in the hallway, a few feet apart. Our strip show continues until we're standing in my darkened bedroom with only a stream of moonlight coming in through the window.

I take a step back, wanting to see him, needing to take in the whole of him, and knowing he needs the same thing from me.

To know this is real.

To grasp how far we've come in a few short hours.

We pull off our last layers of clothing with our eyes locked on each other's. It's an oddly intimate feeling to be stripped down physically and feel exposed emotionally too.

But hasn't that been par for the course tonight?

I am the first to break our stare. My eyes roam over every sculpted edge of his physique. Shoulders and biceps and abs right down to that sexy V of his hips. And then there's his hard and engorged dick set atop a pair of muscular thighs. Good thing I already know how it feels or I'd be afraid it looks too good to be true.

When I crawl my gaze back up him again, I'm met with an arrogant smirk asking me if I like what I see.

Oh, I definitely do.

"You're stunning," he murmurs after he makes his own languorous appraisal of me. And then he steps into me, his palms running down my flank and then cupping my ass as our lips meet once again. "Simply fucking stunning."

I ache. From the command in his touch. From the soft scrape of his stubble. From the heat of his body as he lays me on my bed. From the way he whispers my name in the dark.

Need builds. It's just as poignant and ravenous as earlier but now is more reverent in nature.

His fingers find their way between my thighs. His groan as he tucks two fingers into me is a seduction in and of itself and only serves to make me wetter.

His fingers start to move. Slow at first. In tandem with his other movements. His lips close over the peak of my breast as his fingers push in and pull out. It's a luxurious pace, much like our kissing, that elevates me to a heightened state of arousal where my orgasm is floating on the fringes, almost within reach, but not quite close enough.

"Spread your legs for me, Ash," he whispers in my ear before tugging on my earlobe. "Let me admire what I fucked into oblivion earlier. What I made sore." The slide of his tongue along the curve of my shoulder. "Let me kiss it and make it all better."

His words are unexpected and yet so very expected. He's a man always in control. A man used to his orders being obeyed. A man who always has his eyes on the prize.

And I'd be lying if I said it didn't turn me on.

So I do as he asks when he leans upon his haunches between my thighs.

He sucks in a sharp breath when he sees me, his hands running ever so slowly and softly up and down my inner thighs.

That smoldering ache I had? Now it's a raging wildfire of need.

His mouth follows the path of his hands, lacing kisses from the curve of my knee to the top of my pussy. And when he kisses me there, when he slides his tongue up and down and the warmth of it hits me, my entire body convulses with desire.

He breathes in through his nose. "God, I love the fucking smell of you," he murmurs before he closes his lips around my clit. I gasp as my hands fly out to grip his hair. "The taste of you." He hums against me so that the vibrations can be felt before leaning back upon his haunches. "The fucking feel of you." With his bottom lip between his teeth, he lines his cock up to my entrance and then thrusts his way into me.

More.

It's my first thought.

It's greedy and crass, but it's true. I had this feeling only hours ago, I'm having this feeling now, and I know I'll want him all over again soon enough.

But when he begins to move, thoughts aren't possible other than focusing on how good it feels when the crest of his cock adds its friction against each and every nerve I have.

"Ledger," I moan through the mounting pleasure swamping me.

His mouth meets mine again, the motion causing him to go even deeper inside of me. His tongue and lips own my mouth much like his cock does my pussy.

"Show me what you do," he murmurs against my lips. "Teach me how to pleasure you, Ash. I want to know." He takes my hand and moves it between my thighs. "*Show me.*"

I wait for the awkwardness to hit when he sits back up to watch how I work my fingers over my clit. I'm slow at first. A little clumsy from being watched. But his groan spurs me on. The way his tongue licks over his bottom lip adds to it.

And when he starts moving, when his sizeable cock begins to work in and out of me, I forget about how he's watching me and get lost in the rhythm. I get lost in the feel of it. Of him inside and my fingers outside.

My body soars with sensations. Bit by bit. Inch by inch. Thrust by thrust.

My breath quickens. My muscles tense. My back arches. My toes curl.

"Ash." My name is a panted breath.

The coil in my core twists tighter. And right before it snaps, just as I tighten around his cock about to fall over the edge and into blissful oblivion, Ledger grabs the back of my neck and forces me to do what he commands, "Look at me."

And I do.

Amber eyes meet mine. They're clouded with lust and determination and everything that's Ledger.

Only Ledger.

The orgasm hits me like a tsunami. Hard, fast, and relentless. It surges through me, touching every part of me as it goes. It ebbs for a beat before coming back to wrack my senses again—a little gentler than the wave before it.

I'm lost in its warmth, in its swell, when Ledger's fingers tighten on my hips and his gritted groan fills the room. I have enough of my faculties to open my eyes and appreciate something I wasn't afforded earlier at Connor's—the glorious sight of Ledger Sharpe coming undone. Of witnessing what I do to him. Of feeling the power of the moment.

His lips find mine again. Softer, gentler, desire sated for the time being, before he collapses on top of me.

Ledger's weight, half on me, half off me, is a welcome feeling. My hand runs lazily up and down the line of his spine, our hearts pounding against one another's.

I don't know what happens in two months or even tomorrow, but I know seeing you again brought me right back to those summer nights I spent with you.

A soft smile plays on my lips because those will be my words to live by. That will be the mantra I repeat.

"I guess you're right."

I can feel his mouth curve into a smile against my shoulder. "*About?*"

"It was definitely better the next time."

When he leans back to look at me, his grin is blinding.

CHAPTER SEVENTEEN

Asher

L EDGER'S BROAD SHOULDERS FILL THE WINDOW FRAME AND BLOCK the early morning light coming into the kitchen. The steam from his coffee curls up above his shoulders.

I study him as he takes in my farm and its fields, the early morning mist weaving itself through the rows.

How did this happen?

I keep thinking I'm going to shake my head, and last night, this past week, will all be a dream. How does fifteen years pass and you still have a connection with someone as strong as ours feels?

It's the weirdest thing to feel like you know someone when you truly don't know much about them anymore at all. Their likes. Their dislikes. How they take their coffee. What their late-night fridge raid choice is. Their taste in music. The hobbies they like or the company they keep. What they're like after a bad day.

All things I used to know about the man standing in front of me, yet now feel like a complete mystery.

And yet none of those things mattered last night. Nor do they in this moment that I need to enjoy instead of overanalyzing.

I don't know what I expected to happen after that incredible sex, but waking up beside him, seeing him standing in my kitchen, definitely wasn't one of them.

"You've expanded quite a lot," he says and then hisses when the coffee he takes a sip of scalds his tongue. "I don't remember there being lavender on the slopes over there."

"We had a fire burn through here about six years ago," I say as he turns to look at me. He has a way of doing that right at the perfect time to show me I'm being heard. "The house was saved, but almost everything else was lost. The Lavender. Machinery. Tools. Cars."

"I had no idea. I'm sorry."

I shrug and take a sip of my own coffee, recalling the devastation and the weight it put on Pop's shoulders. How it felt like he aged so quickly during that time. "It was a disaster. The lavender was burned through and the heat of the fire somehow triggered the seeds of an invasive species called mallow to crack and sprout."

"Seeds? Where did those come from?" He takes a few steps toward me.

"We learned that lesson the hard way. Apparently, they can lay dormant under the soil for years, and then extreme heat like a fire, can trigger them to imbibe, crack, and then grow." I shake my head, remembering Pop's despair. "The mallow took over the fields. Stole water nutrients from the new lavender seeds we were trying to propagate. They'd start to grow and then die. We tried everything but ended up having to use a ground clear."

"Which means the soil was poisoned and couldn't grow anything for a certain amount of time, right?" he asks.

"I'm impressed," I tease. "How does a man who lives in a concrete jungle know about ground clear?"

"We have a family home in Sag Harbor. We've had to use it there."

Of course, he has a house in Sag Harbor. Just a small reminder of what different worlds we live in.

"So you understand why we couldn't grow in our existing fields. It forced us to buy more land." I point to the slopes he was referring to. "Gran and Pop were so stressed taking out a second mortgage on this house to pay for it when they didn't have any viable lavender to harvest and profit from. Their anxiety was a constant around here, regardless of how hard they tried to hide it."

"Understandably."

"It took us a full two years to get up and running and back to our prior capacity, but the repercussions of that year are still being felt to this day."

"Two years." He whistles. "That's a lot of time to be without your commodity."

I nod. "It was. And of course, Pop couldn't stomach the thought of letting Danny or George go since they're like family, so he made the sacrifices instead . . ."

"Sounds like the man I knew." He smiles softly. "Did insurance help?"

"It did some, but not enough to cover the cost of buying new land and waiting out a year to be able to reseed again."

"I can imagine. I'm sorry that happened." He looks out the window and then back to me. "And now it's all yours."

"It is."

"And how do you feel about that?"

I hold his gaze and ask myself about how to answer his question. A question I've asked myself numerous times over the past few months.

"Is it what I envisioned I'd be doing with my life? No," I say with a reticent smile, "but you already knew that. At the same time . . . it's where fate has led me to be. Is it a daily grind? Definitely. Especially when I'm learning on the fly and don't have enough confidence in myself to be certain I know what I'm doing or how to do it. The Fields was Pop's area of expertise, and while I helped out in between taking care of Gran and doing its social media, I was never knee-deep into the details."

"And now it all rests on your shoulders," he murmurs.

I nod but rise abruptly from my chair and move toward the coffee pot, uncomfortable with the questions that logically should come next. Why are you not sketching anymore? What happened to going to college and conquering the world? Why are you still in Cedar Falls?

They're all valid in their own right, but ones with answers that will give away too much. That Asher Wells—the Wells family, in general—is even more penniless now than we were back when his father accused us of being just that. The last thing I want him to know is that I'm struggling and that losing the farm and this house is a real possibility if we don't have a strong harvest this year. That I'm doing everything in my power to get up to speed and figure out how to reinvent the wheel here so we can turn a profit and stay afloat.

But he doesn't ask, he doesn't pry, and while I'm grateful that he doesn't, I wonder what he's thinking right now. What it is he sees when he looks at me, as he stands here in my kitchen in the early morning hours.

Does he regret coming here last night? Is he simply being polite by having this chat when he really wants to go? Was last night as incredible for him as it was for me? Because last night was incredible, but now there's a sense of reality setting in, and what the heck do we do now?

My unspoken questions mixed with the weight of his stare on my back has nerves suddenly firing to life.

"Speaking of work falling on shoulders, I'm sure you have plenty yourself that you need to get to. Don't feel the need to stay on my account," I ramble as I fiddle with the coffee filter, grab the sponge to wipe down the counter, and then straighten the dish towels on the counter. Anything to keep my hands busy.

"Asher?" His voice is closer than I expected. I never heard him move.

"Hmm?" I ask as I move toward the refrigerator.

He hooks an arm around my waist to stop my progress. "You're doing it again," he says.

"Doing what?"

"Being skittish."

I look up to meet his eyes. He's right. I'm acting like a stray dog who's afraid of everything. This is not me.

"I don't do this morning-after thing very well, is all," I finally say.

"No?"

"No." I smile to cover my flushing cheeks. "In fact, I don't do it at all so . . ."

He angles his head and studies my face. "What do you mean you don't do it at all?"

I can see the moment he understands what I mean. That I'm not one to have overnight company. I swear he stands a little taller and his chest puffs out a bit more.

"Am I the first guy to ever sleep over here?"

"Until a few months ago, I didn't exactly live alone." Pop would have died of embarrassment if he'd walked into the kitchen and found a random man with bedhead drinking coffee. I think I would have too. After the conversation *we* had with Gran the other day, I venture to say that she wouldn't have been at all embarrassed.

Ledger's grin widens. "So, is this making you uncomfortable? Me standing here, drinking your coffee, making small talk?"

"Not uncomfortable, no." I try to take a step back, but Ledger holds me in place, raising his eyebrows as if to tell me he's not satisfied with my response. "I just . . . I just don't know what that means or how this ends, or . . . *whatever*."

He reaches out and tucks a piece of hair behind my ear. "Well, it—or *whatever*—means *we* had a good night. The fact that I'm not rushing out is a good sign. One that means I want to see you again."

"There was a question?" I tease despite the ridiculous amount of relief I feel from his words.

"Not at all." He presses a chaste kiss to my lips. "And how it ends is I finish my cup of coffee and then head into work because I have to figure out new and clever ways to kiss Mayor Grossman's ass—"

"I warned you."

"You did." He nods. "And when I walk out that red door over there, we'll both spend our day thinking about the incredible night we had, all while trying to wipe the goofy smiles off our faces—that people will question what they are there for. Then, we'll touch base later and see how we feel about seeing each other again. It's as simple as that."

"What? You mean there's no three-day rule about calling?"

"I think fifteen years covered that for us."

I laugh. "Should I worry that this is something you have down to a science because you do it a lot?"

"Not a lot. No."

My eyes stay locked on his, and I hate that the thought of him standing in someone else's kitchen, having morning coffee irritates me. It's ridiculous. Of course, he's done that before. He's extraordinarily handsome, wealthy, and educated. "The perfect catch," I murmur out loud before I realize I have.

"The perfect catch?"

"Yep. I bet you're the perfect catch for all those high-society, Park Avenue regulars in Manhattan."

Like I once aspired to be.

"Hey. *Don't.* That look on your face is saying too much." That I'm not good enough for him. That I don't fit in his world. That his dad was right. He brushes the most tender kiss to my lips and rests his forehead against mine. "I don't care about the high-society ladies in Manhattan, Asher. Those women are perfect on the outside and boring on the inside. I prefer things a bit more complicated. A bit more real. And with more history to them." He sighs and leans back, searching my face to make sure I've heard him. When he's satisfied, he rubs his thumb back and forth over my lower lip. "I do have to get to work, though."

"So is this the part where you kiss me goodbye?"

"It's a hard job, but somebody has to do it," he murmurs seconds before his lips slant over mine. The kiss is the perfect amount of soft yet demanding. He's definitely in control—of the angle, the intensity, the length—and he's somehow perfect at all of them.

When the kiss ends, he walks toward the door and then stops to look back at me. There is a lopsided smile on his lips. "This is the part where you start thinking about me all day."

CHAPTER EIGHTEEN

Asher

"Meet me in Bear Valley? That's it? After you leave the whole of Cedar Falls talking after last night, that's the text you're going to send me?" Nita says as she meets me on the sidewalk in Bear Valley, where I've been waiting for her to meet me.

"It worked, right?" I give her a quick hug. "You're here."

"I am here. You're just lucky my babysitter was available today or else you'd be standing here with that smug grin on your face waiting forever."

"Remind me to thank her."

"Noted."

"And screw the town for talking." I shrug as we begin to walk slowly down the sidewalk. And I mean that, sincerely. I refuse to let their stupid gossip affect anything about what happened last night in a negative way. "At least I've actually earned the gossip they're dishing on me this time around."

"True," she says and then nudges me. "So . . ."

"So . . ." I toy with her. "Dare I even ask what the gossip is about?"

Nita laughs. "Wayne's curious how a man can last that long."

Wayne? *The man who knocked on the bathroom door at Connor's.* "Poor Mrs. Wayne then."

"I know, right? And Judy Jensen is grumbling over how it's you who pulled in the new, wealthy, eligible bachelor in town when she clearly has more to offer him than you do."

"Fuck her," I say as I point to a cute shirt displayed in a storefront.

"My sentiments exactly," Nita says as she angles her head to look at it.

We window-shop. This is our thing, the way we spend time together and unwind. When you struggle financially, there's not much else you can do, so we've fallen into this routine where we head here or there and stroll around while we talk.

"Nah," she finally says as we move to the next window. "That color washes me out."

"What about Carson?" I grimace. "I need to call him and apologize."

"He's fine." She rolls her eyes and swats at my arm. "He came back into the bar. One minute nursing his bruised ego. The next lying about how he knocked the guy—er, Ledger—out cold."

"Which didn't happen, by the way, but if people believe that then they should also believe I was bringing Ledger back to consciousness with a little mouth-to-mouth," I say coyly with a flutter of my lashes.

Nita bursts out laughing. "Personally? I think every woman in town is jealous of you, so you just keep on doing what you're doing because you know what? *Screw them.*"

"I'm not going to argue on that one."

"So, because there is in fact gossip and you did in fact disappear from Connor's, can I assume the two of you worked through your differences, then?" She leans in and looks closely at a diamond pendant in the jewelry store display.

"In so many words, yes."

"And the answers you were looking for were satisfactory and that more than kissing happened—according to Wayne, that is."

I laugh and point to a yellow diamond ring that sparkles. "Wayne is correct, yes, but you already knew that."

"So what changed your mind? Or rather tipped the scales for you?"

"I decided that maybe this is what I need right now. *Maybe he is.* That I'm walking into whatever this is with the knowledge that he has a life, that I have a life, and in two months he'll be gone."

"So, enjoy the time you have, void of any expectations?"

"Yes."

"How very mature of you."

"Or stupid of me," I mutter.

"It's only stupid if you forget to keep your heart locked down. Something that I might add that you're pretty damn good at."

At least I have her vote of confidence on this.

"Oh, *look.*" She tugs on my arm to go inside an apothecary store. There are soaps and lotions and a million other things to sniff and sample and fawn over. "Talk about pamper central."

I'm mesmerized by the scents running into one another and the décor and the product packaging. I pick up a tin and smell the candle inside. "Definitely pamper central."

"I could buy one of everything in here."

"I wouldn't complain about that," a woman says as she approaches us, smile big, eyes kind. "I'm Sarah. Owner and jack-of-all-trades here. Just let me know if you have any questions. Everything is locally sourced and made in my own garage," she says.

"Oh. Wow. That's incredible." Nita picks up another sample jar and smells it.

"Thank you. I was laid off from my corporate job and was struggling with how to make ends meet. I fell back on what I knew best to save the day—making soaps and oils. It's something my grandmother taught me when I was little. It was our bonding time. Who knew it would save the day?"

"It's amazing how that happens sometimes," I say. "Congratulations. By the line at the cash register and the boxes stacked for UPS to pick up, it looks like it was the right decision."

"It definitely was." Sarah smiles before being pulled away by a customer's question.

"I'm going to get a little something to take to Gran when I see her later," I say. In less than ten minutes, I've purchased the gift I picked out for her, and we're heading back out the door.

"I definitely need to come back here."

"I know. It's a treasure trove."

"You should tell her you grow lavender," Nita says. "Maybe do a trade. Lavender for free products."

"I wouldn't complain about that," I say, looking back over my shoulder to note the store's name. *Just in case* I need to know it in the future.

"What are we doing here, anyway?"

"Besides having some girl time?"

She narrows her eyes and stares at me. "What are you up to?"

I point to the little boutique at the end of the street. "I hear they're having a huge sale this week."

Nita's eyebrows shoot up. "Hell. I wasn't going to ask for details about last night—"

"Yes, you were."

"You're right." She laughs. "I was. But if we're playing hooky to come here to buy you lingerie, I don't think I need to ask."

"Not lingerie." She narrows her eyes and tries to understand. "More like needing to up my bra and panty game."

"He was that good you're going back for seconds, huh?"

"Or fourths or fifths." I slide a look her way just in time to catch her mouth shock open into an O. "So yes, I need something more than my practical T-shirt bra and boring panties."

"Otherwise called lingerie." She laughs. "There's more to lingerie than garters with stockings and scraps of lace, Asher, although I'm pretty sure Ledger wouldn't mind you adding those to your repertoire either."

I roll my eyes as we cross the street. "So you're really not going to ask about last night?"

"Oh honey, you bet your ass I'm going to ask. I want all the details. His skill level. Your orgasm count. Size and shape are important details too." She hooks her arm through mine as we enter the shop. "And every damn detail in between."

I laugh. I can't help it because *Ledger was right.* I have the goofiest smile plastered on my face.

CHAPTER NINETEEN

Ledger

Nine Years Ago

"DON'T GO ANYWHERE, LEDGER." CALLAHAN AND FORD dart glances my way as they make their way around the conference room table toward the door. Both of them just as curious as I am as to why our dad has requested that I stay behind when they get to leave.

I lower myself back down into my seat as Callahan mouths the word "sucker" to me before flashing a grin and heading out the door.

Fucker.

My dad moves toward the floor-to-ceiling windows that frame the conference room. His daily uniform is in place: starched, white dress shirt, a solid, bold-colored tie, gold cufflinks that my mom gave him on his birthday the year she passed, and dark gray slacks.

I look at him expectantly, my knee jogging as the collar of my own dress shirt feels like it's tightening around my neck. And I wait.

No one rushes my father. He speaks when he wants to, and when he chooses to, you best be listening.

"It wasn't good enough," he says in a calm tone, his back still toward me.

What in the hell is he talking about?

"Dad? *Sir?*"

He turns to face me, his head angled to the side—much like I do when I study someone—and my palms grow damp with anticipation.

"Professor Blackman recorded your presentation for me."

He had my mock proposal presentation recorded so he could critique it? *What the actual fuck?* Is there any place his far-reaching arms can't touch? My professor at Wharton? Jesus fucking Christ.

"*You know Blackman?*"

The muscle tics in his jaw as he takes his time answering. "It's a small world, Ledger. That's something you best remember."

Now that the shock has almost worn off, the anger starts to fire. "What do you mean it wasn't good enough? Blackman said it was excellent. The content. The packaging. The presentation." I'm top of my cohort. Top of my fucking class. *What in the hell does he mean it's not good enough?*

"I would have fired you." He shrugs with indifference as if he didn't just rip me apart. "It was sloppy and meandering. Your figures need work. Your presence needs to be more commanding." He takes a few steps toward me as I try to keep my face stoic, despite how his words devastate me. "What have I always told you?"

"Set goals. Meet goals. Adjust the goalposts. Start over again," I say, repeating the mantra he has drilled into my head.

"Good." He nods and crosses his arms over his chest where he stands a few feet from me. "Tell me what yours are right now."

I struggle momentarily to come up with them. "Graduate Wharton. Take my place beside you here at Sharpe."

"And after that?"

"*After that?*" I ask.

"Yes. *After that?* Where do you reset the goalposts to?" If someone were to overhear us, they'd think my father was talking about the weather. Only my brothers and I know this tone means anything but that. He's getting irritated.

Well, so am I.

Why aren't Ford or Callahan in here getting the third goddamn degree? Callahan is the one who dropped out of Wharton, for fuck's sake, and is already working here. Why doesn't he have to reset his goalposts? Ford is busy being Ford, gladly flying under the radar without the pressure of being the oldest or the ease of being the youngest.

"After that, son, what is next? Take the company from me? Work on taking us internationally? Make Forbes magazine before you're forty? Carry on the family name? *What. Is. Next?*"

"Dad. Yes. To all of that," I stammer out.

"Not good enough, Ledge." His voice rises in pitch. "Not for you, anyway. Do you want to shame the Sharpe name with your laissez-faire attitude? My firstborn. My protégé—"

"Callahan is already working here. Ford will be soon too." I shove up out of my chair, needing to move. To pace. To not be sitting down while he stands tall over me. "Did you have this talk with them too? Did you demand to know their goals?"

"No." The chill is back in his voice, and it infuriates me.

"No? Why the hell not?"

"Check your tone."

I squeeze the bridge of my nose and bite back the retort on my tongue. When I turn back around, I hope he sees the love and frustration in my eyes. The want to please, but also the need to be my own man. My respect for him but not how he goes about things sometimes.

"I ask this of you, son, because I know you're capable of it. I demand this because nothing less than perfection is good enough." His tone softens for the first time in this conversation. "The three of you are my legacy, but you, son . . . *you* have something special that money or education can't buy. I'm looking to you to uphold the Sharpe name in more ways than I ever could."

I hate that my throat burns with emotion as I nod in response.

"I want a status report every Monday morning from you. What your goals are for the week. Which ones you completed last week. Structure and planning equal success."

"Yes, sir."

He walks over to where I stand, puts a hand on my shoulder, and squeezes. "We didn't do all this work, all of this posturing, for you to be second best, son." When his eyes meet mine there is so much pride in them that it makes my chest ache.

Is he a hard son of a bitch to work for? *Definitely.*

Is he a perfectionist to the nth degree? *Indisputably.*

Does he love the three of us unconditionally? *Yes,* each in our own way.

So why does a lump form in my throat at his praise?

Because he's my idol. Because when your idol criticizes you, it's hard not to be overwhelmed.

"I won't let you down, Dad."

He nods and pats my back. "Expectations are a funny thing. They can weigh you down or they can make you shine. What will your response be?"

CHAPTER TWENTY

Asher

"GRAN? YOU AWAKE?" I knock on the door to her room and push it open to check for myself.

She's propped up in her bed, her eyes closed like she's sleeping. Her hair is like a halo of silver around her head and her complexion is flawless, including the wrinkles that illustrate a life well-lived. My beautiful gran.

She's had a rough couple of days, so I'm glad she's resting now. Resolved not to disturb her, I tiptoe into the room with a fresh bouquet of lavender to replace the one dying on her windowsill, as I do every few days.

"Asher. You're here."

Her lopsided smile is wide when I turn to face her. "Did you think I'd miss a chance to hang with my favorite person?"

"Pop was your favorite person," she says and doesn't even try to hide the tears that well in her eyes. "He snuck you candy, let you eat ice cream for lunch, and called you in sick to school to go fishing with him. I could never compete with that."

"You didn't have to." I take a seat beside her and press a kiss to the top of her hand. "You gave me spa days in your bathroom, let me sit on the counter while you made pies, and snuggled with me whenever it thundered."

"I don't want to be sad, Ash. Tell me something happy."

"Well . . . I may be seeing someone."

"Mr. Handsome." My eyes meet hers, and I nod. "I knew something was going on when you came here the other day. You never could keep a secret from me, you know."

"Guess not."

"It was in the way he looked at you. Words can fool, but eyes can't lie." Gran's wisdom at its finest. "He looked familiar. Was he a high school friend?"

I nod and hope she doesn't catch the lie. Maxton's words not only hurt me that night, but they devastated Gran and Pop too. She said as much the other day when I asked her what she remembered. It agitated her just talking about it. The last thing I need to do is upset her when she's had enough pain over the past few months. "Something like that."

"And he treats you well?"

"Yes, but we're just in the seeing each other phase. That's it."

"Uh-huh," she says in that way that says she doesn't believe me.

"Do you want to get outside for a bit? We can take a stroll in the gardens? Get some fresh air?"

"No." She pats her hand over mine. "I'm too tired today. Everything hurts." She yawns. "I'm sorry."

"Don't be." I press a kiss on her forehead. "I'll leave you be so you can rest."

"Hmm." She smiles softly as her eyelids start to droop. "I remembered something about that night. The one you were asking me about the other day."

"Oh?" There's not much more she can tell me considering her reiteration of events was basically word for word how I remembered it happening.

"When Pop came inside after talking with that . . . *horrid man*, he had something in his hand. A tan envelope."

"What was in it?"

"That's the thing. Pop told me it didn't matter. All that mattered was you. I never saw it again."

I stand there beside her as her breathing starts to even out and her eyes flutter closed. "Will you take him some lavender for me too?" she whispers, her voice already drugged with sleep.

Pop's headstone. She wants me to take him lavender too.

My heart squeezes in my chest.

"Of course, I will. I promise to bring both of you lavender always."

CHAPTER TWENTY-ONE

Ledger

"That won't work."

"Why not?" Hillary asks, hands on her hips, a crease in her brow.

"Because if we put local craftsmen in the hotel who already have a store in town, they'd be getting less profit after we take our cut. Grossman will accuse us of stealing from them or taking advantage of them or some shit like that," I say and sigh in frustration.

"Then let's find people who don't have brick-and-mortar stores. There have to be locals we can showcase. Ones that are just starting out or who can't get representation in local shops."

"That's an angle." A shitty one, but one nonetheless.

"Don't sound so enthused." She chuckles. "I think it's worth a shot. Maybe use one of the shops as a *locals-only* fare. Give it a catchy name. Place it off the main lobby next to the gift shop."

"Get someone to work on that and see what we come up with. Quality is key."

"As is everything."

"Where are we on the school library thing?" I ask, frustrated that we even have to deal with bullshit like this. The look on Hillary's face says she feels the same way since she should be elbow deep in the details of the resort's construction—contractor problems, supply chain issues, decisions that have to be made on the fly.

Hillary updates me over the next hour. On her meeting with the school district superintendent over a donation that S.I.N. can make to give the library a facelift. Then we moved to her follow-up meeting with the director of the assisted living facility. They're willing to accept our generosity of a new HVAC system, but have to cut through some red tape first.

It's amazing how much money talks.

Then again, I've never known anything otherwise.

One meeting rolls into another. Union issues with the staff in our Aspen resort. A possible property acquisition in California Wine Country—a market we've wanted to move into for years. It's still a long way off, but it's a rarity something comes up for sale there, so I welcome the first step. Conflicts with supply chain at our resort in the Virgin Islands.

And it doesn't matter how much shit like this, the details, the complications, and the nitty-gritty of our business generally turn me on, my mind has a hell of a time concentrating this week.

Asher.

Jesus.

The woman.

Last night.

This morning.

How can each time get better with her?

That's a stupid fucking thought considering I was a fumbling teenager the first time we were together . . . and yet, usually the memory of something is better. Call it selective amnesia or wishful thinking, but my memory of her doesn't hold a fucking candle to the Asher I left behind in the farmhouse this morning.

Focus, Ledge.

Ha. That's funny.

"You're knocking down fires all over the place today," Callahan says in greeting when he answers the phone. "We should have you vacate the office more often. Your productivity level seems to go up."

"Fuck off."

His chuckle rumbles through the line. "Nah. It's too much fun giving you shit."

"Tell Sutton she needs to keep you on a tighter leash," I say, referencing his wife.

"Oh, I don't know. I like how tight she grips me."

"Yeah. Yeah. When are you two leaving to take on Japan?" I ask in reference to the property we're buying from Takashi. Callahan and his wife will head there and manage the transition of the resort.

"After we close escrow."

"Yes. Sorry. Every day here feels like ten."

"That bad, huh?" He chuckles. "At least you'll get to escape back to the city next month for the gala."

"Shit. Yes. *That*," I say, my mind completely blanking on the charity gala we're sponsoring for the Alzheimer's Association, something we've done every year since Dad's diagnosis. "I've been preoccupied with this bullshit."

"*You forgot something?* How unlike you. And here I thought you were counting down the days until your return to civilization."

"Like I said, I've been busy." I pull on the back of my neck, confused over my sudden desire to make up an excuse as to why I can't go back. *Seriously, Ledge?*

"Or preoccupied. Everything okay?"

"Yes. Yeah. Sure."

He laughs again. "What's up with the three-word answers? That's your tell."

"My tell?"

"Yeah, when you're lying about something." He pauses. "So, what exactly are you keeping from me?"

I shake my head and practically flip the phone off. This is the problem with having brothers who are as close as we are. They know too much about you even when you don't say a word.

"I'm not keeping shit from you. I'm just trying to get this whole shitshow here sorted out and fixed. You know how much menial crap like this drives me crazy," I deflect.

"It's a necessary evil though."

"I mean, we've always had to grease palms in one way or another for a new project, whether it be in discounted room rates for an inspector or whatever, but this ask is flat-out ridiculous."

"Bribery. Extortion. Blackmail." He makes a noncommittal sound. "Sounds about right. The question we should be asking though is *do you think it will work?*"

"Only time will fucking tell, but I swear to God, if we do all this shit and Grossman moves the bar again for us to jump over, I'll be fucking pissed."

Set the goal. Meet the goal. Adjust the goalposts.

If it were Dad in Grossman's shoes, he'd definitely move the bar.

"Agreed. That's why you need to move as fast as possible and get shit finished before new ideas can materialize. We need Harrison to double-check the contract to ensure there is nothing else they can legally pull on us."

"Thanks, *Dad*."

"Now you know how it feels."

Both he and Ford swear I'm just like our father. They tease me about it relentlessly.

But after the revelations of the past week, the thought sits differently with me now.

"Hey, Callahan?"

"Hmm?"

"Remember that last night we were here? In Cedar Falls?" I ask.

"You mean when Dad had a deal go sour, and we had to get home right away so he could salvage it? That night?"

"Yeah." My chest constricts.

"What about it?"

My mouth opens, my need to tell him everything—finally, after keeping it quiet for so many years—eating at me. But I don't say a word. I find myself shoving up out of my seat and walking to the window to look outside, one hand fisted, my jaw clenched.

"Ledge? You there?"

"Yeah. Never mind." *I can't do it.* As much as I want to tell him, I can't ruin his vision of who our father was. I can't tarnish a memory simply to make myself feel better.

Like that night and its aftermath, I'll have to stomach this one alone.

"You sure? Because it sounded important."

I smile simply because I'm hoping it will carry over to my voice. "Not important at all. I just happened to drive by that old field we used to go hang out and drink at."

"It's still there?"

"It's about a quarter of the size because it has houses on three sides now, but . . ." I continue rattling on about a field neither of us cares about. Because I'm afraid if I stop, my brother, my triplet, will pick up on something in my voice that tells him otherwise.

"I swear I thought you were going to tell me you ran into Asher and either hit it off or found out she has six kids or something like that."

"Uh . . ." I'm caught flatfooted by his comment, rattled by a moment of uncertainty.

"You're fucking kidding me," he says. "You *have* seen her, haven't you?"

I scrunch my nose up, wanting and not wanting to tell him simultaneously. "Yeah. It slipped my mind. I just so happened to run into her at a bar."

"You didn't forget to tell me shit." He snorts. "You've always been so damn secretive when it comes to her. Back then, it was like she was everything and then suddenly, *poof,* she was nothing. It was like she'd dropped off the face of the earth, and now you tell me you ran into her, and that's all you're going to give me?" he asks. "Because that screams to me she's either dog ugly now and you ran the other way, or you guys fucked like rabbits." I don't respond. "So, which one was it?"

Fucking Callahan. I hate that a smile breaks onto my lips. I hate that I want to confide in him so badly. I hate that I still want to keep whatever this is with Ash close to the vest.

"Neither," I lie.

"Uh-huh." Spoken like only an annoying little brother can.

"She's fucking gorgeous is what she is."

"Ohh." More sounds from the asshole. "Why so sensitive?" His laughter fills the line.

"Are you trying to be a prick?"

"Only if you're trying to evade the question."

"We talked for a bit. Agreed to meet up at a later time to catch up. That's all."

"Liar."

"Go away."

"*And she's fucking gorgeous,*" he says, mimicking my tone.

"She is. Full stop."

"When Ledger pulls out the *full stop,* you know he means business."

"I'm going now, Callahan."

"Oh, I figured you were *coming*." His chuckle fills the line. "And hey, Ledge?"

"What?" I snap.

"This is when you act like the *old me* since I'm now an old married fucker."

"*Act like you?*" But the minute I say it, I start laughing, because I know what he's going to say. Him and his penchant for telling me I have a stick up my ass.

"Yeah. Sleep with the woman. Skip some work to fuck off with her. Your lists can wait. Live a little outside of the office."

"I'm going now, Callahan."

"I bet you are."

I glance at the clock. Let's see how long it takes for Callahan to tell Ford and for Ford to call me.

CHAPTER TWENTY-TWO

Asher

"So is this the *touch base later* and see how we feel about seeing each other again portion of the day?" I ask.

"It is." God, I love his voice and how it wraps around me. "Did you have a good day?"

"I did. I worked on sorting some of Pop's stacks. I took Gran some fresh lavender for her room. Then I came back here and surveyed the lavender with George to see how close or far we are on harvesting the different species."

"And what was the consensus?" he asks.

"One is getting close. A few others have at least four more weeks." I look out the window at a car that drives by the farm. Traffic on our road is few and far between, but the car keeps driving past. "What about your day? Were you busy conquering the world?"

"Not all of it."

"Just a hemisphere then?"

"Something like that." He chuckles. "Any regrets?"

His question catches me off guard. We've seen each other a couple times since that first night, so the fact that it comes out of the blue has me sitting up a little straighter.

"Should I be worried why you're asking me that question?"

"No. It's nothing. Callahan was giving me shit the other day about something and it led me to think, which led me to wonder if . . . I don't know. If you had any regrets about . . . *this.*"

"No." It's a question I can answer without hesitation.

"No?"

"You?" I ask.

"Definitely not."

"Whew, glad to know we're on the same page," I say dramatically, followed by an awkward silence where I want to ask when I can see him again but fear coming off . . . needy? Too clingy?

"I had every intention of asking you if you'd let me take you to dinner tonight, but I completely forgot that Hillary—my project manager—set up a working dinner with Espies."

"The owner of the Cedar Mountain Resort?" I ask, referring to the swankiest ski resort between here and Billings.

"That's the one. We're trying to create exclusive packages for the guests. Luxury deals they can't get anywhere else."

"Luxury," I murmur absently.

"Yes. Luxury. Decadence. A destination to lose yourself in. That's our brand. That's what S.I.N. is known for."

"It's attractive marketing. Have you met Espies yet?"

"No. What is it that I should know?" Ledger asks cautiously.

"He's a decent guy." I almost say *indulged trust-fund kid*, but figure that's an insult to Ledger as well, so I refrain. "Just steer clear of talk about hunting. Or trapping. Or anything to do with dead animals. It will unleash a conversation domination topic where he'll show you a picture of every animal he has killed in the past twenty years, along with a very detailed story to go with each one. From spotting to shooting to skinning."

"Um . . ."

"It's okay, city boy. You don't have to respond. The topic of hunting is commonplace here, but Espies takes it to a whole other level."

"Thanks for the heads-up. I'll definitely keep clear of that."

"And if you're trying to win his favor, take a bottle of Don Julio. That will make him happy."

"Noted." His soft sigh fills the line. "I'm sorry about . . . tonight."

"Don't be." I look around the office. "I have plenty of work to keep me busy."

We say our goodbyes, and I'm left staring at a blank computer screen with nothing but my own thoughts.

It's for the best. His meeting. Us being apart for the night. Some distance so that things are left with a little perspective.

I laugh. *Who am I kidding?* I miss him.

As ridiculous as that sounds, I do.

"No time like the present to tackle more of Pop's stacks," I mutter to myself.

But there is a thought that keeps coming back to me. A thought I haven't been able to kick since meeting Sarah in Bear Valley the other day.

I fell back on what I knew best, to save the day . . .

I twist my lips and stare into the night beyond the windows. Those words repeating in my head. I study the lavenders' silhouettes. The dark shadow of Pop's unfinished barn. The craggy oak tree towering over the south quadrant.

Ideas start to form. Begin to tumble. Take shape.

Luxury.

Decadence.

A destination to lose yourself in.

That's when I see a light in the darkness. A way to make this work. A way to fall back on what I know best to save the day.

Screw Pop's stacks.

I open my laptop and begin to plan.

My dreams are wild. Lights strung from tree to tree. Lavender tied and drying in rows from the barn ceiling. Tables end to end between the lavender rows, adorned with flameless candles and woven fresh flowers. Laughter— *so much laughter*—floating on the night air.

And love.

Definitely an abundance of love.

I awake with a start. My heart is pounding, but the smile my dream caused is still on my lips.

My cell rings again.

I scramble through the darkness, fearful something has happened to Gran, only to see Ledger's name on the screen.

"Hello?"

"You're sleeping. I'm sorry," Ledger says. "I forgot you're a farmer."

"Whatever," I say and roll my eyes as I sink back into my bed, pulling my comforter around me that still smells of his cologne. "It's okay. Hi. How was your meeting?"

"It went well. Hunting was in fact brought up, but with Hillary's help, I was able to steer the conversation as far away from it as possible."

"Thank God for Hillary."

"You can say that again. She's a lifesaver." He sounds tired, and the rasp to his voice tugs on parts of me. The lonely parts of me that love having him around.

"Definitely," I agree with a laugh.

"So what did you do tonight? Flirt with random guys to make me jealous? Streak down Main Street to start more gossip? *Think of me?*"

My smile widens—it seems to be a permanent fixture when I talk to him. "All of the above."

"That's what I'd expect." He chuckles. "So glad you haven't changed."

"Never."

But I have. So much has changed over the years.

Pieces of life that don't matter. Events that changed me. A loneliness I could never put words to.

Silence settles between us.

"Talk to me, Ash," he murmurs. "Tell me why you gave up your dream to move to the big city. Tell me about the boys who broke your heart. Tell me . . . *everything.*"

"That's a tall order."

"Perhaps. But I want to know."

So I tell him about college, Gran's stroke, helping take care of her, and how the money ran out for me to return.

"That was a big ask. To give up your dreams to care for her," he says without judgment.

"It was, but when you've lived your whole life and only two people have ever loved you, you don't hesitate to sacrifice for them since they've sacrificed so much for you."

There is a brief silence, then he clears his throat. "Three people. I loved you too, Asher."

His admission has tears springing to my eyes. Maybe I'm just feeling vulnerable talking about all of this when it's so much easier to shut down.

When your own damn mother doesn't want you, it's hard to open your-self up to more hurt.

"Don't get quiet on me now. Don't run away."

"I'm here." *I loved you too.* Past tense. I'm not sure why that hits me so hard, but it does. "What else was on your list of questions? Oh. Yes. My love life." His sigh is heavy in response. "You asked," I warn.

"I'm beginning to think I shouldn't have." He chuckles.

"Don't worry. There hasn't been a lot or anyone meaningful, if that's what you're asking. A couple of seasonal visitors, a few local guys—but none of them lasted longer than a couple of months."

"Is it bad if I say that makes me happy?"

"Are you saying you thought I slept around?" I tease.

"No. That's not—I didn't—"

"Relax, Ledger. I was just teasing you."

"Talk about sticking my foot in my mouth. Jesus." He snorts. "Why only a couple of months though? Is it because you're picky or because you like the chase but not the after?"

It's because none of them made me feel how you did.

"Maybe a little bit of both," I lie. "First, it's not exactly easy to date someone when you remember that he picked his boogers and wiped them on your desk in third grade."

"Jesus," he coughs out.

"Small-town life at its finest. And truth be told, I'm not exactly the eas-iest person to take home to Mom and Dad. I have no parents, and up until recently, I lived with my grandparents, and a lot of men can't handle the fact that I have a mind of my own and freely speak it. They think it's cute at first and then, after a month or two, try to tell me how things should be."

"I think that's one of your best qualities."

I blush under his praise. "Enough about me."

"No. You haven't told me nearly enough."

"You just don't want to answer the same questions."

"You're happy though, right, Ash? I mean you could always go back to school if you wanted. You could get out of Cedar Falls somehow. Dreams don't have time limits."

"Do I always wonder, *what if?* Of course, I do. Anyone else would do the same. It's like half of me would love to pursue what I once wanted, while the other half is completely content being right here where I don't have to pretend to be someone I'm not."

"I think you're a lot of people, Asher Wells," he says softly. "I'm pretty sure I like all of them."

I smile and snuggle deeper into my bed, allowing his words to wrap themselves around me. "Your turn."

He groans. "I guess I opened that door, huh?"

"You did."

"Lay it on me."

"How did you lose your father?"

He blows out a breath. "Hitting with the hard stuff first, huh?"

"It's easier to get it out of the way. You don't have to talk about it if you don't want to."

"No. It's fine." He pauses. "In a sense, I lost him the same way you lost your pop—in his sleep. But the root cause was Alzheimer's."

"I know for a fact that saying I'm sorry doesn't ease any of the pain, but I am sorry you lost him, Ledger."

"True, but thank you. Especially after everything he did to you . . . I don't expect you to be sorry."

"My feelings for him are irrelevant. I can still have compassion for you, your loss, and understand your grief." I soften my tone. "Was it a long ordeal?"

"No. Fortunately, I guess. If there is such a thing." He exhales a weighted breath. "But his demise was jarringly quick. It started with him forgetting a few things at first. Then blanking on major life events. Then . . . everything."

"That had to be rough."

"It was. My brothers and I struggled with it. Still do."

"And how are you managing . . . with everything . . . with the lie he told you?" I don't know how to phrase it.

"Honestly? I wish I could block it out, pretend it never happened so I could keep that idyllic image I've always had of him in my mind, *but it did*. We're proof of it." He starts to say something and stops. I give him a minute to gather his thoughts because I can't imagine how I'd feel if it were Pop who was the one who had done this. If his lies were the ones who tore us apart.

"We would have broken up at some point anyway. Those are the years where you find out who you really are. Besides, you were heading to college that next month with a whole new array of cute co-eds to make your way through."

"You think so?" he asks.

"We were from two completely different worlds, Ledger. Your dad was right in that respect. It's a long shot to think we would have lasted."

"Hmm." It's all he says but I'm wondering if he's thinking the same thing I am. *Would it be able to work now?*

"And what of the women who've broken your heart? Or rather the women whose hearts you have broken?" I chuckle. "I'm surprised you don't have a penthouse in the city, a gorgeous and cultured wife with two-point-five kids to fill it up with laughter and love."

His sleepy chuckle vibrates through the line. "I have the penthouse, but no wife. No kids. Not yet. Not till I'm at least thirty-eight-ish."

"You say that like you have marriage on a schedule," I joke.

"Not a schedule per se, but a ten-year plan, yes."

"So, you think you can schedule when you plan on falling in love?" *You didn't schedule ours when we were teenagers.* "Like it's some task to conquer after a board meeting?" My tone is a mixture of disbelief and confusion.

Not because I'm hoping to be that person he falls in love with (well, maybe), but because it sounds so clinical coming from a man that is more than passionate in other ways.

"Look, it's not like that. You make it sound so cold and calculating. I'm a planner. That's what I do. I set goals and have to meet them before I can move on to the next ones. That's all, and I have a lot of goals to check off before I want to settle down."

"You can't plan for love, Ledger. It's either there, or it isn't. And sometimes it isn't there and then it grows into love." My comment is a stark reminder that there is so much about him I don't know. The boy I once knew is still there, but like me, has been changed by his life experiences.

"I don't do well with unknowns and things I can't control," he says, and I can tell he's frustrated that I'm not understanding him. "I was always somewhat like that, but after the events of that night—the threat I thought was real—I changed. For a while, I lived in a constant state of unknown where so many things were out of my control, and the only way to take that control back was by planning."

I try to put myself in his shoes, to understand the fear of the accusation and the constant threat of being prosecuted looming over a teenager's head. Just like his father's words scarred me, I know they scarred Ledger even deeper.

So I'll give him this. I might not understand it. I don't have to agree with it. But I have to respect it because I wasn't there during those years. I wasn't witness to the aftermath of his father's cruel deception.

"So, no, love hasn't been on my radar, Asher. I date. I see women for a bit like you do men. But I don't tie myself down to someone with a label, if that's what you want to know."

"Never? You've never let someone get close to you?" I ask, finding it impossible to believe that a man like Ledger hasn't been in love time and again.

"My heart was broken one time," he says, and a small, selfish part of me hopes that he's talking about me, while the other part is jealous of whoever it was if it isn't. "I don't even think she knew how bad she broke it, but truth be told, it was pretty well shattered. Maybe that influenced my dating decisions after? I don't know. But I'd really love if we could move right along and off this topic."

I laugh. "You started this line of conversation. Not me."

"Hey, Ash?"

"Yeah?"

"Remember we used to do this all the time? Talk for endless hours on the phone about anything and everything? Talk until one of us fell asleep? Talk just so we knew the other one was there?"

His words are like a warm blanket cocooning me. "We did, didn't we?"

"Mm-hmm. And you always fell asleep first."

"I did not."

"Yes, you did." He laughs.

"Tell me more about your meeting," I say.

And so we talk like the years have evaporated.

There is an ease to our conversation.

A comfort that is hard to find.

And yes, I fell asleep first.

CHAPTER TWENTY-THREE

Asher

Sixteen Years Ago

"Ledger?" His shoes crush the dead leaves on the ground as he makes his way into the clearing. I'm on my feet the second I see the angry red mark on his cheek. "Oh my God. What happened?"

He shrugs his arm out of my grasp and walks to the creek's edge. Hands on his hips, shoulders moving up and down with his anger-fueled breaths.

I wince at his rebuff, uncertain what to do or what to say. Clearly, he's pissed off. Obviously, he got in some kind of fight—or at least was punched.

I'm not exactly good at dealing with bruised egos.

"Did you get in a fight with one of your brothers?" I finally ask.

"No." He bites the word out, and I retreat a step.

"Are you okay?"

Another sharp, "No."

I shift on my feet. I twist my lips. I figure it's best to just leave him alone. Obviously, something happened and, as much as I want to know what, I don't deserve to be snapped at for asking.

What wisdom would Gran give me right now? Give him space? Leave him alone? Feelings take time to verbalize?

I decide to wait him out, so I take a seat at the base of the old willow tree and lean against the trunk.

It's our spot.

He can't be mad at me when I'm sitting in our spot, right?

"Is this what you deal with here? In your own town?" he asks and then turns to face me, his eyes alive with anger.

"What did you do?" I ask, dread filling my stomach.

"I broke some fucking guy's nose is what I did."

"*You what?* Ledger." I struggle to find words. "What do you mean you broke someone's nose? Who was it?"

"Some prick talking absolute shit about you."

"What did he say?" I whisper and take a deep breath as I brace for an answer that I guarantee I've heard different variations of during the sixteen years I've been on this earth.

His stare is unrelenting, and his clenched jaw only serves to highlight the red on his cheek.

I can't look at him. I don't want to meet his eyes and see that he looks at me differently now that he's heard the shit said about me.

She's a whore, just like her lowlife of a mother was.

She's a bastard who even her own mother never wanted.

She kind of looks like so and so. Do you think he could be her dad?

Could you imagine wanting to kiss her? She might be your half-sister. Disgusting.

I've heard them all. I've cried over them.

I focus on the wind rustling through the willow tree above. The white petals of the wild daisy in my hand as I pluck one off at a time. The chirp of the birds flitting about overhead.

Anything other than letting him see the shame that is eating me whole. Anything other than finding out he believes any of it.

I was able to keep him away from it all last summer. I was an idiot to think I could do the same this year.

It's too hard to speak, so I keep staring at what's left of the daisy blurring from my welling tears and brace myself for what comes next.

Ledger's ridiculously expensive tennis shoes come into my view as he steps up to me and squats down. I still can't look at him.

"You don't deserve this, Ash. None of it. You couldn't pick the mom you got any more than how fortunate I am to be born into my family. It's all a crapshoot. It's all . . ." He growls in frustration and hucks a rock as far as he can throw it. It hits the water with a loud plunk. "It makes me so mad that you have to deal with that. That you have to hear that utter crap."

I shrug. "It's not a big deal."

"Yes, it is," he practically shouts at me. "It's horrible and wrong and—"

"And I've lived here my whole life, so for the most part, after sixteen years, they pretty much don't say it to my face. At least there's that."

He shakes his head. His hands are fisted. His teeth are gritted.

"What did they say?" I ask again.

"Nothing." He plops down beside me, his arm going around my shoulder and pulling me against him. "It's nothing."

"Which one was it? Bastard-child Asher? She's a slut just like her mom? She's a homewrecker and needs to go?" I shift so I can face him, our knees bumping against each other's. "You'd think after all this time they could think up new ones." I emit a self-deprecating laugh to hide how I'm crumbling inside.

"It wasn't anything." And the way he says those three words and the glance he gives me says it all—the slight was too harsh even for him.

"Tell me."

"No."

"Ledger. I need to know so I can protect myself." He looks out toward the creek, and I grab his hand. "Please."

"It was just something about how easy you must be, because you're just like your mom, and questioning if I'm afraid I'll catch something."

I blink the tears away, hating that he won't look at me.

I will not let their words get to me.

I will not let him pity me.

I will not . . .

"Forget about it." I grab his face and press a kiss to his lips. At first, they remain rigid and angry before slowly softening and kissing me back.

It's like little explosions of warmth happen all over my body when Ledger kisses me. Little acknowledgments that he sees the real me. Likes me for me. It's the only time I know I'm looked at and not judged. It's the only time I can let my guard down.

When the kiss is over, I rest my head on his shoulder and we sit like this for some time, lost in our thoughts.

I don't ask who made the comment.

Needing to know isn't a necessity.

Because whoever it is today, it will be a different one tomorrow. And even a different one the time after that.

Gran and Pop have taught me that no one else defines my worth but me.

But it still hurts like a bitch, regardless.

"Thank you for defending me. You didn't have to. I'm sorry you got hurt," I whisper and press a kiss to his cheek. "Do you really have to leave next week?"

He links his fingers with mine and sighs. The topic we've been avoiding the last few days is his inevitable departure back to Manhattan and his fancy prep school. We did this last summer—said goodbye before school started—and somehow stayed in touch. His coming back gave me something to look forward to. His calls, while he was gone, helped the time pass. I just hope we can make it work this time too.

"I'll be back next summer. We can talk all the time on the phone and text and Skype, just like we did this year. We'll make it work, Ash."

"I don't want to let you go."

He chuckles as we fall into our routine. "You have to, though."

"On one condition." I quirk an eyebrow at him, going for humor to mask my sadness.

"What condition is that?"

"That you promise me you'll come back next year. That you promise me you won't forget me." My voice breaks on those last words. All I can think about is the rich, sophisticated, beautiful girls at his prep school back home. Ones who have moms and aren't called sluts. Ones who would gladly enjoy Ledger's kisses and attention just as much as I do.

How can I compete with that? How will phone calls and texts beat sitting beside them in class every day?

He reaches out and runs a thumb over my cheek, his smile soft, his eyes warm. "You're my lavender girl. How could I ever forget you?" He presses a kiss on my lips. "Stop worrying. They're all pretentious and ridiculously shallow," he says, reading my mind. "And I'll make sure I talk about you so much that they're all jealous of you." Another tender kiss. "I won't forget you. I wouldn't be able to even if I wanted to."

CHAPTER TWENTY-FOUR

Asher

I'M DAYDREAMING AGAIN.

Then again, is it daydreaming if it really happened and you're simply replaying it in your head over and over because it was that good?

Dinner at Bessie's Diner. Making out on the porch swing on the veranda in the moonlight. Talking on the phone into the early morning hours. My time spent with Ledger has made me feel like a teenager again in some senses and a cared-for woman in others.

"Asher?" I look up to see George standing in the doorway. "Wow." He scans the office. "I don't think I've ever seen it this . . . uncluttered before."

"I've made progress, right?" My smile beams because I have, and I'm not ashamed to welcome the praise. It's been taxing and confusing and a huge learning experience as I've gone through each piece of paper or receipt or napkin with scribbles on them, and tried to figure out its importance. Is it a recurring bill? Is it a monthly supply invoice I need to budget for? Is it, is it, is it . . .

"I'm impressed. Can I show you something?"

"Not if you're going to ruin my good mood."

A smile breaks over his face. "It won't. I promise."

"Whew," I say, rising from my seat and closing the lid of my laptop. I'm nowhere near ready to have anyone see what I'm working on yet. Not until I know I can actually make it happen.

I follow George down the steps and toward the fields. "How's Angel doing?" I ask him about his wife.

"Good. Stressed over the new resort. I don't know." He runs a hand through his hair and tries to pull off a smile that looks as if it's nothing, but . . .

"About the resort?"

He nods. "She's in charge of catering over at Lakefront," he says, referring to another smaller resort on the lake. "She thinks The Retreat is going to wipe out their business, and she's afraid she'll get laid off."

I don't even know what to say. It's definitely a concern of many businesses around town. "Maybe it'll do the opposite. Maybe it'll be the only affordable place in town to hold events if The Retreat is too expensive."

"Maybe." He doesn't sound too sure.

I pat him on the shoulder. "Let's hope so."

He nods as we round the corner, and when I look up, my feet falter. "George." His name is a gasp as I take in the barn.

"She looks good, doesn't she?"

I look from the barn, to him, then back. The weathered wood of its exterior looks brand new. He's kept its patina charm but has not stained it to look like it was just built yesterday. "You guys did all this?"

"Yep. We power-washed it down then sprayed on a treatment to protect it from bugs trying to find a new home." Pride shines in his eyes.

"In two days. You did *this*?"

He nods, his grin widening. "The fields are behaving themselves, so we've had some time. It looks good, huh?"

"Wow." I take a few steps closer, shocked how such a simple thing has virtually given the ranch a facelift.

"You're happy with it?"

"Happy doesn't begin to describe it."

"Okay. I wanted to make sure you were good with it before we started on the inside."

"By all means, George." I shake my head, unable to take my eyes off it.

"That's it, then. See? I told you it was good news."

"Very good news. I mean . . . thank you." I'm honestly in awe.

"What are you planning on doing with this, anyway?"

"Making this a destination, George."

"A destination?"

I nod. "I'm still figuring that out, but I want other people to enjoy this place. To find happiness here. To make memories here."

But when I turn back toward the house again, my smile is so wide my cheeks hurt.

For the first time, I really think I might be able to pull this off.

What do you think, Pop?

I hope it makes him proud too.

A sample business proposal I found on the Internet is beside my laptop. It feels confusing and impossible with its mission statement and graphics and pricing structures. Now it's up to me to translate all of that where my cursor blinks on the blank screen in front of me.

I have to start somewhere, right?

A knock on the door startles me.

"One sec, Geor . . ." But my words fall off when I look up and find Ledger standing in the doorway.

Seeing him is like a sucker punch to the gut and a jump-start to my libido.

Every freaking time.

He's wearing casual clothes—blue jeans, a pale green V-neck that fits just right—and flip-flops adorn his feet. There's something about seeing his choice of shoes that makes me smile.

This is as casual as Ledger Sharpe gets, and he wears it well.

Then again, he wears everything well.

"Hi." His grin could light up the room. "*George?* Should I presume that's the man who just drove out of the gate in his truck?"

It's the first time I notice the fading sun and the color streaking across the sky indicating that it's well past seven in the evening. "I completely lost track of time."

"Working on something important?" he asks. The sun is at his back, creating a halo around his silhouette.

"Yes. No. *Maybe.*"

"You can't go wrong with that answer." He laughs as I rise from my seat and move to him. "Want to talk about it?"

"Just a pipe dream that I'm trying to figure out if I can make a reality."

"Tell me more," he murmurs as I step into him and press my lips to his.

Partially as a distraction and mostly because he and that glorious mouth of his are all I can think about.

And just like that, the budget numbers and figures and graphics I've been trying to piece together all afternoon slip from my mind.

There is only him. Only Ledger.

"We need to stop this before I forget my surprise for you," he murmurs against my lips before kissing me again.

"Only if you promise we can start where we left off later."

"It's a deal."

"Wait. Did you say surprise?"

"Go for a walk with me?" he asks cryptically and holds out his hand.

I look at him and then look at his hand. "Here? On the farm?"

"Yep."

We take off in a slow stroll toward the back part of the property, walking near the end of the Folgate. There's a breeze, which makes the lavender look like it's at the bottom of the ocean, its leaves floating back and forth like water. A tide of purple.

There is a lot to be said about The Fields, but one thing that's always held true is its sight, scent, and the tranquility that comes with each of them, leaving an indelible mark on you.

It was my short-lived time at the Pratt Institute that made me realize it.

It was returning home to take care of Gran and nurse the pain of losing my dream that reinforced it.

"It's beautiful here," Ledger says.

"It is. And so very far from your normal, everyday life."

"True," he says with a nod, "but that doesn't mean I don't recognize beauty when I see it." He looks at me in a way that says he's talking about me.

I blush like an idiot and look around, curious what this whole walk thing is about. *What is he up to?* But rather than give me any clues, he just swings our hands back and forth.

"When did that happen to the barn?" he asks. "I'm usually an observant person. Did I miss that it's always looked like that or has something changed?"

"I figured this place needed some curb appeal." I'm not ready to tell him about my idea yet. I need more time to figure it all out. The last thing I want to do is make an ass out of myself for aiming too high. Especially with someone like Ledger who brings and transforms resorts to life for a living.

"It looks great. What else have you got in mind?"

"I'm figuring that out," I say, more than grateful when he doesn't push for more. "What about you? Any headway with the mayor and his ridiculous demands?"

"Some. We've hired local contractors who want to work with us. It's a costly move given the cancelations with outside companies already contracted. But we're making it work and trying to make it right since we did overpromise and under-deliver."

"That's admirable."

He shrugs. "It's the right thing to do. Did it give Grossman the right to blackmail us over it? Force me to be here for two damn months? No way in hell, but we pride ourselves on standing by our word—so we will."

Two damn months.

In that whole comment, that is what I heard the most. What my mind fixated on. I knew this was the scenario. Ledger told me the time frame that first night at Hank's almost three weeks ago, but hearing it now after . . . everything, makes it hit a lot harder.

He's going to leave again, Asher.

It's no surprise. You knew that. Enjoy him while you can . . . *but guard your heart.*

Easier said than done because, despite my resolve and the short few weeks we have been involved, I already know my head and heart aren't on the same page.

It's ridiculous. How could what some would consider puppy love as a teenager suddenly come back with a vengeance upon seeing that same person as an adult?

Get a grip.

This isn't love.

This is lust with a side of history thrown in.

And as if Ledger timed the reveal of his secret to stop my over-analytic mind, I look over to see why Ledger has stopped walking. In the middle of the clearing, he has a blanket laid out. On one of its corners is a basket with a few bottles of wine beside it.

I look over at him and simply shake my head. Words escape me.

"This is the place, right? Where we used to go and get lost in nothing but each other?" he asks as if my silence is a bad thing.

"Yes." The single syllable is laced with surprise, affection, and . . . love. "How—I mean—what—"

"You deserved a date. Especially one without the town watching your every move. This—our old stomping ground—fit the bill. At least we won't have to worry about Pop catching us fooling around."

"Oh my God," I say as I step forward, stretching our hands across the distance between us. "Do you remember that time—"

"When my hand was up your shirt and your hand was down my pants and Pop came out—"

"With a flashlight?" I laugh. "There's no way he didn't know what was going on."

"None. At all." Ledger's smile is wistful, and it strikes me that it's a rare look from him. He's always steadfast. Always intense. Something else looks good on him. "I don't think I've *ever* moved so fast in my life."

"My favorite was the sweatshirt you balled in your lap to hide your hard-on."

"I totally forgot about that." He laughs.

"How could you? You stammered out excuse after excuse about why you couldn't stand and take a walk with Pop when he asked you to go check out the new tire swing—"

"No. It was the new tractor because he said city boys needed to learn how easily accidents can happen on a farm. I'm pretty sure he wanted to add me to that statistic by pushing me under the tire simply to prevent me from touching you again."

"As any father would."

We both laugh, and I realize it's the first time I've thought about Pop and truly laughed at his memory rather than feeling sorrow.

I'm healing.

Minute by minute. Day by day. Memory by memory.

And I think a huge part of it is having Ledger here to talk about him with.

As we approach the blanket, he stops when I squeeze his hand. "This was very thoughtful of you and just what I needed. Thank you." I step up on my toes and press a kiss to his lips. His hands slide up the length of my spine before fisting in the hair at my neck as he deepens the kiss.

My body reacts to his touch, to his lips, to everything about him in a way I don't remember doing for anybody else before. Nothing is ever enough. His touch. The groans of pleasure in the back of his throat. The feel of his muscles tensing beneath my palms as I run my hands up and down the plane of his chest.

"If that's what I get for a picnic in a field, you can bet your ass I'll be planning something more elaborate next time."

CHAPTER TWENTY-FIVE

Ledger

Fifteen Years Ago

"A SHOOTING STAR. LOOK." I POINT TO THE LAST REMNANTS of it as it dies out with its fall.

"Make a wish," Asher says, squeezing my fingers currently laced with hers.

"That's ridiculous. No one believes that shit."

"Fine. Then I'll make one for you."

"Go ahead."

I turn my head so I can look at her. We're lying on a blanket in the middle of the lavender fields staring at the stars. Or at least she is while I'm trying to figure out when to make a move. A guy only has so much restraint when the girl he's with is like Asher—gorgeous, funny, unique.

A girl who looks at me like I'm a normal boy instead of the prep-school trust-fund kid whose father is part of New York City's elite.

Hell, she's never asked for a damn thing. Not once. I have girls back home asking for fancy shit when they can afford it themselves. And then there's Asher who has nothing and asks for nothing. If she did, I'd give it to her in a heartbeat. Without question. It's not like Dad ever checks what we spend money on anyway.

If he did, we'd be majorly screwed for all the money we shelled out for beer on this trip.

Asher closes her eyes and scrunches up her nose. It's freaking adorable.

"What'd you wish for?" I ask when her nose un-scrunches. Apparently, that's her wish-making face.

"I'm not telling you." She swats playfully at me, but her eyes remain fixed on the sky above. "If I do, it won't come true."

"C'mon. I wanna know." *What does a girl like Asher wish for?*

"No."

"Pretty please?" I lean up on my elbow so I can stare at her and so she can't ignore me.

"No."

"Ah, there's a smile," I say, putting my hand on her hip and rocking her back and forth. "You know you want to tell me."

"I need the wish more than you want me to tell you," she says drolly.

"You *need* it?" I draw the word out. "Then that means it's me, right? Since you *need* me."

"Oh, geez." She rolls her eyes. "Did you seriously just say that?"

"Yes. And I'm pretty sure I'm right."

She pats the top of my hand still on her hip. "For your ego's sake, I'll keep letting you think that."

"Don't you worry about my ego. It's doing just fine." I flop back onto the ground, look up at the stars like she is, and huff. "You're no fun."

Crickets chirp all around us and beetles make their distinct clicking sound, but the only thing I really hear is Asher's even breathing beside me.

Feeling slightly and ridiculously dejected because she won't tell me, I fall quiet.

"I wished that I'd get a chance to make my mark somehow." I'm just about to ask what she means when she continues, her voice barely audible. "That people will look at me and admire me, what I've done, what I've made of myself instead of looking at me and feeling sorry for me because I'm Lydia Wells's, the town floozy's, daughter."

Her voice breaks, and it fucking kills me. I'll never understand how she feels because we're polar opposites. Whereas she has pressure weighing on her because people expect nothing from her, I have it because they expect too damn much from me.

We're from completely different worlds, and yet somehow . . . *we work.*

"Ash." I lean back up on my elbow and run a hand up and down her arm. I don't even know what to say. How to respond.

She shakes her head and musters a smile I don't believe. "It was stupid. Forget I said anything."

"No. It's important," I murmur and press a kiss to her lips. "And I want you to know I already do look at you like that." Another kiss. "You are Asher Wells, my lavender girl, and maker of her own destiny."

Then another one.

And later when we see another shooting star, I make my own wish: for Asher's wish to come true.

CHAPTER TWENTY-SIX

Asher

"DID YOU SEE IT?" LEDGER ASKS, HIS FREE HAND POINTING TO the sky as a star streaks across it before burning itself out.

We're lying on the blanket. His arm is wrapped around me with my head resting on his arm. Two bottles of wine have been consumed, a charcuterie has been devoured, and we're both just soaking in the tranquility of the evening. Of the perfection he created in bringing me here tonight.

"I did," I murmur.

"Are you going to make a wish? I seem to remember you were quite big on that back in the day."

My smile is bittersweet. What's is like to be young and naïve and think the world will treat you like you deserve?

"I think I'm too old to make wishes, Ledge."

"What? No. You're never too old for wishes"—he squeezes his arm around me—"or dreams. You need to make one."

I feel silly but close my eyes and scrunch up my nose anyway.

But I remember that last wish I made. And how not long after Ledger up and left Cedar Falls abruptly—once I'd given myself to him—and the gossip that burned through town in the days and weeks to come. That Ledger had gotten what he'd wanted from this small-town girl before going back to his hot, socialite girlfriend. That I'd ruined the summer for every other girl there who'd had their sights set on Callahan and Ford because they'd left too. That I was trash just like my mom, trying to screw my way up because I'd never amount to anything otherwise, so I deserved the cruel words and harsh judgment. I'd earned it like a badge. And I'd proved them right—I'd never amount to anything.

And yet, with my eyes clenched shut, I wish.

I wish that this were real. I wish this never had to end. I wish the same wish as I did before, fifteen years ago.

When I open my eyes, he's still there, still looking at me like he did back then. But this time, there's something more in his eyes. Adoration. Lust. Respect. Desire. *Hope.*

Important things for any woman to see. To know that someone feels that way when they look at her.

I reach out and cup the side of his face, needing to touch him. Needing to know he really is real.

He turns his face into my hand and presses a kiss on my palm. *Be still my heart.*

I rise onto my knees, his eyes narrowing and full of curiosity as he watches me lean forward and press a kiss to his lips.

He tastes of the wine we just drank and the certainty that I need as I slowly move to straddle him while I deepen the kiss.

His body is warm beneath me, and the summer night air has the slightest hint of a welcome chill to it.

He kisses me back with the same gentle demand that I do him. His hands are in my hair, on my cheeks, cupping my face. Our tongues dance against one another's, and our bodies heat up as we make out in the moonlight between the lavender rows.

"Asher," he murmurs against my lips, a reverent sigh between kisses.

Leaning back, I strip my shirt over my head, wanting to feel the intimacy that comes when his hand runs over my skin. Needing to feel it.

I look down at him, my moonlight boy, and know this is my favorite look on him. Eyes heavy with desire and his smile soft and a little crooked.

"What?" he asks.

"I just want to look at you." I lean down and press a kiss to his lips. To his chin. To his neck. "I need to touch you, Ledger," I murmur against his skin. My hand runs down the front of his chest. "To taste you." My lips follow their descent as I crawl back to where his cock is hard and pressed against the seam of his jeans. His stomach muscles tighten beneath my lips when I make quick work of his zipper, free his cock, and stroke it with my hand. "To devour you."

The hiss of his breath fills the night air as I slide his cock between my lips and take him all the way to the back of my throat. His thighs tense. His guttural groan is the only thing I hear as he reaches down and cups my chin.

I look up at him through the moonlight night as his eyes turn dark and his eyelids grow heavy with desire. And with my gaze locked on his, I give him the pleasure he deserves. With my tongue licking over his crest and my lips suctioning around his shaft and my hands stroking every thick, hard inch of him.

It's a heady feeling sucking Ledger off. To know that drop of precum that hits my tongue is because of me. To watch a man usually so measured in his actions, lose himself in the sensations I create.

"Ash." My name is a strained rasp in the night as he fights to hang on to his control, and I provoke him to let go.

By letting his cock hit the back of my throat. By using my fingers to work their magic around the base of his shaft. By humming to add a vibration to the onslaught of sensations I'm already creating for him.

He hardens and swells as his hand moves to my hair and fists there.

I suck harder and stroke faster, my own body aching for his release so he can shift his focus on me. So I can enjoy this body of his.

Because when it comes to Ledger, I can't seem to ever get enough. Not his touch. Not the sounds he makes when he's about to come. Not the way he makes me feel, physically and emotionally.

"Ash." He struggles in indecision. "Fuck." One hand still in my hair. "Yes." The other hand pulling on my arm for me to come ride him. "Now."

A yelp escapes my mouth as he hauls me up and makes quick work of my jeans in an awkward dance of desperation and laughter, all while trying to kiss the breath out of me.

It's my turn now to moan in ecstasy. At the way he stretches me when I sink down ever so slowly onto him. At the feeling of fullness he creates. At the ever-burning ache that I fear will never be sated.

"Ledge . . . so good," I murmur against his lips as his fingers dig into the flesh at my hips while I adjust to him.

"Good God, you're going to be the death of me," he groans out.

I begin to rock my hips.

At least I can ensure he dies a happy man, then.

CHAPTER TWENTY-SEVEN

Ledger

"THE PROTESTORS ARE BACK AGAIN," HILLARY SAYS WHEN SHE pokes her head in my office.

"Seriously?" I barely even glance up from my laptop. That's how much I don't fucking care about who's protesting now. "What do their signs say this time?"

"Let me see." Hillary moves to my window and peeks down below. "*Preserve our lakefront* is one. *No unions here,* which is rather comical considering there isn't a union happening. *Big city greed means small-town ruin.* Wow," she says as she turns to look at me with raised eyebrows. "That's a new one."

"Rather catchy, don't you think?" I lean back in my chair and try to switch gears from Takashi getting squirrely on details to the debacle front and center. "Is there a website they go to find these slogans?"

"Who knows. Catchphrase.R.Us perhaps?"

"How about GoFuckYourself.com."

"I vote for that one." She chuckles and looks back out the window again. "They need to make up their mind though, because they change their message daily."

"Which is why I think the mayor is behind this."

"He really does have a hard-on for you, doesn't he?" she says as she moves away from the window and takes a seat in the chair in front of my desk.

"The question is *why?* My guess is that visibility is key when you're running for reelection."

"My guess is he needs to lose simply on principle."

I laugh. I love Hillary and her dry sense of humor. She's been with S.I.N. going on ten years now and has been an incredible asset.

"While I have you, where are we in 'project town involvement'?" I roll my eyes to emphasize how thrilled I am about this.

"We've passed out flyers to all local businesses, placed an ad in Cedar Falls and Bear Valley newspapers, and notified the City of Commerce. Maybe we'll get some submissions from local artists and craftsmen so we can feature their work at the resort. Maybe we won't."

"It's a crapshoot. The big question is, what do we do if we only get ugly shit for submissions?"

Hillary laughs. "Then we don't take it? Or we put it on the back walls and not front and center. We paid a fortune for our interior designer. The last thing I want to do is have to ugly up their esthetic to accommodate this new *glitch* from Grossman."

"Agreed." I take a sip of my water as she rises from the chair. "And thank you." She stops and looks at me. "I know you have a crap ton on your plate, trying to get this done on time and under budget, and then I added this to it. You're doing a great job."

Hillary has the oddest expression on her face as she looks at me.

"What is it?" I ask.

"Do you know I worked for your father for over eight years and while he was a kind man, he was also more than demanding. He paid me well and understood when I needed time for my kids or whatever, but not once did he ever say something like what you just did. Thank you, Ledger." Her voice is soft, her eyes sincere. "I truly appreciate it."

And when she walks across the hall to her office, her words echo in my head, and I smile.

About the time I turn back to my laptop and type answers Takashi isn't going to like, a little pair of legs—whose torso is hidden behind a picket sign—comes walking into my office.

"I think you took a wrong turn," I say.

"It's me, though. Tootie." She sticks her head out from behind the cardboard and offers me her toothless grin.

"Did you think I'd want you walking in here with *that* sign?"

"It's my cover," she says, leaning it against the wall and crossing her arms over her chest.

"Your cover?" I ask.

"Yep." She takes a stroll around my office space, touching almost everything in the process. The walls, the windowsill, the corner of my desk. It's almost as if she's assessing it, which is ridiculous. "I needed a way to sneak in here. I figured this was the best way."

Hillary walks back toward my office with a perplexed expression, perhaps wondering how Tootie got past her, but I just hold up my hand to stop her. I nod to let her know it's okay.

"Does your mom know you're here?" I ask as Tootie finishes her survey and helps herself to the seat Hillary vacated minutes ago. She takes a moment, making a show of wiggling her butt in the chair to feel out if it's comfortable.

The purse of her lips tells me she finds it suitable.

"Yep. I told her I was going to come sweet-talk you into coming over for dinner, but don't come. *Ever.* My mom burns toast like it's an Olympic sport. I wouldn't subject you to her cooking. Not even my enemy."

"Thanks for the warning."

"Anytime." She folds her hands in her lap as she tries to scoot her tiny body to the back of the chair. "Besides, people are talking."

"About?"

"You."

"They are, are they?"

She sighs heavily. "I mean, I try not to listen, or at least I say that I try not to, but you know I do."

"Of course, you do. Should I ask what they are saying or are you going to tell me in your own sweet time?"

The little giggle she emits has me shaking my head. "They say you *have* a woman."

"First lesson in life, Tootie. If you ever date a man who says he 'has a woman', dump him on the spot."

"Why?"

"A man does not *have* you. You are your own person with your own thoughts. He can enjoy you and your company. He can want to spend time with you and laugh with you. At no point does he ever *have* you. Got it?"

"I think you're going a little deeper than is needed. Should I rephrase?

I'll rephrase." She clears her throat and sits a little taller. "They, the people in town, say that you are *enjoying* the company of a woman."

Smart-ass.

"It's none of their business what I'm enjoying," I assert. *To an eight-year-old.*

"You're right. It's not. But it's a small town, so technically everyone thinks it is their business." She looks down to where she's started picking at her yellow fingernail polish. "Are you going to explain to me why Mayor Grossman wants to screw you over?"

I choke on my next breath. "Tootie."

"What?" she asks innocently enough. "Would you rather me say fu—"

"Nope. Screw works. Screw is just fine." Jesus. This kid. "Why do you say he wants to screw me over?"

"He was at the coffee shop when Momma was talking to Ellie May about the man she wants to . . . er . . . *enjoy*." She winks and grins, but her cheeks turn pink. "And the mayor was sitting behind me talking and talking and talking about how he needs to keep the pressure on you because it looks better for him."

And there is the answer Hillary and I were just asking the question to. I look up to see Hillary across the hall nodding, clearly hearing Tootie's whirlwind conversation.

"He's not exactly in my fan club."

"You have a fan club? How did I not know this?" She sits up a little straighter. "Do you charge a membership fee? Have a paying Patreon club where you reveal extra tidbits? How. Did. I. Not. Know. This?"

"It's an expression, Tootie. A turn of phrase. It's not a real thing."

She waves a hand at me. "And to think you got me all excited about nothing."

"Was there more you wanted to say about the mayor?" I ask.

"You need to kill him with kindness. That's what Momma says to do when Alex teases me." She rolls her eyes dramatically. "A fist to his nose sounds better in my opinion, but apparently killing him with kindness works even better."

"Sure. Yes. Okay." There's no way I'm going to tell her I vote for bopping Alex in the nose. *But I do.*

"What did you ever do to him, anyway?"

"Your guess is as good as mine." I shrug. "He's just an opportunistic . . ."

"Asshole? Is that the word you were going for?"

It's Hillary's turn to cough out a laugh.

"Something like that." I fight my own smile. "Why are you trying to help me, Tootie Tootie Bo Footie?"

Her grin is ear to ear from the nickname. "Somebody has to because, in case you didn't know, it's a dog-eat-dog world out there, Ledger."

"Clearly." I nod, trying to keep a straight face. And then it dawns on me. "Hey, do you want to help me with something?"

"Like be a secret agent or something?" She sits up straighter.

"Nothing quite that intense." I laugh. "In an effort to kill the mayor with kindness, Hillary and I," I say, pointing to Hillary, "are working on upgrading your library at school."

"You are?" Her eyes widen.

"We are. So I think you're the perfect person to help us decide what exactly it needs."

"You mean like a reading couch and a moon pod and wobble chairs and another set of Harry Potter because it's *always* checked out? That kind of stuff?"

"Exactly that kind of stuff."

"A way to a woman's heart is through her books. That's for darn sure."

I just stare at her, blinking. There's nothing else I can do.

She crosses her arms over her chest and purses her lips, clearly in deep thought. "Do I have a budget, or do I get carte blanche?"

Where does she come up with this shit?

"How about you just make a list—"

"It would be much easier if I created a Word doc and gave you links to where to buy the items."

I stare at her dumbfounded. "What?"

"Yeah. It's what I do for Momma at Christmas. She says it's much easier for Santa if he has web links because he has so many kids to get toys for. That way he gets me exactly what I want."

Can't fault Momma for that one.

"Okay. If you're okay with doing that—"

"Kids are fluent in computer these days. Don't doubt my skills."

"I won't. I'm not. I definitely do not doubt you."

"Good." She stands and gives us a resolute nod. "I need to get back to Momma. She probably thinks I got lost somewhere and am in some kind of peril. She listens to too many true crime podcasts." She rolls her eyes. "But I'll get on that right away as I'm assuming you need progress to get the mayor off your back?"

"Something like that. Thank you for the help."

"You know, if this thing with the woman you *enjoy* doesn't pan out," she says as she stops to pick up her sign and then looks over her shoulder at me, "I'm available to take her place in about twenty years. Later."

And with that, Tootie skips out of my office and down the hall.

I meet Hillary's eyes across the distance. "I want to be her when I grow up," she says.

CHAPTER TWENTY-EIGHT

Asher

THE DAYS PASS QUICKLY.

I hate to admit that I would do anything possible to slow them down, to eke out more time with Ledger each day, but it's true. The clock still turns. The hours still fade. The days turn to night.

And as much as it hurts to admit, I know he has a life to get back to in New York City. He is rarely on the phone when we are together. In fact, I'm rather positive he makes a point to be unplugged. But on the off chance he has to take a call he's waiting for, I'm immediately reminded of his stature and importance in a world so very foreign to me. Facts and figures roll off his tongue in a no-nonsense tone that has to be intimidating to anyone on the other end of the line, but to me is a turn-on.

There's nothing sexier than a man who is sure of himself.

But it's those times when he's fixing a problem or negotiating with God knows who, that I'm reminded he does have a life that's real, a penthouse that's most likely posh, and a social life that's probably active to get back to.

My chest aches at the thought.

So I find comfort in the rhythm we've fallen into. Days spent working on our own. Evenings spent getting to know each other again even though it feels like we've never been apart. Late nights enjoying each other's bodies and learning each other's pleasures.

But there seems to be an unspoken line we're both toeing. One that has us taking a step back for a break every day or two, almost as if both of us are afraid to get too close.

I think it's futile.

Yet I still play the game.

And I still attempt to convince myself this is simply infatuation.

"Oh my God, Ash," Nita says as she walks toward me, her hands out, her face up to the sky. The look of amazement she gives me when she finishes twirling under the softness of the lights causes goosebumps to chase over my skin. "This. Is. Amazing."

She keeps moving. Around the clearing where George and the guys finished stringing lights back and forth from tree to tree to the barn in a zigzag pattern. They are muted and cast a soft glow in the darkening night. To the various antique and well-worn pots we've gathered from garage sales from neighboring communities. With flowers spilling out of them, they add a touch of color to the patinated barnwood they sit against.

She moves inside the barn. From the ceiling's rafters hangs row after row of lavender bundles drying amidst several shabby chic chandeliers that lighten the all-wood interior.

She runs her hands over the newly stained railing that leads to the barn's loft. Over the piles of décor items I've yet to put out.

"Do you like it?" I ask, not caring whether she does or doesn't, because I do. It's been so long since I've been able to take ownership of something and see it to fruition that I forgot how good it felt to do so. With every thought and placement, that familiar hum returned to my veins like when I used to sketch.

There's a creativity to this. A freedom to invent and inspire and bring a vision to life. I never realized how much I was missing this feeling, how happy it made my heart and the calming it did for my soul, until I started this project.

Who knew falling back on what I knew best would mean both the lavender and my sketching?

"I'm stunned. Literally stunned," she says, her feet continually moving as she takes everything in. "You are going to be booked for weddings and events and . . . so many things."

"That's the plan." *Luxury. Decadence. A destination to lose yourself in.* Ledger's words were the driving force behind the feel of it. Sarah from the apothecary's comments were the ones that flipped the switch on in my head. "And then once we get our feet under us, I'm thinking we create another outbuilding over there," I say and point in the distance.

"For what?"

"So we can make our own soaps or oils to sell to places like Sarah's apothecary. So we can have people come out here to be hands-on and make it themselves." I shrug and smile shyly. "More pipe dreams."

"*This* is not a pipe dream. *This* is you falling back on what you know best. The one constant in your entire life. *The lavender.*" She grabs me in a quick hug and makes a squealing sound as she turns around and takes it all in again. "You could do weddings over there by the tree."

"That's what I was thinking too. Have the ceremony out there and the reception in the barn."

"It would be so beautiful with the lavender as a backdrop and the breeze blowing through it. Gran and Pop would love this, wouldn't they?"

My smile is bittersweet. "I already showed Gran some photos. It made her cry happy tears. She couldn't believe this was our farm. I already talked to the staff about how we can get her here when it's finished so she can see it."

"There won't be a dry eye in the house on that day."

I nod because I already have it planned in my head. Getting Gran here. Letting her see her beloved lavender again. Sneaking her over to visit Pop on the way back.

Pop. He already knows what it looks like, because he's been here beside me every step of the way, guiding me.

"Fingers crossed I get approved for my loan so I have the capital to buy the rest of what I need. Tables and chairs. I want to add a bathroom for guests and a kitchen onto the back of the barn so I can accommodate a caterer. Pave the dirt road coming in here for easier access." I scrub my hands over my face, having already visualized it a hundred times. "If I'm denied, this is all for naught."

That's my biggest fear. That if I leverage the farm for collateral for this new loan, I'll not only be risking my family's blood, sweat, and tears, but also my home.

And then, what if I don't get the loan? I know from experience that it's almost crueler to have the dream and get it yanked away from you when you've had just a taste of it than to simply dream it and never get a chance to experience it.

"If you don't get approved, you'll figure it out somehow. It's about time you get to reap the good luck around here." She stops and lifts an eyebrow.

"Then again, you did find Ledger so that seems like maybe you've cashed some of that in."

"For the time being, anyway." I try to joke about it, but Nita knows me well enough to know what I'm doing when I change the topic—avoidance as usual. "I've also been working on a proposal to offer special deals to clients of The Retreat. Receptions. Parties. Whatever. The resort would get a booking commission, and I'd get more traffic. Once I'm finished with it, then I'll present it to the person in charge there."

"You mean Ledger?" she says sarcastically as she slides a look my way as if I'm crazy.

"No. *Not Ledger*. I don't want him to have anything to do with this."

"You know that sounds crazy, right? He owns the damn resort, yet you think he's not going to know?"

"I don't care if he knows after my proposal has been accepted, but not before. No way. I want to get the partnership on my own merit. Not because he gave me a handout."

"A handout and a hand are two different things," she asserts.

"Promise me you won't say anything to him if you see him."

"Fine. Whatever. But how are you going to keep all of this from him when he comes here?"

"He's seen the outside of the barn but not the inside. I'll say I added the lights because this part of the property is darker, and I wanted to brighten it up." I shrug. "He's a man. He doesn't notice details until you point them out one by one."

"True." She laughs. "Where is the man of the hour anyway? Why's he not here screwing your brains out between the rows of lavender?"

"That was three nights ago," I say nonchalantly as her grin widens.

"You're serious, aren't you?" I nod and she sighs. "Jealous with a capital J. So what exactly is going on with him?"

"What do you mean?"

"I mean I've known you for a long damn time, Ash, and this is just different."

"Different *how?*" I ask but already know her answer. Because I can't put my finger on it and neither will she be able to.

"The amount of time you spend with him without feeling smothered. Your want for more than just the damn good sex you're having. The fact that you're taking a chance on this"—she points to the barn and the lights around us—"when you've been so willing to just settle. It's nothing I can definitely pinpoint, but it's there and I love it."

My smile is soft as I shake my head. "I hate when women say it was a man that gave them confidence and all of that bullshit, so I'm not going to say it, but I don't know, Nita. Something in me has changed with Ledger here. I don't know if it's self-assurance or if it's that I don't give a crap about anyone in town or what they say about me . . . I'm just more like the old me I was before I got called back here."

She nods. "Hold on tight to it, okay?"

Let's hope I can.

"It's so weird to think he and I have lived two completely different lives over the past fifteen years, and we meet up again and . . ."

"And it's magic."

"I wouldn't go that far. It's just . . . us." It's as though we picked up things from where we left them. The friendship. The ease of communication. The laughter. Everything is still there but just . . . *so much more* than before. Perhaps that's the sex, but I don't think so. It's as though there aren't the same restrictions as there used to be. No more father and grandparents interfering. No more me caring what others thought. No more me worrying about everything other than just us.

"Well, I'm happy for you. I truly am. No one deserves someone to treat them like a queen more than you."

"Does that mean you'll be here to help me pick up the pieces when he leaves?" I ask off-the-cuff but mean every word of it.

"You know I will be." She reaches out and squeezes my hand. "But something in me thinks instead of breaking you apart, he'll have made you whole again."

I stare at the lights swaying on their thick black cable and take a deep breath. Ledger's always had such a profound effect on how I see myself. Desirable. Lovable. Leave-able . . . even if that hadn't been true from his perspective in the end.

But therein lies the problem with Nita's story.

I know how bad it hurts to lose Ledger.

CHAPTER TWENTY-NINE

Asher

Ledger: Are you free next Saturday night?

Me: No. I have an appointment to watch paint dry.

Ledger: Look at you with the jokes.

Me: Anything for you, dear.

Ledger: Cancel the paint appt. We have plans.

Me: Are you sure? I was really looking forward to it.

Ledger: Smart-ass.

Me: What do I wear?

Ledger: I'll get back to you on that.

Me: Okay. I'll be naked until told further.

Ledger: No complaints on that front.

Me: Smart man.

CHAPTER THIRTY

Asher

I CAN'T SLEEP.

My mind is in overdrive, and my excitement building over my new endeavor has created insomnia. The kind of restlessness that only a good bout of sex with Ledger can seem to fix by tiring me out.

I contemplate texting him. He might still be working since I know he had a conference call with someone overseas that he had to stay up for, but I decide against it.

He might ask more questions about why I suddenly can't sleep. And I don't want to have to lie.

Instead, I opt to wander through the house and selfishly admire the changes I've been making to the décor to make it more mine.

I've been scouring garage sales, estate sales, and online markets for others' trash that I can make my treasure. It's taken some time, but that's okay. I think it would be too hard to change it all at once. That would feel like I'd tried to erase Gran and Pop completely.

Rather, I make a change, get used to it, and then move to the next. Little by little I'll make it mine while preserving elements of what was once theirs.

The office. I realize I left the desk lamp on, and when I head in to turn it off, I'm met with one more of Pop's stacks.

I stare at it for a beat.

Just tackle it and get it over with. Clean the slate. Rip the Band-Aid off. Keeping it isn't going to miraculously bring Pop back to life.

I smile and know I'm right. With a deep breath, I take a seat and prepare to face it.

Within an hour, I have broken the big stacks down into sub stacks.

I've gotten it down to a science now: receipts for taxes go in one place, invoices get filed alphabetically, and payroll info by the employee is kept in binders on the shelf. I have a file for miscellaneous items I'm afraid to throw out in case it's important but that I'm not quite sure of its relevance yet.

And then there is a stack of silly Pop things that I'm just not ready to part with. A Post-It note that Gran had written "love you" to him on. A ticket stub from the last movie we saw together. I never realized Pop was such a sentimental guy until I started this project.

It makes me love him even more . . . *if that's even possible.*

I'm singing out loud to the music pouring from the speakers and doing a little shimmy with it as I add the items to my "Reasons Why I Love Pop" file. I do one shimmy too many and accidentally drop one of the papers in between the two hanging files. I reach in between them and scratch my fingers around where I can't see to try to feel for it.

I find it, touch it . . . but there's also something stiffer than a receipt there too. Figuring it's another *lost between the crack* item, I pick it up to put it in its proper place. But when I pull it out between the drab green hanging files, I'm met with a tan envelope with worn edges.

My heart stops in my chest.

"When Pop came inside after talking with that . . . horrid man, he had something in his hand. A tan envelope."

I know it's *the* envelope without any other proof than its color. It has to be. For the briefest moment I contemplate letting sleeping dogs lie and not open it. I already know that Maxton Sharpe was an unscrupulous asshole. Is there going to be something beneath this seal that paints Pop in a different light? In my heart of hearts, I know nothing could change my opinion of him . . . and yet I still hesitate.

But curiosity gets the better of me as I move to the desk, take a seat, and slide my finger under the seal. With a deep breath, I remove the lone object from inside.

An uncashed check.

Made out to Pop.

Signed by Maxton Sharpe.

With a date of that fateful night.

Made out for forty thousand dollars.

I stare at the faded blue rectangle and am not exactly certain how I feel. Surprise? Indifference? Disgust?

This is what saving his son from what he felt was a disgrace from dating me was worth to him? This is all he believed I was worth?

Tears blur my eyes, and those damn insecurities Maxton cemented into my psyche that night rear their ugly head. But for all the *right* reasons. For *Pop* reasons.

He didn't cash it.

We've always struggled financially. This money would have gone a long way for a family like ours whose ends didn't always meet.

He sat on it, holding on to it for years, long after the check was invalid.

I think of the college experience I missed out on. The dreams that slipped through my fingers.

He could have deposited it into a savings account. He could have used those funds to help pay for my college.

And what if he had, Ash? How would that make you feel knowing the price of your destroyed self-esteem was what put you through college?

I blow out a breath and lean back in the office chair, trying to process the dueling emotions inside of me. Regret and relief. Time passes. Moments tick by in the early morning hours as I play with the check's edges. Study the scrawled penmanship. Stare at the name in the memo section—*Asher.*

Would life have been easier if Pop had cashed this check? Used the money for me? Used it to get better care for Gran? Used it to unburden the finances after the fire?

Of course, it would have been.

But I look around at everything I have—consider the times we struggled that brought us closer. The memories we made because we had to be more creative. The Fields and everything I'm aspiring to make it . . . and I know I wouldn't have wanted it any other way.

Did I miss out on a dream?

Yes, I did.

Dreams change. Isn't that what I told Ledger that first night at Hank's? The irony is I said it to deflect the conversation. To give an excuse about why I didn't go to college.

And now I'm sitting here believing it.

Dreams do change.

And I'm damn sure going to make this one a reality come hell or high water. It's the least I can do to honor Pop for being the man he was. For having integrity. For building me up when someone else tore me down.

For loving me how he did.

After some more reflection, I tuck the check back into the envelope and file it in my "Reasons Why I Love Pop" file. Where it belongs.

And as I trudge upstairs, finally tired and ready for sleep, there's one question left that's plaguing me.

To tell or not to tell Ledger about the check.

He's struggling enough with loving and idolizing a man who hurt him. Do I want to add to that pain, or do I want to keep it to myself?

Both options are wrong.

Now I need to decide which one is the lesser of two evils.

CHAPTER THIRTY-ONE

Ledger

"Napa's a crapshoot," Ford mutters. "You think there's red tape in Cedar Falls? It's got nothing on Napa."

"Great. Then maybe we abort that project and just focus on the ones we have for a while," I say. The three of us are on one of our weekly conference calls to make sure the right hand knows what the left hand is doing.

"Did I just hear Ledger say he's taking a break from his quest for world domination?" Callahan teases. "Is the air too fresh there? Is it messing with your brain cells? *Abort the project?*"

"I don't think I've ever heard those words fall from his mouth before," Ford says.

"It must be all the sex," Callahan says. "It's rotting his brain."

"Either that or he's getting none, and it's all the jacking off that's causing his lapse in judgment."

"Are you two done?" I ask, glancing toward my office door, expecting Asher any second. "I have shit to do. Clearly, you're both in dereliction of your duties while I'm gone if this is the shit you're worried about."

"Oh. Are you puffing your chest right now? Trying to show us you're the boss?" Callahan chides as if we were twelve. "One hundred bucks Asher just walked in."

"One thousand," Ford says and, sure enough, when I glance back to the door, Asher's standing in its opening.

All thoughts leave my head. Instead of her usual jeans and tank top, she's standing there in a pale-yellow sundress. It hugs her chest and then flows to above her knees, showcasing one shapely pair of legs. White strappy sandals only add to the sexiness of the look.

"Earth to Ledger," Ford says.

"He's too busy picturing how he's going to fuck her on the desk after everyone leaves." Callahan laughs.

"Fuck off. I'm going now."

I end the call to their dramatic protests and kissing sounds.

Such assholes.

Assholes, though, with a *really* good idea.

I glance at the desk, then up to Asher, and smile.

Definitely a good idea, but one that will have to wait.

Who knew when I asked her if she wanted to come see the resort's work in progress, I'd be preoccupied during the entire tour by the swing of her ass? By her cleavage on display? And by the feedback she is giving?

Who knew that could be sexy? Intelligent suggestions, realistic questions about how things will work, and thought-provoking inquiries I don't know the answers to just yet.

"So this really is going to be finished in a month? That feels like not enough time with so much left to do." Asher turns to look at me, and there is something about her question that has my feet faltering.

Finished in a month.

"What?" she asks when I just stand there and stare at her.

"Nothing. I just lost my train of thought," I say and shake the thought away. "The last month is always chaotic. The big stuff is typically done by then, but it's the many tiny odds and ends that need to be tied up all at once."

She runs a hand over the quartz countertop in the spa as she walks through it. "Do you ever miss your end date?"

"Sometimes. Not often. I'm not a fan of opening if it's not perfect." I shrug, enjoying seeing her here in something so luxurious. It suits her. "Sometimes we have to, though. The guests would never know . . . but I would."

"A perfectionist."

"To a fault." Just like my father.

A month ago, that would have filled me with a sense of pride. Now? I'm still struggling with how it makes me feel.

But I have the best distraction I can think of. *Asher.*

We move through the resort. I show her the gift shops with empty racks because the merchandise is en route. We go through each wing with me spouting more information that I'm not sure she even cares about, but she lets me without looking bored. She sighs when she sees each of the four pools. She sinks down onto a couch in front of a soon-to-be working firepit, which has been placed in a dome-shaped room made completely of glass.

"It'll be incredible when it's snowing outside and you can sit here by the fire. You'll be warm but feel like you're outside."

"That was the hope," I murmur, my eyes never leaving her while she looks at everything else.

Finished in a month.

When that month passes, what then, Sharpe? What happens to what-ever this is? How do you hold on to something that isn't yours and who has a life of her own here?

It's not part of the ten-year plan.

She's never even been on the plan and yet . . . I don't know. I just don't know.

What if I don't want to move that goalpost just yet?

Confusion swirls in my head. Things I want. Those I thought I wanted. And then *her*—the unexpected.

I shake my head as I study her. She's snuggled into the chair, her neck resting on its back, her eyes closed.

Asher.

She makes me feel things.

Want things.

This was supposed to be a fun way to pass the time while I'm stuck here. A relationship rooted in physicality.

Who the fuck was I kidding?

And how can a connection that began over seventeen years ago still feel just as strong?

I run a hand through my hair, about to give in to the need to go over and kiss her to quiet my head, but luckily find my senses because seconds later, there are footsteps nearing.

"Excuse me, Mr. Sharpe?" I turn to find Nate, Hillary's right-hand, standing at the entrance to what we at S.I.N. have dubbed the Snow Globe room.

"I told you, Nate, it's Ledger."

"Okay, Mr. Sharpe," he says and smiles.

"What can I do for you?"

"I know this is Hillary's realm, but I wanted to keep you up-to-date on where we stand with the list of items from our morning meeting." He holds up a clipboard with a list on it.

"I'd appreciate it."

"The plants have been delivered, and our landscape architect will be here tomorrow to start his process with his crew. All of the fixtures and furniture for the spa will be delivered on Friday. I have a crew ready to start the install on Saturday. I have the local electricians we hired from town almost done with the finish electrical." He looks up to meet my eyes. "The only things we have left—well, left on today's list at least—are getting the fire marshal out here to test and sign off on the fire alarms. Oh, and also scheduling the painter to come back for touch-ups in a few weeks."

I run over my mental checklist to see if he's missing anything. He's not. "Thank you, Nate. That's all great."

His smile is full of pride as it should be. This is his first project with us and even though I clearly scare the shit out of him, he's doing a great job.

"Cool. Thanks. Are you okay if I work on the rest of this tomorrow, or—"

"Sure. On one condition . . ."

"Promise you'll be there? At the tree?" Her gray eyes search mine.

"On one condition."

"What's that?" She angles her head to the side, her bottom lip between her teeth as she waits for an answer.

I hold my hands out to my sides. "That you'll love me forever," I yell, hoping this incredible high she gives me lasts forever.

The memory flashes through my head the minute the words are out of my mouth. A scene I've replayed numerous times in my teenage years but didn't remember the words to until right now. *On one condition . . .*

I glance over to Asher, but her back is to me.

"Mr. Sharpe?" Nate asks, pulling me back to the here and now. "You were saying? The condition?"

I smile. "All I was going to say is sure, go home, so long as you have a good night."

"That's the condition?" Confusion blankets his face.

"Yes. That's the condition."

A grin breaks out on his always-too-serious face. "Yes, sir. I will."

I watch him as he walks down the foyer toward the lobby, other staff and construction members milling about.

This time when I look over at Asher, her eyes meet mine, and there is a wistful smile on her lips.

She remembers it too.

There's nothing I can say at the moment. Even if I knew the right thing to say, I don't think it would help.

And just as soon as the moment is there, it's gone when more voices are heard down the hall. But our eyes hold for a brief second more. Another moment where we acknowledge what once was while trying to figure out what exactly this is.

"You want to see more, or am I boring you to tears and you want to be done?" I ask in an attempt to get us back to whatever we were before those three little words.

Her smile is genuine as she holds out her hand to me. "Show me everything."

And I do. I spend the next thirty minutes trying to impress her. It's ridiculous that I want to, and yet it's true.

I want her to be impressed with this. More importantly, *with me.*

I've never cared what people think. I'm a Sharpe. That's impressive enough for most people in and of itself.

But she doesn't care about that.

She never has.

So I'm hoping I can impress her by just being me.

Jesus. I sound like a sap. A whipped fucking sap when in reality we never really defined whatever this is between us so does it even fucking matter?

"That was impressive. *You,* Ledger Sharpe, *are impressive,*" Asher says as she quickly glances around the outside of my office before grabbing my shirt and pulling me into her. Her lips meet mine in the most tender of kisses. She tastes like spearmint and smells like sunshine.

This woman.

Christ.

That yellow sundress.

Those sexy lips.

Her body rubbing up against mine.

Her praise.

I glance at the clock, and then reach back and grab the phone off my desk while Asher's hands are still on my hips.

"Yes, Mr. Sharpe?"

"Hey, Bernie. Are there any protesters at the front gates?" I ask, counting on the fact that he'll give me the rundown like normal.

"Right now? None, sir. According to my log, you and a . . . Miss Wells, are the only ones left on the premises."

"Great. Thanks. I wasn't aware. I guess we've been so wrapped up in our discussion that I lost track of time."

"It must be serious."

"It is." I glance at Asher. It's about to be *real* serious. "Can you inform me if anyone else arrives?"

"Are you expecting someone in particular?"

"Not at this time, but you never know."

"Agreed. Not a problem, sir."

And if Bernie has any inkling that I'm asking to be alone so I can fuck Asher on my desk, he doesn't let on. But he's a smart man. I wouldn't put it past him.

I hang up the phone and when I turn to Asher, she has one eyebrow raised and a mischievous smile on her lips.

"*Can you inform me if anyone else arrives?*" she asks coyly, running a fingernail down the middle of my chest. "Why is that, Mr. Sharpe? Do you have plans?"

My lips are on hers in a second, my hands sliding up the bare skin of her thighs to grab her ass beneath her dress. "I have a lot of plans."

"Is that so?" she asks between kisses.

"Fucking you on the desk." I nip her lip. "You riding me in the chair." I delve my tongue between her lips. "So many fucking plans."

"Yes, sir, *Mr. Sharpe.*"

CHAPTER THIRTY-TWO

Asher

ON ONE CONDITION.

When he said those words today it was like being back on that moonlit night when the world seemed right and life seemed fair.

He remembered it too.

What he said.

The moment we shared between us.

But there was something else that glanced through his eyes. Uncertainty? Confusion? I'm just not sure.

The mature thing to do would be to say something about it. To put it out in the open so maybe both of us can proceed with parameters in mind.

But I don't want to be mature. I don't want to ruin this time I have with him because I'm more than aware this time is limited.

One more month.

Four more weeks.

And then what?

Do we cut each other out of our lives as we did back then? His work responsibilities will be over just like his summer vacations once were. The difference this time around is I'm not content to be a phone call and a text message away for nine months of the year while I pine for his presence the other three.

I deserve more than that.

I deserve better than that.

This whole thing has gotten complicated despite things between Ledger and me being so easy. I've become the queen of lying by omission.

To Gran when she asks for more details about the man I'm seeing. To Ledger by not telling him about the check.

And my own internal justification is the same thing that is conflicting with me—that Ledger will be gone sooner than later.

"Is there a reason you've been staring at me for the past minute?" Ledger teases as his eyes narrow at me from over a container of Kung Pao chicken.

Get a grip, Ash.

"I wasn't staring."

Quit mind-fucking this to death.

"You were zoned out. Should I worry that it's because I have food on my face or something in my teeth?"

Just enjoy his company and figure the rest out later.

"No. Sorry." I smile and move the food around in my take-out container. "I was lost in thought."

"You're probably thinking, *Ledger is getting rather pudgy around the middle since he's been here for weeks and hasn't worked out properly.*"

"I think you've worked me out just fine, thank you very much."

His grin is lightning quick as he sets his food down, crawls on all fours, and presses a chaste kiss to my lips. His eyes darken with desire when they meet mine. "I'd be more than happy to work you out again shortly."

Just enjoy his company.

"*Shortly?* I think you're losing your edge, Ledger Sharpe." I take his hand in mine and place it between the V of my thighs.

His groan is an aphrodisiac in itself.

"*My edge?*" He snorts. "I don't think that's what you were saying a few hours ago."

Snapshots flash through my mind.

My bare ass on his pristine desk. My legs spread wide. My fingers tugging on his hair. His amber eyes looking up at me from between my thighs as he slid his tongue up and down my slit before pushing it inside me.

The decadent intensity.

The mind-blowing pleasure.

The utter bliss of the orgasm that slammed into me heightened by the thrill and fear of being caught by someone walking into The Retreat and catching us.

And then of course, there was the sex itself. How Ledger bent me over his desk with my sundress bunched around my hips. How he pushed his magnificent cock into me while my pussy was still fluttering from the climax he'd given me moments before. How he held my shoulder with one hand and gripped my hip with his other while he teased and toyed and ground into me over and over until we were both left spent, breathless, and momentarily satisfied.

My body aches from the memory. From the promise of more of him.

Because it's always momentary satisfaction when it comes to Ledger. There's always a want for more. A need for more. A desire for one more taste or touch or kiss of his.

He's the best kind of addiction in the worst kind of way. One you want to have but fear the withdrawal from.

"A few hours ago? Did something happen?" I ask coyly with a bat of my lashes and a taunting smile. "Oh, yes. I completely forgot."

"*You forgot?*" he says in mock shock as he grabs my leg with his free hand and tugs me down to the floor where he is. My laugh is smothered by his lips. "Then I guess I better help you remember."

My gasp is sharp when he nips my shoulder. "The food though . . ."

He grinds his clothes-clad cock between my thighs. "Fuck the food. It's better reheated."

"Definitely better reheated."

CHAPTER THIRTY-THREE

Asher

I RUN THROUGH THE SLIDESHOW I'VE CREATED. THE NEW PICTURES I've taken of The Fields are simply stunning. I've stared at them over and over and still can't believe it's the same place I've trampled every inch as a child.

I swear it's the magic of photography but every image feels soft and romantic and like a place I'd personally want to hold an event. Granted, the images purposefully neglect to show the items getting the loan would provide, but they still highlight a complete and beautiful backdrop for an event.

I glance around the waiting area. Funny how I was here the other day and didn't notice these chairs. I welcome the distraction of thought though, because my knee keeps jogging up and down and my palms are so sweaty that I have to rub them on the only pair of slacks I think I own. This is a big deal in general, but it's an even bigger deal to me. I want to be in and out of The Retreat before Ledger comes back from his working lunch.

"Miss Wells?" I glance up and smile at the lady standing in the hallway. She gives me a peculiar look, one that says *why are you meeting with Hillary when you were here the other day with Ledger?* But I simply smile back at her. "Hillary will see you now."

"Thank you. Okay." I rise on shaky legs with my laptop and a printed copy of the presentation in my hands and follow her.

Hillary gives me a similarly curious look when I walk into her office, but doesn't say a word until I take a seat.

"I'm assuming there's a good reason why you specifically asked to have this meeting with me when Ledger is out of the office?"

Hillary is an imposing figure. She's tall with hard features and unrelenting eyes. It helps that I've seen her laughing with Ledger before, or else my nerves would be more rattled than they already are.

"Yes. For me, it's a good reason. For you, it may put you in an awkward position, and for that, I'll apologize ahead of time."

"Continue," she says with a nod as she clasps and unclasps her hands in front of her on the desk.

"Luxury. Decadence. A destination to lose yourself in. That's your brand. That's what S.I.N. properties are known for," I say, repeating Ledger's description that has stuck in my head ever since I decided to make this work. "And at The Fields, we not only share that vision, but we want to offer an opportunity for your guests to experience it with more of a small-town feel to it. Whether it be a wine tasting event beneath the stars in a fragrant field of lavender, or a family reunion with live music, or a wedding ceremony and reception, we can accommodate your needs."

With a deep breath, I continue my presentation for Hillary, struggling at times when her stoic expression gives me nothing to feed off of. When I'm finished explaining the premise, I move on to explain my future aspirations of producing lavender products for purchase.

I force myself to slow down several times, but I hope my excitement for this new venture is more evident than my nerves.

And when I finish, Hillary leans back in her chair, lips twisting and stare implacable. "Why exactly would our clients prefer your farm instead of this multi-million dollar resort they're already paying for to hold their event?"

"Some may. Some may not. The Fields simply gives you another option for those guests who wish to get more of an authentic small-town experience. As you'll see when you read through the full proposal, I've listed comparative studies of other high-end resorts and similar partnerships, complete with a breakdown of the typical S.I.N. demographic and how this partnership can meet their needs."

Another nod. "And you didn't bring this to Ledger for what reason?"

I stare at her, blinking for a beat, assuming the answer is quite obvious, but I explain anyway. "If you should want to partner with The Fields on this, I'd rather the partnership be based on merit than obligation. As you're aware, Ledger and I know each other personally. I want this opportunity because it's valid and good and beneficial. Not because he feels obligated to make it."

"And you think I'm able to separate my decision even though you are my boss's girlfriend?"

"I'm not his—we're not . . ." I clear my throat and shake my head. *Shit. I wasn't expecting her to be so blunt.* "Clearly, you're a damn good business-woman, or else you wouldn't be in charge of this resort. So yes, I think you are more than capable of making an unbiased decision on what is best for your resort when it comes to partnerships or outside opportunities. I also know that Mayor Grossman is holding you guys to the fire when it comes to incorporating the town somehow in The Retreat."

"And you think this would help with that?"

"I think Sharpe International is undeniably receptive and astute and already has things in the works to fix Grossman's requests. People are talking around town, and I think the tide might slowly be turning in your favor. Adding The Fields to your . . . guest options isn't going to affect him one way or the other. But what does it hurt? The Retreat gets a booking fee for simply offering the opportunity. Your guests get a unique experience."

"And you get business."

"Yes. That is the point, after all," I say without apology. My nerves have given way to confidence now. I'll be doing this with or without the resort's partnership.

"How are we supposed to tie this into The Retreat?"

"You don't. We're a lavender farm. You're a large upscale resort. It's simply another adventure they can take like the skiing or the outdoors packages you are offering through your concierge services."

"And the venue area is ready to go?"

"It will be in the next month." *I hope.* If I can secure the loan. Let's hope the questions I was answering with the bank on the way over here are another positive step in doing just that.

Silence falls in the office as Hillary flips through the paper version of my presentation. My pulse races and my knee begins to jog again.

This is the first time I've ever had the opportunity to take a chance like this in my adult life. The Fields was always Gran and Pop's. It always had to be run their way because you don't fix what's not broken. But now it's essentially mine, and until this moment, I didn't realize how bad I wanted this.

How much I needed something more to define myself with.

"It's not a bad idea by any means," Hillary muses, her eyes still looking at my proposal. "Your numbers are fair and your ideas sound."

"Thank you."

"I'm currently reviewing several other proposals to complement the packages Ledger and I are securing. I'll definitely take yours into strong consideration when I make my decision." She looks back up and gives me an all-business smile. "I don't mean to sound cliché when I say *I'll be in touch*, but I'll be in touch."

"Thank you." I rise from my seat and reach across the desk to shake her hand. "I appreciate your time."

It's not until I am clear of the building that I think I actually exhale.

Now it's time to go spend some time with Gran to take my mind off waiting for an answer.

CHAPTER THIRTY-FOUR

Asher

"IT LOOKS NICE."

"What does?" I ask Nita as I plop down on the couch across from where she's seated.

"The house. You're slowly making it yours."

"You mean I've taken down all of the embarrassing photos that Gran and Pop had hanging of me everywhere?"

"Well, there's that." She laughs. "But it feels more like *you* than like them now."

"I know. It's been a gradual process and a hard decision to make to start doing it, but I had to come to terms with the fact that Gran isn't coming home and Pop is gone. I figured if I'm updating the barn, I might as well incorporate more of me in here as well."

"And how does that make you feel?"

"Proud. Sad. Resolved. Pop and I never specifically talked about what I'd do when they were gone, but he always told me he loved my 'Ash style.' And so, now it's both them and me. What they built with a little bit of me thrown in."

"Well, it looks great. Bright and clean with pops of color. I like it, and I think he would have too." She shimmies her shoulders to add some levity. "It's like I'm looking at an all-new Asher in so many different ways these days."

"Well, this *all-new Asher* is getting antsy waiting for Ledger to do whatever it is he's going to do."

"Hey. I didn't expect to hear from you until later. What's up?"

"So . . . I know you're going to be pissed, but just go with it," Ledger says.

"Just go with what?" Why am I going to be pissed?

"With the surprise I have for you. It's not meant to tell you I don't like you just how you are—but rather meant to spoil you."

"Um . . . okay." I walk to the window of the farmhouse and look out to where George is messing with something, my curiosity more than piqued. *"Should I be worried?"* I tease.

"No. Not in the least. I just wanted to do something special for you."

Cue my heart skipping a beat. *"Okay."* I draw the word out. *"When should I expect said surprise?"*

"You'll know soon."

"What does he mean, *you'll know soon?*" Nita asks.

"Your guess is as good as mine."

"But it has to do with the secret date he's taking you on tonight?"

"Yes. I asked him last night if he could give me some suggestions about what I should wear. That phone call was his answer."

"Sexy, rich, and mysterious. Are you sure I can't make a play for one of his brothers?" She laughs.

"Whatever." I roll my eyes and then hold my hands out to my sides to showcase a pair of old running shorts and a plain black tank top. "Well, if whatever he has in store doesn't show up soon, this is what he's going to get for my date attire."

Nita laughs but then sinks back into my couch and looks at me wistfully. "It's exciting though, isn't it? To have a secret date and a handsome man planning it."

I look at her and twist my lips. "I think this is the most romantic thing someone has ever done for me. That's not saying much considering a close second is Brad Wheelan sneaking Valentine's hearts in my lunch box every day for a month in sixth grade."

"Seriously? Brad? As in Brad, Brad?" she asks, her eyes widening.

"Yes. That Brad," I say. The same Brad who is now married to his husband and living happily with two adorable sons.

"Well, I think—"

A knock on the door interrupts her and makes me jump. The windows are closed and the air conditioning is on, so the fact that someone drove down the driveway and I didn't notice, startles me.

"Are you expecting company?" Nita asks as I pull open the front door.

"Hello?" I ask the woman standing on the front porch. Her hair is pulled back into a sleek bun, her entire outfit is black, and her makeup is flawless. She looks completely out of place on my doorstep.

"Asher Wells?"

"Can I help you?"

Her smile widens, and it's only then I see a rolling clothes rack to the right of the door, another two women standing beside it, and some very large portable cases.

She holds her hand out, and I shake it. "I'm Millie Paulsen and these are my assistants, Jayne and Fran. We are your glam squad." She gives a sassy wink. "Ledger has sent us to get you dressed and made up for your evening out tonight."

I glance back to Nita who is mouthing the words, *Oh my God*, in response.

Personal stylists? Seriously? I've never experienced anything like this in my entire life.

"I—I can't aff—"

"Honey, do you actually think a man is going to send us to your doorstep and expect you to pay for it? If that's the case, it's a requirement to dump his ass. But that isn't the case with this." She gives a nod and a quick smile. I have a feeling the woman is a force that no one disagrees with. "Shall we get started?" She may ask the question but is already moving past me and into the house before I respond.

Jayne and Fran are right behind her, doing the heavy lifting by pushing the wardrobe cart and travel cases into the house. It's only then that I see the gowns hanging from the rack. In the quick glimpse I get, their style covers the gamut and tells me whatever our destination is must be pretty fancy.

I hold a hand to my stomach as nerves and excitement bloom.

Holy shit.

All this for me?

Definitely the most romantic thing someone has done for me.

The last few hours have felt like a blur. I've been primped and styled and glamorized in a way I never have been before. After a small fashion show where I tried on every dress, the blue beaded one with the sexy neckline and mid-thigh slit was voted as the favorite.

And I was secretly happy about that as it was the one I felt the best in.

Nita just sat back and observed the entire time, shaking her head and with a grin on her face.

She looked like how I felt. Stunned. In disbelief. Adored.

It's a feeling every woman should feel at some point in their life . . . and a feeling I can't remember having since . . . since that last night with Ledger fifteen years ago.

The thought has me smiling softly and closing my eyes to prevent the tears that are welling from falling. The last thing I want to do is ruin my makeup. But how crazy is it that it's been the same man, both times?

When I'm certain the sentimental tears are gone, I open my eyes to find the driver of the car Ledger sent for me turning into the gates of the airport.

I glance around, expecting him to stop me at the small terminal of the local airport, but he keeps driving.

Through the gates.

Across the tarmac.

Up to a black jet with the words, Sharpe International Network, emblazoned on its tail end.

"We're here, miss," my driver states as he pulls to a stop.

CHAPTER THIRTY-FIVE

Ledger

SHE TAKES MY BREATH AWAY.

It sounds cliché, but when Asher steps out of the SUV, she renders me breathless. The blue dress she opted for hugs her every curve. It's sexy but classy—just like her. Her hair is in some kind of loose but intricate something or other that has me wondering how I'm going to keep my hands out of it and not mess it up when I kiss her.

Because I will be kissing her.

In fact, I don't know how I'm going to keep my fucking hands off her.

Her makeup only adds to the full effect. It's definitely more than I'm used to her wearing, but she's still my Asher.

"Stunning." It's all I can say when she looks my way and her eyes hit mine. The smile she gives me. The look in her eyes. How her body intuitively turns to me. "Absolutely stunning. You. The dress. *Everything.*"

When I press a kiss on her cheek, I swear my stomach flips over. Something about her, about this moment and bringing her to see my brothers tonight, overwhelms me.

She's incredible in every sense of the word. Asher in her everyday life stuns me. But she . . . fits. *And I'm not sure what to do about that. Yet.*

How do I merge our two very different worlds together?

Because I'm starting to see that it may become an absolute necessity.

"Look at you," she says, luckily breaking up my thoughts and tugging gently on the lapel of my tux. "Handsome as ever."

"Well," I say, hands in my pockets as I rock back on my heels. "I know what a picnic in the field got me"—I shrug—"so I figured why not aim a little higher this time and see what happens?"

She snorts, and it's so very Asher—dressed to the nines and yet still so very much *her*. "Guess you'll have to wait and see."

I hold my elbow out for her to put her arm through. "Shall we?"

"You're not going to tell me where we're going yet, are you?"

"Nope." I want her to see the skyline of the city she loves and see her reaction as she figures it out for herself.

When I step to the side to let her up the stairs first, she stops and simply takes in the entirety of the jet in front of us. "Holy shit," she murmurs.

"What?"

"This is normal for you, Ledger Sharpe, but this is insane to me. Utterly insane."

Her face is a mixture of awe and disbelief that has me rooted in place as she starts up the stairs to board.

We've had a private jet at our disposal our whole lives. Many of the kids I grew up with at prep schools either owned one like us or used one when they traveled.

I thought this would be a cool treat for us. To get away. To go to where I love. To just be together.

Never in a million years did I think I was going to enjoy her taking in things, being spoiled by things I'd always taken for granted as much as I am right now.

When I reach the top step and see her studying every single detail of the plane's interior, I can't stop smiling.

She deserves so much more than this.

"Hey, Asher?" I ask as I come up behind her and wrap my arms around her. "Promise me you'll let me spoil you all night long?"

She turns, and her grin is mischievous as hell. "On one condition . . ."

The phrase stops me. Thoughts, ideas, and memories collide that have me smiling.

"Oh yeah?" I ask, eyebrows raised, more than willing to meet whatever condition she's going to offer. "What's that?"

"You let me join the mile-high club."

"Deal. Check, please. Done. Where do I sign up?"

When she throws her head back and laughs, I know it's a sound I could listen to forever.

CHAPTER THIRTY-SIX

Asher

THE CITY'S SKYLINE IS SIMPLY INCREDIBLE. I CAN'T STOP STARING at it, just as I couldn't when I looked out the jet's window and realized where Ledger was taking me.

It didn't hurt that I was still recovering from one of the most mind-bending orgasms I've ever had either.

Who knew private jets had bedrooms or that having crew members just on the other side of its door could enhance the adrenaline pumping through your veins when you're bent over and being fucked from behind?

And who knew how masterful Ledger could be at *not* ruining my hair or dress while ruining other parts of me in all the best kinds of ways?

"It's going to be hard for you to come and not make a sound, isn't it Ash?" Ledger murmurs as he runs the tip of his nose down the length of my spine exposed by the open back of the dress.

I gasp as he pushes in deeper, my body already more than primed, and my arousal already on high alert knowing Sally, our flight attendant, who so generously served me a glass of wine just moments ago, is on the other side of the door.

And there is no doubt she knows exactly what is going on in here right now.

Ledger reaches around to my front, his fingers dancing over the slick flesh there and adding the friction I need to push me to the brink.

I drop my head down as pleasure swamps me. "It's going to be hard not to mess that hair up." *He places an open mouth kiss onto my shoulder.* "To not flip you over and watch you." *Another kiss on the other shoulder.* "To not hold my hand over your mouth to quiet your scream." *Faster strokes over my clit.* "To watch you sink your teeth into your bottom lip when you come."

He pulls out so that just the tip of his cock is in me, teasing me like that for a few moments, before slamming into me again in one smooth stroke.

"Ledger." His name is a moan. A plea for more. A rasp of appreciation.

"But I sure as fuck am not going to complain about this view." Another withdrawal out. "How your pussy stretches around me." Another push back in. "How it grips me so fucking tight." A grind of his hips. "The sight of how goddamn wet you are."

His fingers work faster.

"Do you hear that? How wet I make you?"

His hips move harder.

"Yeah. Right there. There's that spot that gets you."

His hand grips tighter.

"I want you to come for me Ash. Don't hold fucking back."

Sensations build. Pleasure mounts.

I come in a torrent of sensation. All thoughts are abandoned as my body rides each wave as it hits me. And before I can catch my breath, Ledger's sharp hiss fills the small bedroom as he empties himself in me.

For a few seconds, it feels like the world stands still. It's just Ledger and this moment and pleasure. Simple, shameless pleasure.

I jump when his lips meet my neck again, seconds before the warmth of his breath hits my ear as he chuckles. "Welcome to the mile high club."

The mile-high club was definitely all it's been cracked up to be.

Then again, it simply might be that it has everything to do with Ledger and nothing to do with the plane.

But here we are. In the city I left in a rush twelve years ago, thinking I'd be back, to never end up returning.

Sounds of the gala carry on behind me. Small talk. Polite laughter. Loud exclamations from people who haven't seen each other in forever. Praise how divine the canapes are. Thank-yous murmured when champagne glasses are refilled. The lowering of voices before the catty comment.

I turn from the skyline and focus on the lavish party before me. I definitely fit the part with this stunning dress and glam makeover, but while I wait for Ledger to come back from the restroom, I feel a bit out of place.

"Ash Ash Bo Bash. Is that you?" I turn to find someone who looks just like Ledger but most definitely isn't, seeing as he has a stunning woman on his arm.

"Once a teenager, always a teenager," the woman says before stepping forward with a warm smile and her hand extended. "Asher, so nice to meet you. I'm Sutton Sharpe. And this brother is Callahan."

"Hi. Nice to meet you," I say and then turn toward Callahan with surprise on my face. "You're the first one to get hitched? Never in a *million years* would I have guessed that one."

Callahan gives me a lightning-quick grin before kissing my cheek. "Never in a million years did I think I'd ever see you again. With Ledger no less. The years have been kind to you." His smile turns genuine. "You look beautiful."

"Thank you." Nostalgia hits me like I didn't expect, seeing another Sharpe brother again.

"And truth be told, I was surprised I was the first one too, but this one," he says, looking adoringly at his wife, "she's a force to be reckoned with. She got me hook, line, and sinker. I'm a lucky man."

"You are," Sutton says unapologetically but then winks at me.

"There she is," another voice says as Ford joins us on the patio. "It seriously is you, isn't it?"

"Crazy, huh?" I say, feeling a little more comfortable now that I semi-know some people.

"Completely." He gives a quick shake of his head as if he's trying to reconcile the past with the present, much like I am. "Out of all of us, *you still chose Ledge?*" he teases.

"Hey. I heard that," Ledger says as he steps beside me, puts his hand on my waist, and pulls me into him.

When I found out we were going to the annual Alzheimer's fundraiser that he and his brothers host, I was curious how he'd act around them. Would I be a friend he brought along, or would I be treated as his date?

The kiss he presses to the side of my temple and the words "I'm glad you chose me," murmured in my ear, definitely say the latter.

We talk for a bit about nothing of importance. It feels like déjà vu most of the time as memories come back fast and furious.

"The dinner is about to start," Ford says. "Shall we head to the table?"

And the dinner is lavish. Filet mignon and truffle oil potatoes. A choice of various desserts. Expensive wine flowing like water.

Just like the Sharpe brothers are hoping donations will be—flowing heavily into the charity.

When Ledger, Ford, and Callahan's speeches are finished, and they've been accosted by people wanting to be seen by them, I make my way back out to the patio and the view of the skyline I love. I told Ledger to take his time doing what he needs to do as I truly don't mind the fresh air or the time to simply sit and admire its beauty.

I'm just about to reach the doorway when I get stuck behind a group of five or so women all talking furiously about some guy named Theodore and how one of them saw him with someone who wasn't his wife the other day.

"Excuse me. May I get by please?" I ask when there is a break in their conversation.

"Oh. We're sorry," the one in the silver dress says before narrowing her eyes at me. "I don't believe we've seen you before."

"What family do you belong to?" the one in the gaudy black dress asks, who looks like she uses a Sharpie for eyeliner. Clearly money can't count for taste.

"Family?"

"Yes, dear," green dress says. "Who are you? A Rothschild? A Montgomery? A Vanderbilt? *Who?*"

"A Wells," I say with a smug smile to match the ones they are giving me. "We're not from these parts."

"Oh," black dress says as she blinks her way through her tangled lash extensions. "Then who are you here with?"

"Ledger Sharpe."

"Sure, you are," gold dress says with an eye roll to her friends. "I'm sorry, but personal assistants are all hanging in the adjacent room. I'm sure you'd be more comfortable chatting with like-kind and commiserating about how miserable we all are to work for. Besides, I hear the food in there is great too."

For a brief moment, I'm brought back to the farmhouse. To Pop standing toe-to-toe with Maxton Sharpe. To the harsh words that fueled my inadequacies for way too long.

"I'm sure the food is good in there. Leave it to the Sharpes to treat everyone with kindness." My smile is smug. "And for the record, I'm actually Ledger's date, but I'll make sure to tell his PA when I see her." I smile, having no clue if he even has a PA here in New York.

"Oh. I wasn't aware," green dress says. "So you're with him for the money then? Take it from us, it isn't exactly the easiest life fawning all over your husband most days to stroke his ego."

"Not the money, no. I own my own business and can support myself just fine." I stand a little taller. "And in case you didn't notice, the Sharpe men don't need anyone to fawn all over them. It just happens naturally to everyone around them. Besides, fawning is beneath you." I glance over my shoulder to see that Ledger is still otherwise engaged. *I'm glad you chose me.* "Enjoy the rest of your night. *We* truly appreciate your donations tonight."

With that, I walk away with my head held high and a smile on my lips.

CHAPTER THIRTY-SEVEN

Ledger

TONIGHT HAS BROUGHT ON A MIX OF EMOTIONS FOR ME. It's the first time I've been home since facing the reality of what my father did—the lies and deception that kept Asher and me apart. It was easier to push it to the back of my mind when I was away, but now being here—at something we do in his honor—has made it harder to ignore.

There's hurt. There's betrayal. And there's a burning need to share it with my brothers, but an even greater desire not to taint their view of the man he was since we, as humans, tend to canonize the ones we love after their death.

And to have to go up there and speak about him tonight without highlighting any of his flaws felt rather hypocritical.

Especially with Asher sitting there staring at me.

Is that why I asked her here tonight? Because I knew it was going to be tough for me? But then again, what kind of an asshole does that make me? Jesus Christ. Why didn't I think of this before? I invited her to celebrate the honor of the man who said horrible things to her.

Talk about throwing salt in the wound.

How could I have been so selfish? How could I have been so blind?

I need to find her.

I need to apologize.

She saw the New York City skyline and probably assumed I was taking her out, just the two of us. Not to this.

What an asshole.

"You okay, man?" Callahan asks with a firm pat on my back as I scan the room looking for Asher.

"Yeah. Fine. Good," I say and shake the thoughts away.

"A three-word answer. That means you're lying."

"What's he lying about?" Ford asks when he steps up.

"Beats the shit out of me." Callahan shrugs. "My money is on it being about Asher."

"Asher?" Ford asks with a raise of his eyebrows as if he's surprised. "What's the deal there? You going to break that ten-year plan of yours? I believe it's item six point five under section two that states 'I will not fall in love or get married until age forty.'"

"Let it go. Don't do this tonight."

"Why? If the roles were reversed, big brother, you'd jump at every chance you had to harass the hell out of us," Ford says.

"So, what gives?" Callahan asks. "Is this a permanent thing or a temporary thing?"

"Because if it's permanent, then you know Callahan and I have to vet the adult version of her."

"Take her out for a night, grill her with questions to see if she's worthy of our big brother. Make sure she—"

"Leave it be," I say quietly. I'm not in the mood for this, *for them*, especially when I screwed up royally tonight and need to fulfill my duties so I can get the hell out of here.

"Nope. Not gonna happen." Ford's grin is a taunt in and of itself. This isn't the time. This isn't the place.

And it sure as hell isn't any of their business considering they don't know the whole story.

"Look. Asher and I . . . it's nothing major," I say for them to let it go; all the while, those three words feel like they're burning a hole through my gut. "It's just a fling that will be over in three or four weeks when I'm done with my penance in Cedar Falls and get to come back home. Simple. Easy. Done."

CHAPTER THIRTY-EIGHT

Asher

"LOOK. ASHER AND I . . . IT'S NOTHING MAJOR," LEDGER SAYS to his two brothers. I'm listening intently, and my feet falter a few feet away from the trio. "It's just a fling that will be over in three or four weeks when I'm done with my penance in Cedar Falls and get to come back home. Simple. Easy. Done."

And there it is.

The answer to the question I've been too damn afraid to ask.

Or more like too chicken to ask.

My heart drops to my feet. There's no other way to describe it. Our silence on what *this* is between us was for a reason.

To him, it's just a fling.

To me, it's . . . I swallow down the swell of emotion that surges inside of me. Emotion I'd prefer to ignore at this point.

I take a few steps back behind the corner so I can gather my wits. So I can take a deep breath and fight the tears burning in my eyes. So I can convince myself that I was stupid to think this might be anything other than a short-term, convenient affair with incredible sex.

Because good sex doesn't mean love, regardless of what our past held.

"Asher. There you are," Ledger says when he turns the corner to find me standing there preparing to face him.

"Hi." I hope my smile is convincing. "I was just stopping to give my feet a break. They're not exactly used to wearing heels all night."

"That bad?" he asks, but when he steps closer, he brings his thumb and forefinger to my chin and holds my face still. His eyes search mine. "I've hurt you, haven't I?"

How did he know I overheard him with his brothers?

I scramble for a response, but he beats me to it.

"I apologize for bringing you here to celebrate a man I'm sure you're not too fond of. Truth be told, I'm not entirely sure how I feel about him right now either. I was selfish to make you sit through that. To make you come here. I wanted you here for me and didn't think of how it would make you feel."

"It's okay. I'm glad I could be here for you," I murmur, partially relieved he doesn't know I overheard him, partially not.

"Thank you." He brushes his lips gently over mine in that way that makes me simply want to melt into him. Even after hearing his proclamation. "But this wasn't much of a date in the city you love. Let me make it up to you."

"Ledger—"

"Shh." He kisses me tenderly again. "There's nothing more I'd love to do."

He grabs my hand and starts heading for the elevator. "Ledger? We can't just leave. You're the host." He enters the empty elevator car and holds his hand out to me. "You have to be here."

He tugs me so I land against him, and the second the door closes, his lips are on mine in a searing kiss filled with greed and lust and about ten things in between. "My brothers can handle it," he murmurs against my lips. His hands go up to thread through my hair and then stop when he realizes the epic number of bobby pins stopping him. "We have to be back to Cedar Falls by six a.m."

"But it's almost eleven at night. Where—"

"We're in the city that never sleeps, Asher. My city. We might as well take advantage of every waking moment we have."

His city. For the moment we have.

We gorge on ice cream sundaes at Serendipity 3 in our fancy clothes. We stop by a drugstore after that, Ledger giving me a piggyback ride through the aisles, to buy a pair of flip-flops because my feet are sore, and I don't want my heels to hold us back. Ledger holds my hand as we walk through the city, guiding me through sidewalk traffic as I stare up at the buildings towering above me. We take silly selfies in Times Square. He patiently waits while I window-shop in the darkened storefronts on Park Avenue. My stomach turns as he shows me the observation deck of the

Empire State Building. We stroll through what he deems is the safe part of Central Park.

It's exhausting and rejuvenating and I allow myself to focus on the here and now. Not the fling or the time limit Ledger imposed unknowingly earlier.

And when our bodies are exhausted and the moon disappears from the skyscraper-lit sky, we begrudgingly make our way to the airport and the waiting jet. We're greeted with welcome smiles from a crew whom I'm sure expected to already have been to Montana and back by now, but you'd never know it.

We're in the air within minutes. And soon after, Ledger reclines our joined seats and pulls me against him. He covers me with a blanket and wraps his arms around me so that I rest my head on his chest.

We lie like this for some time, but it's when he presses a kiss to the crown of my head and murmurs my name that the truth collides.

I don't respond to him, letting him believe I'm asleep.

Tears well in my eyes, and I'm not sure why. Is it that I just need a moment or is it that I'm hiding from him?

I'm glad you chose me.

Now that there's quiet and my mind can reflect, the events of the night have caught up to me. And that's comforting. I love spending time with him. He makes me feel incredible.

That's also scary because . . . because of how *much I love him.*

The acknowledgment jars me.

But I already knew this, didn't I? That Ledger was easy to love?

Maybe I hadn't realized that I was *in love* with him, but somehow it happened. Little by little. Discussion by discussion. Kiss by kiss. Laugh after laugh. I'd fallen back in love with Ledger Sharpe. I can't chalk it up to lust anymore. To simple attraction. The want to see him every waking minute. Because yes, there's all that, but there's also a need deep in my soul to be with him. There's that tug on my heart every time I see him and the emptiness that fills it when we're not together.

I lie there in stunned silence for some time, sorting through my thoughts, my options, and how each one will devastate me in one way or another. And when Ledger's breathing evens out and his soft snores fill the plane, I dare to look up at the only man I've ever loved romantically.

A man who, for a small moment in time, I thought I had a future with. The man who publicly claimed me tonight, suggesting *he* was glad *I* chose *him*. And to think I believed it was all true.

I'm going to let him go.

I'll enjoy the time we have left. I'll love him within the confines of my heart alone.

This time, I'll end it on my terms.

Because for once in my life, I won't be taken by surprise when someone I love leaves me.

This time, I'll choose to be on my own again.

CHAPTER THIRTY-NINE

Ledger

"TELL ME SOMETHING, SON."

I look over to my dad who's sitting on the bow of the sailboat. The sun is bright in Sag Harbor today, but the ocean breeze has tempered the heat. He looks old. That's my first thought. My second is how long will I have him with me this time?

His episodes are more often than not these days. Bouts of forgetfulness followed by confusion over where he is typically rules our time together.

But the water has always made him happy, and so my brothers and I have been trying to make a conscious effort to have him on it as much as work permits.

"What is it, Dad?"

"Have you ever done something you thought was for good reasons, that you meant well by it, but that never really sat well with you as time wore on?"

I stare at my dad, his silver hair blowing in the breeze and his unrelenting eyes staring at me. "Are you talking about work? Sure, we've all done something we did and then second-guessed it. That's how it goes sometimes . . ."

"No, I'm talking about something I did to make sure you . . . I was scared you were going to make poor choices."

"Dad, I'm confused. What are you talking about?"

"It's okay, Callahan." He smiles, and I let his confusion over him thinking I'm my brother stand. As we've learned in the past, correcting him only serves to agitate him.

"What poor choices are you talking about?" I ask, knowing damn well Callahan sure as hell made many.

"I should have trusted you, son. I should have known you had the best head on your shoulders of the three of you and that you would've made the right decisions."

"Okay." I'm lost but just smile and nod because that's the only thing I can do when he starts talking in the confused circles his damaged mind spins.

"I'm sorry for interfering. I'm sorry for thinking I knew better than you did. I'm sorry for lying in order to make sure you didn't make a mistake."

"It's okay, Dad. Whatever you did, I'm sure it was with good intentions." What in the hell is he talking about?

"Thank you. I'm so sorry, Ledge. I just needed to say that to you."

I jolt awake with a pocket of turbulence, my heart racing, and my brain in overdrive. I'd completely forgotten that conversation with my dad in the months leading up to his passing. I'd chalked it up to confusion and the disease stealing his memory and him thinking I was Callahan.

But he wasn't.

He was talking about me. About the lie he told. About what happened in Cedar Falls.

I know this deep down in my soul. *He was apologizing.* Making amends. Righting wrongs before he passed.

How does that make me feel? Relieved that he had a conscience? Upset that he had to have one over what he did in the first place? Content that his guilt ate at him over the years?

I just don't fucking know.

Is it enough to forgive him? No. But maybe it's enough for me to try and put it in the past and not let it eat a hole in my gut every time Asher smiles at me.

And then there's the woman lying against me. The one I brought with me tonight.

How her face lit up when she realized we were in Manhattan.

How I breathed easier knowing she still loves the city.

Because it will make it easier when . . . when I what? When I ask her to move there with me?

Is that what this was tonight?

A test? A trial run?

For her or for me?

I look over to find her inches from my face. Those dark eyelashes against her pale skin. Those lips that all but break me when they turn up in a smile.

I lean down to kiss her. She responds. Even in her sleep, she responds to me. But I know the minute awareness hits her. Where we are. That my hand is running up her thigh. That I'm kissing her.

It's in her sigh.

In the way her hand reaches out and runs down my cheek.

In the soft utterance of my name.

"I need you, Asher. God, I need you."

And without another word, and with our lips still teasing one another's, Asher shifts, pulling her dress up over her hips so that she's straddling me. Her body fitting on top of mine, my cock pushing into her, as if we were meant to be.

We kiss like that's all there is left in the world. Her taste the only one I've ever craved. Her lips the only ones I want to feel.

We make love in gentle movements charged with emotion as she grinds her hips over mine in the engine-hummed cabin of the airplane.

We become one without words. Whatever needs to be said is done through soft sighs and measured actions.

A kiss to her collarbone. A shudder of pleasure. A grind of my hips. Her forehead against mine as she bites back her moan.

In the sky, on this plane, time doesn't matter. It's just her. It's just me. It's just *us*.

It's when we land that the clock will start ticking again. It's when we hit the runway that this dream will begin to dissipate.

I know this.

I despise this.

So I focus on her and fall under her spell. The scent of her skin. The demand in her touch. How her breath catches every time I bottom out inside of her. The way she grips her muscles around me as if she never wants us to be apart.

A sentiment—*a desperation*—I feel too. One that also scares the shit out of me.

And when she starts to climax, I thread my fingers through her hair so she's forced to lean back and look at me as she does.

So I can watch what I do to her. So I can see the emotion in the depths of her eyes I think we both feel but haven't spoken. So I can remember her forever, just like this.

As mine.

There is no greater pleasure for me than her.

None.

CHAPTER FORTY

Asher

"N O NEWS IS GOOD NEWS, RIGHT?" THE LOAN SPECIALIST AT Cedar Falls First and Trust says to me.

"That doesn't make me feel any better," I say drolly.

"I know, but just give it some time. You already have a large debt—"

"But those loans—those mortgages—are under my gran and pop's name. This one would be under my name, on my credit—"

"—with their farm as collateral. So, they go hand in hand."

I pinch the bridge of my nose and sigh. "I know. Thank you. I appreciate it. I'm just antsy and want to get started."

"I'm sure it will be fine," she says.

"Okay," I say, sounding less than convinced. "I look forward to hearing back from you."

When the call ends, I place my head in my hands. I feel like I'm waiting on everything these days: the loan approval. Hillary's answer. Each day to tick by so that we get closer and closer to the end of the month.

But the brochures I had made look incredible and have even got the stamp of approval from a smiling-through-her-happy-tears Gran. The new signage has been ordered and will be ready to put in place by next week.

I don't know why I feel it is so critical for me to do this, for me to succeed at this, right now in my life, but it is.

I've managed to sort Pop's stacks, make sense of them, and organize them by how they make sense to me. I have a clearer picture of The Fields's debt and have spreadsheets and a budget in place so I can start paying them down. I've made the house more *my* home than Gran and Pop's.

Now all that's left is to officially make the next chapter of The Fields my own. Past and present combined.

And maybe it's more than just proving to Pop I can do it, proving to myself that I'm capable. Maybe I'm trying to be in control. Maybe I know I'll need something to throw myself into when I'm faced with a heartache like I've never known before.

. . . it's nothing major . . . it's just a fling that will be over in three or four weeks . . .

Did I really think he was going to stay? Of course not. But maybe I figured that we'd make it work somehow. That we'd find a middle ground.

But did I even think that would work? If I was about to throw myself wholeheartedly into a relationship with someone who clearly couldn't divorce himself from New York City because of his business, would I have jumped headfirst into turning The Fields into a destination location like I am?

Maybe I knew all along.

Because realistically, this was never going to work before it even started, no matter how much I told myself differently.

CHAPTER FORTY-ONE

Ledger

"DID YOU EVER THINK YOU'D GO BACK TO COLLEGE?" I RUN A finger up and down the length of Asher's spine. She's lying face down on my bed, her cheek on the pillow, and turned toward me. The early morning sun coming in through the blinds makes a halo around her hair. Her eyes are sleepy, her cheeks are flushed, and I don't think I've ever seen her more beautiful. *At peace.*

She shrugs. "For a long time, I did. Of course, I'd love to, but I simply don't think it's in the cards for me. I mean, what would I go back for? It's not like I still sketch, so I don't have a portfolio to get admitted with and . . . there's The Fields."

"Business? Marketing? I don't know. There are a lot of degrees that would be beneficial in running The Fields."

"But in the end, does it really matter if I have a degree to run it? I mean, unless I apply for a job in the future that is. If that's the case, then that means I've run The Fields into the ground."

"I know. But it was always something you wanted so badly. Maybe just simply doing it for yourself is more than enough of a reason to go back."

"Pipe dreams are for kids without responsibilities, Ledger. That's not me anymore."

We stare at each other for a beat before she suddenly shifts in bed so that she's seated and the sheet is pulled around her chest.

There she goes again. Changing the subject off of her. I can't help but feel like she's trying to distance herself from me. I've felt like this for the past week or so. She's suddenly busy when before she made time.

But it's more than that.

And I can't quite put my finger on what *it* is.

"What about you?" she asks, breaking through my thoughts. "What's on that ten-year plan of yours?"

Shit. I'd forgotten I'd mentioned that to her a while back. I shrug. "It's just goals, timelines, things I want to accomplish."

She nods. "Like . . ."

"Like moving into the Asian market, which we're currently in contract on a new project. Like getting a write-up in Forbes." I twist my lips and then chuckle. "It's stupid really, but it's a goal . . ." my dad mentioned it, and I have always felt like I needed to live up to it. "It's just one I've had since I was in grad school. To be noticed for my work and not just for being Maxton Sharpe's son."

"I can understand that. What else is on there?" she asks, her fingers plucking at the sheet, her lips twisting.

Why won't you look at me?

"I don't know. I haven't looked at it in a long time to remember," I lie and don't know why.

Because you don't want to talk about the personal side of it. The married at forty *part.*

And why is that, Ledger?

"Huh."

"Asher?"

"What?" Her fingers don't stop with the sheets.

"Look at me."

"Hmm?" Her eyebrows are lifted and her smile is in place when she faces me. She leans down and presses her lips to mine. "I've got to get going. Work's calling."

"Don't go." I reach out and grab her hand. "Let's play hooky today. We can drive . . . I don't know where, but we can drive somewhere and eat ice cream cones while sitting on the hood of the car and just be together."

Who am I right now? When have I ever cut out from work to play hooky? When have I ever wanted to do something without a set purpose?

Her eyes darken. "I'm sorry." Another press of her lips to mine. "I can't."

"Tell me why not?" I ask, my hand on her neck, pulling her back toward me.

"Because . . . *I can't.*" She looks at me, and I'd give anything to know what she's thinking. There's something she's just not telling me.

"Asher?"

And this time when she meets my lips, she doesn't stop. She silences my question as she straddles my hips and then slowly kisses her way down my body until her lips wrap around my cock and suck me into forgetting.

Each lick of her tongue, every suck of her lips, each scratch of her fingernails against my balls, all drug me with desire and push the worry to the back of my mind.

But forgetting only lasts for so long.

I'm not about to complain about the incredible blow job she just gave me, but as she walks along the path to her car in nothing but my T-shirt down to her mid-thighs, my mind won't stop.

Not because I have to go to work.

Not because I have meetings.

Not because I have to meet with Hillary or any other person on the face of the earth, but rather, *because I can't.*

Asher was always generous with affection. With kissing. With touching.

It's everything else she guards like a fortress.

And right now, she's building walls faster than I can knock them down.

She starts her car and gives me a little wave before driving off. I watch till I can't see her anymore and then jump when I see Tootie standing at the edge of my driveway. Her arms are across her chest and a lone eyebrow is raised in dismay.

"Jesus, kid. You scared the hell out of me."

"I thought you weren't the type to have a woman who comes over and then sneaks out about the time that school starts."

"I never said that." I run a hand through my hair, not really ready for Tootie. I haven't had my coffee yet.

"Momma calls that the walk of shame."

"It's not a walk of shame when you plan on seeing the woman again."

She makes a mock puking sound in her hand. "Oh, please."

"Please what?"

"People only say that when they're in love. Gag. Gross. I'm gonna puke." She coughs. "Are you in love with Asher?"

I stare at her for a beat, my heart pounding, my eyes darting, and then begin laughing. "You should be in the theater. You're a great actress."

She straightens up and smiles. "I know. I'm a real Bette Davis. At least according to my grandma, but I have no idea who that is so I just smile and pretend I do."

Whew. Subject changed. Topic over.

Why does that bug you so much, Sharpe?

She shrugs. "So, you plan on seeing her again then? The lavender lady?"

"Yes. Not that I have to give you an answer to that question."

"Did you not get enough sleep?" she asks, cocking her head to the side. "You seem a little grumpy."

I scrub a hand over my stubble. "I'm fine. Just need coffee." *And more Asher.*

"Momma's a dragon before her coffee too."

"Most adults are," I say to make conversation and lift a hand to wave to her mother who's watching the two of us from their kitchen window.

"But not Asher, right? Because she didn't look grumpy." She holds something out to me. "Here."

"What's this?" I ask taking the thumb drive from her.

"*This* is a thumb drive," Tootie says very slowly and loudly as if I'm senile and can't hear her.

Little brat. I give her a sarcastic glare. "What's on the thumb drive, silly? Remember, no coffee yet. I'm still in the dragon stage."

She giggles. "It's the links to all of the library items. I didn't know your email, so I couldn't shoot it over to you that way."

Shoot it over to me?

I smile and nod. "Thank you. You're awesome. You did a great job."

"How do you know that when you haven't opened it yet? It could be nothing, and I could be incompetent."

"I highly doubt that, kiddo."

"So, there. You have it. And I'm thinking naming it after me could be my payment for all my hard work."

This time I laugh. "Do you now?"

"Yep." She puts her hands on her hips and offers me a huge grin as a selling point.

"I'll keep that in mind."

"Good." She takes a few steps away and then turns back to face me. "Do you know who Jason is?"

"Jason?" I shrug. "No clue. That's a pretty common name. Why?"

"No reason."

"What are you not telling me, Tootie?"

"He was bragging at the café the other day about finally getting you back or something like that. I thought it was weird." She looks back to her house. "I gotta go before Momma gets mad. She's burning toast for breakfast again. *Pray for me.* Later, Sharpe."

"Later, Tootie."

Jason?

Who the hell is that?

CHAPTER FORTY-TWO

Asher

"Wow." I look over and see Ledger pulling up to the curb on the street behind me. His elbow is propped on the open window, and a smile is wide on his face as he takes in the cherry picker that is currently hanging a new sign over the entrance to The Fields.

"You like it?" Pride warms me. Especially because it's praise coming from him.

"It looks incredible." He parks his car and walks over to where I'm standing. "This is starting to look like a whole new place with all the changes you've been making."

I so desperately want to tell him *the why* behind it but still haven't heard from Hillary. It's imperative for me to get this partnership on my own merit. I've always been looked at through a different lens in this town, and the last thing I want with this first venture of my own is for it to be assumed I slept my way into it.

"I'm trying." I shrug. "It definitely needed a makeover. That, and I wanted it to feel like it was somewhat mine. I know that sounds silly, but . . . it's always been Gran and Pop's. Updating it, bringing a little more life to it, makes me feel like I've contributed to it somehow."

"I can understand that. It's admirable." He pulls me against his side and presses a kiss to my temple. "I'm proud of you. I truly am."

"Thanks." I glance back at his car and then to him. "What are you doing here? I thought you had a busy day."

"I did. I do." He nods. "But I wanted to see you more."

My heart lurches in my throat. I always want to see him, but as of late, protecting my heart is of equal importance. Telling myself to enjoy the time we have left and not stress about what comes next is one thing. Actually listening and believing it, is a whole other thing. In fact, it's brutal to want someone so badly—to be with him and enjoy him and laugh with him—while acknowledging that each second we spend together, I fall a little harder for him. *And hate that one day he'll be gone.*

"You know how to make a girl feel special. I'd never complain about a visit from you." I smile while admiring the sheer beauty of him.

How am I ever going to let him go?

"Do you have time to break away for lunch?" he asks.

"I can't," I say, as much for self-preservation as I do for truth. "These guys will be here for the next hour hanging new signage. I have to be here. Can we meet up later?"

"I have a dinner meeting."

"I can leave the key under the mat for you for when it's over?"

CHAPTER FORTY-THREE

Ledger

THE HOUSE IS QUIET WHEN I OPEN THE FRONT DOOR TO Asher's house. The kitchen light is on, its funky chandelier creating crazy shadows on the white shiplapped walls as I make my way up the stairs.

I stop in the doorway.

She's asleep, lying on her side, with her hair fanned out across the white pillowcase. Her shoulder is bare, the pale pink of her lips parted, as her even breathing fills the room.

I welcome the blissful silence. Normally I can't stand the quiet, but here, on the farm, there is something about it that makes it ring differently for me. *Or maybe it's just Asher who does that.*

Quieting my head is an impossible feat most days. My thoughts never stop. To-do lists are constantly being added to. Facts are thought of, figures are worked through. Details are being defined.

It's how I work.

It's who I am.

And yet this is the only place I've ever been where the silence soothes rather than grates. It's even more potent in the mornings when I wake before Ash and simply enjoy watching her sleep. Holding her. Loving her—*fuck.*

Is that why I was so angry with my brothers at the fundraiser? Did they see it when I refused to?

I love her.

How did *I* never see it before? I'm in love with Asher Wells.

The same girl I was in love with fifteen years ago.

The question is, what am I going to do about it?

I undress, unable to take my eyes off her, slip into bed behind her, and pull her against me.

"I love you," I whisper against the back of her head.

I love you, yet I have no fucking clue what to do about it.

CHAPTER FORTY-FOUR

Asher

"Miss Wells?"

"Yes. Hi. This is Asher."

"It's Hillary from Sharpe International."

My heart leaps in my throat. I take a step back from the entrance to City Hall and away from other Cedar Falls citizens as they file into the meeting. "Hi. How are you?"

"Good. Thank you. Over the past few weeks, I've taken serious consideration of your proposal. I've gone over the details and market comparisons. I've weighed whether its added value is beneficial for our clientele . . ."

I sigh with anxious anticipation.

"And I wanted to let you know that we've decided to move forward with your proposal."

"You have?"

"Yes, we have." She pauses. "Of course, it's contingent on you completing the improvements you outlined in your presentation. An asphalt drive and parking lot. Chairs and tables for both a ceremony and reception. A kitchen to house caterers."

"Of course. Yes." I'm stunned. I'm thrilled. I'm terrified. *Holy. Shit.* "I don't even know what to say right now."

"I have a feeling it will be a hugely successful option we offer to our guests. Nothing says wealthy clientele like ones who pay for luxury and then want a little piece of grandiose country thrown in. The Fields will be perfect for that."

"I'm thinking that's a compliment?"

She laughs. "Yes, that's a compliment. It means it's luxurious but at the same time classic Cedar Falls."

"So, what do I do now?"

"Legal will be drawing up contracts in the coming weeks, and then we'll go from there."

"Okay. Yes. Thank you for taking a chance on me. I—"

"I look forward to visiting it myself. I'm sure it will—Oh, shoot. My apologies. I have to cut this short. I have to take this call. We'll talk soon."

And before I can ask the question—*does Ledger know about it?*—she hangs up.

I want to do a mini-jig on the sidewalk but settle with an ear-to-ear grin.

Then, of course, reality hits. The loan. *My loan.* I still haven't gotten an approval yet.

I tap my cell phone against my chin as I accept the high but fear for the low.

I'll cross that bridge when I come to it.

I'm not going to let anything ruin my mood today.

CHAPTER FORTY-FIVE

Ledger

MAYOR GROSSMAN ACTS LIKE AN ANOINTED KING AS HE WALKS through City Hall shaking hands and laughing like a pompous ass. It's a sight, that's for sure. One I can't help notice as I scan the auditorium. *Where are you, Ash?*

She said she'd be here. *Why don't I see her?*

Tootie's here though. I catch her eye from across the room, and she waves at me. It's when I look back to where Mayor Grossman is still on his *look at me* parade that I get a closer look at the man whose back he's patting and shoulder he's squeezing. There's something about him that I can't quite place.

"Hey, who's that?" I ask the city recorder who happens to be walking next to me.

"That's the mayor's son," she says as she walks past to take her place at her desk. "Jason Grossman."

Jason.

Tootie had said that name too.

While the name hits my ears and falls flat, there is something about the man that I can't quite place. Is he a contractor for the resort? One of the protestors who heckled me last week? Did I see him at Hank's that first night?

Just as Mayor Grossman takes his seat on the dais and pounds his gavel to get the meeting started, it hits me.

No fucking way.

I take another look at Jason. Sure, he's aged some, but I never forgot that smug, condescending mouth of his. Or the nose with a slight crook in it.

Jason. He's the kid whose nose I broke sixteen years ago. The prick who talked shit about and disrespected Asher.

How didn't I see it sooner? The face structure, the same mouth shape, the beady eyes. Jason, the kid I punched years ago for disrespecting Asher, is Mayor Grossman's son.

Motherfucker.

Is that what all of this has been about?

Some kind of long-overdue vendetta put into motion by a pissed-off father? Is it his warped way of trying to get back at me for putting that bump in his son's nose?

Maybe he should have taught his son some manners. Some respect. Then again, I guess the apple doesn't fall far from the tree.

Jesus Christ.

Seriously? This is why we're being put through these ridiculous paces?

Mayor Grossman calls the meeting to order, but I miss half of the bullshit pomp and circumstance he says for posture because I'm too busy trying to figure out what to do and how to play this. Anger has me wanting to call the mayor on this publicly. It has me angling on how I can broadcast that their elected official is a petty, simpleminded asshole.

Logic and professionalism have me taking a step back.

It's as simple and as complicated as that.

As much as I'd personally like to let the whole town know who they are dealing with, I have a feeling they already know. No doubt he's shown his true colors before, and yet, they still elected him.

I, on the other hand, have a business I need to run here. A business that we've sunk a shit ton of money into and can't risk losing our occupancy permit because I stoop to his level. So as much as it pains me, I'm going to have to take the high road on this.

But that doesn't stop me from glaring at Jason until I swear he can feel it. He looks up and meets my eyes. I simply stare at him. I don't make an expression at all other than to let him know that I see him, and understand what all this bullshit is about—to position his dad well for reelection and to exact petty revenge.

"And now to the matter at hand," Mayor Grossman says, pulling my attention to him and the council members on either side of him. "We met last month to discuss the necessary changes that Sharpe

International and The Retreat needed to make to warrant getting a final inspection and in turn, an occupancy permit. Mr. Sharpe, the floor is yours."

I walk over to the lectern, clear my throat, and begin. "I've enjoyed my last six weeks here in Cedar Falls. While I'm a city boy at heart, there is a reason my brothers and I wanted to buy a resort here and contribute not only to the town's future, but also to its overall success." I take the next few minutes to bullshit. About the charm I've found here in Cedar Falls and its citizens who love their town. About the potential to make this partnership beneficial for the town as a whole. About S.I.N.'s philosophy and goal with The Retreat beyond a healthy profit margin.

"That's all well and good," the mayor says when I finish my spiel, "but what about the specific requests this council made?"

Smile wide, Ledger, and prepare to kiss more ass.

"As per your request, Mayor Grossman, and in accordance with our promise, S.I.N. has been contracting local contractors and employing Cedar Falls's citizens and will continue to do so upon opening to the public. In addition, we've made significant strides in two areas we'd like to share with you. We were excited to have the opportunity to contribute to this town we are now a member of. With that in mind, we chose to focus on two aspects that will shape and have shaped this town. We are currently in the throes of overhauling and renovating the Cedar Falls Elementary School Library. It'll be a complete makeover—expanded in size, content, and capacity. Our other focus is the Cedar Falls Assisted Living Facility. Their HVAC system is in dire need of being replaced for temperature control and air filtration. We've made a sizeable donation to get that overhauled in the coming weeks with as little disruption to the tenants as possible."

"And that's been completed?"

"We're not miracle workers, sir. We can't complete projects with such complexities as these two that fast due to scheduling with local subcontractors who are already contracted elsewhere. But rest assured, as you can see in the documentation we provided to you and your fellow councilpersons, contracts have been signed, deposits have been made, and the work is scheduled. Feel free to contact the contractors for verification, but I do believe all the necessary backup has been provided and is already in your hands."

"I see," he murmurs with a nod, eyes steadfast on me as if he doesn't believe me. But the audience is silent now. No more whispers or chuckles like before, and so with the hopes that the tide is turning in our favor, I keep going so I don't lose them.

"In addition to these contributions, we're in the process of contracting local vendors to provide goods and or services to our guests. The hope is that our guests will experience or like something they see or sample in the resort itself—whether it be in one of our many retail shops, art that is displayed throughout the facility, or a package with local excursion companies—and in turn, venture into Cedar Falls to spend more of their money."

"And what companies have you enlisted for this?"

Hillary's assistant, who accompanied me to the meeting, flips through the pages of the handout the council members received and points to the one with said list. "We have provided you with the list in your packet, but would love for the citizens to hear them as well," I say. "Bessie's baked goods will be sold in our coffee shop. Jenner's Juicery will also sell items there as well. Our restaurant and café will be exclusively using ice cream from The Creamery in town. A list of local artists is also provided who we'll showcase in various locations throughout the resort. We'll have inclusive packages for guests with Cedar Falls Ski Resort, Cedar Falls Outdoor Adventures, and—" My mind stumbles when I see The Fields as next on the list. Why is that there? I look up and glance around the room and find Asher. She offers me a reassuring smile, but I stare at her confused.

"Mr. Sharpe? Is there a problem?"

"No. I'm sorry. Where was I? Yes. We'll be offering venue packages with The Fields as well as Mountain High Club."

"That's an impressive list," the mayor says as I look back to Asher, questioning her across the room about what's going on.

It all makes sense now. The barn restoration. The strung lights. The new signage. Her insomnia and late-night work.

Dare I say I'm kind of hurt? That this was all going on and I didn't know about it? That Hillary knew about it and didn't tell me?

Asher did this and didn't trust me knowing about it. She didn't want to share it with me.

It takes everything I have to focus back on the meeting at hand and not walk over to her, pull her outside, and ask her *what the fuck?*

"Does anyone have anything to say for or against The Retreat or Sharpe International that you want on the official record?"

Are we going to do this? Let the townspeople speak or rally together with a mob mentality?

I glance back over to Asher again. I can't help it. And she meets my gaze with equal confusion and hurt that I don't understand.

A throat clears in the microphone, and with a shake of my head, I force myself to pay attention to business instead of personal. "Mr. Mayor. While I understand about profit and tourism, I still feel that Mr. Sharpe and his company, are going to plant the seeds of ruin in our town," the dowdy woman at the microphone says with a definitive nod. "He says he's going to do all these things, but once he gets his permit, he'll do whatever he wants." There are a few murmured agreements from the audience.

She has a point. We're beholden to no one once we have our occupancy permit, but I don't exactly think that's the best thing to say at this juncture.

I look around and am about to take a step to the microphone to defend myself when Tootie walks to the lectern.

"For the record, I just want to say that Ledger will do what he says he's going to do. I cursed in front of him, and he said he wouldn't tell my momma and he hasn't yet." She puts her hands on her hips and clears her throat. "Also, he hired me to tell him everything we wanted and needed in our school library. He wouldn't back out and let me down." Tootie looks over at me and smiles. "That's all."

As she walks back to her seat, the dowdy woman steps back up. "She's a child. She can be easily manipulated."

"I believe him," Asher says, rising from her seat and making her way to the podium once all eyes are on hers. "He's come here to adhere to your ridiculous requests, Mayor Grossman. He's done what you've asked for and then some. He's contributed to the community. He's brought in local talent. He's tried to create residual income for others. What more is it that you want from him?"

Grossman emits a condescending chortle that has me gritting my teeth. "Of course, you'd say that since you're sleeping with him."

"Excuse me?" she says, holding her finger up at me when I rise to my feet in her defense.

"Honey—"

"Asher," she corrects him. "My name is Asher. Not *Honey*."

He clears his throat. "While I'm sure your um . . . *friend* appreciates your unwavering support, I think the city council shouldn't take business advice from someone who can't even secure a bank loan to keep their farm afloat."

There is a hushed silence that falls across the crowd. The kind that says they're digging in for the gossip that's unfolding.

But all I hear from Grossman is *can't secure a bank loan to keep their farm afloat.*

My hands fist. A myriad of emotions flickers over Asher's face as the mayor just denigrated her in front of the town. Humiliated her, just as my father once did.

I start to move toward her, to defend her, to . . . I don't fucking know, but Asher levels me with a look and mouths the word *No*. I never stood up for her all those years ago. I sure as fuck am going to now.

"You want to come at me," I say, my voice loud enough I don't need a microphone. Everyone's heads swivel to look my way. "Then come at me. *That's fine.* But leave Asher out of it."

"I can handle myself, Ledger," Asher says, her voice steely, her expression stoic. "Mayor Grossman here is simply trying to put me in my place where he thinks all *good little women* should be. He'd rather I keep quiet because he's terribly afraid that I might be the result of an affair he had with my mother some thirty-odd years ago." That sends a ripple of murmurs through the audience and causes the mayor's face to turn red and his sputters to become incoherent. "For the record, even if you were my father, I'd refuse to claim you. I've been shamed enough in my life over things I had no control over . . . but I could control that. And I sure as hell would."

And without another word, Asher strides out of the auditorium with the entire town staring at the door she just left through.

It takes everything I have not to chase after her. To remain here in a professional capacity and do the job I'm here to do . . . and not put my personal matters first. *Not put her first.*

The gavel strikes several times as the mayor tries to gain back control of the meeting despite his own ashen pallor. Serves the fucker right.

"Settle down, everyone. Settle down." He clears his throat and tugs on the tie tight over his throat. "We clearly have other things to do than to deal with nonsense and fodder that is unneeded. Are we ready to vote on whether or not The Retreat has met our demands and can now have its final inspection to receive its occupancy permit?"

CHAPTER FORTY-SIX

Asher

I CAN'T BREATHE.

My chest burns as I gulp in huge breaths. My tears sting as I fight them back. I have to get as far away from City Hall and that prick of a man as I can. The ends of the earth wouldn't be far enough.

It doesn't matter that he showed his true colors or that he humiliated me or that I successfully stood up for myself. Those are all things I've learned to deal with being Asher Wells.

It's that I didn't get the loan.

So, I drive.

Down every back mountain road.

Through every stretch of field.

I ignore the calls coming and the texts alerting me from where I threw my cell on the back seat.

My loan was declined. *I was declined.*

The email came in halfway through the city council meeting. *Thank you for your application but we regret to inform you that you have been declined for the applicable loan.* I was stunned. Shocked. Hurt. And there wasn't a thing I could say or do about it in the middle of Grossman's grandiose show.

But he knew I didn't get it. That's the kicker. He knew before I did, or else he never would have said what he said. Goddamn small-town life. I should have thought it through. I should have figured Grossman would know since his daughter-in-law is the bank's branch manager.

So I lashed out. I fired back. I tried to put him in his place and embarrass him just as much as he'd tried to humiliate me.

It's all I could do.

I bang the heel of my hand on the steering wheel and give in to the need to scream at the top of my lungs. The sound is smothered by the wind but does nothing to abate the anger owning me.

It's like I was handed the highest of highs with Hillary's call about being awarded the contract, followed by the lowest of lows, knowing I can no longer afford all the things I still need to meet those contract requirements.

I pull over to the side of the road and stare at some horses grazing in a field until my eyes blur. Then I put the car in gear and drive some more, making a point to be as far away from town as possible.

The last thing I want to see is people.

I wanted this for me.

I needed this for me.

And yeah, sure, it's all set up and I can still hold events, but I practically maxed out my credit card to get it to this point. And my contract is contingent upon these improvements. And, and, and . . .

And so, I keep driving.

CHAPTER FORTY-SEVEN

Ledger

"YOU WANT TO TELL ME WHAT THIS IS?" I ASK HILLARY WHEN I storm into the office, holding up the list of vendors and pointing to The Fields.

I'm worried and furious and feel like I'm going out of my mind because I can't find Asher anywhere. Fucking anywhere, when I looked for what feels like forever. This is a small town. I should be able to find her.

But I couldn't.

And I'm insane with fucking worry over it.

Hillary meets my glare with a measured stare. She never glances down at the list in my hand because she already knows what it is. "It's the vendor list. The title states that too."

"No shit. I'm talking about The Fields being on this list." I walk from one side of the office to the other, unable to sit still.

"I do believe you tasked me with finding local vendors to create inviting packages for our guests, and I did just that," she says cautiously. But there is a smugness in her tone, a defiance in the way she won't back down that has me gritting my teeth.

"And you didn't think to tell me about *this* one?"

"Miss Wells explicitly asked me not to."

"Excuse me?" I shout. "Did you forget who your boss is?"

"No." She pauses and waits for my feet to stop moving and for me to look at her. "As I said, Miss Wells specifically asked that you not know about her proposal. She wanted this on her own merit and not because she's sleeping with the owner."

Her words put fire on my temper in an instant. "Of course, she did," I mutter, needing somewhere to direct my anger because it's still there and it's still raw, but not so much at Asher anymore. Now it's at fucking everyone else in this goddamn town. Here I am thinking—stewing—raging over the fact that she's hiding things from me—dejected that she didn't think she could share them with me—and of course, it's just her being stubborn as always and not needing anyone.

"It's a solid business proposal. Well-thought-out. She did her research. I was impressed with it, with her, but more importantly, it'll be a great option for our guests."

"The proposal?" I ask, my hand out waiting for it. Hillary meets me with the lift of her brows. "*Please.*"

She reaches into her file drawer and hands it over to me. I flip through its pages, and Hillary is right. The proposal is professional, concise, informative, and it doesn't hurt that the pictures look like everything she promises in the text. It's the last page that cites the improvements still in the works that makes everything click.

The loan.

She needs the loan to finish these items.

Without the loan, she doesn't have this. *Fucking Grossman blasted that very clearly across the City Hall meeting.*

The bastard.

Christ. I blow a sigh out and toss the proposal on the desk.

"Ledger." Hillary's smile is faint, and her eyes are soft when I look up to meet them. "Just because you love her—"

"I don't love her," I growl. Saying it in my head is one thing. Admitting it out loud is a whole other ballgame.

She chuckles. "Yes. You do. And that love doesn't give you the right to rush in here like a white knight and save the day for her. She's independent for a reason. Clearly, she's been hurt by life in ways I don't know—but I can see it, because I used to be her. Asserting my independence, needing something that was wholly my own, was a way to take a piece of myself back. It was how I healed. It's what led me to be sitting right here in this office with you. Asher doesn't need fixing, Ledger. She just needs someone to hold her hand if she fails, to celebrate her when she succeeds, and to listen when she speaks. There's so much more said in silence than in a room full of people talking."

I feel helpless. it's a miserable feeling for a man who's always in control.

"I don't want to fix her, Hillary. I just want her to realize she's not alone anymore."

"Have you told her that? That might be a good place to start."

I nod.

Telling Asher that she's not alone anymore is a good start. Perhaps *showing* her too. But fuck, how do I do that if I can't fucking find her? How can I reassure her that I've got her back? That she can trust in me?

"She's independent for a reason. Asher doesn't need fixing. She just needs someone to hold her hand if she fails, to celebrate her when she succeeds, and to listen when she speaks."

Haven't I been listening all this time? Isn't that what I do best with her when we talk on the phone, lie in each other's arms, have picnics—

Fuck, could she be there? At *our* place?

It's the only place I haven't checked.

One place, and I hope to fucking God I'm right.

The wildflowers are bright and the sound of birds is loud as I make my way through the underbrush to the old willow tree.

My chest constricts when I see her sitting there against its trunk, her head back with her face to the sky, her eyes closed.

And if I ever had any doubt before, I sure as hell don't now.

I love Asher Wells.

I'm *in* love with Asher Wells.

Plain.

Simple.

Completely.

I stand there and stare at her. I know she knows I'm here, so I struggle with what to say or how to say it. Hillary's advice circles in my head.

"Thank you for standing up for me today. You didn't need to," I say, feeling like I'm tiptoeing around what we need to talk about but needing a jumping-off place to start somewhere.

"Yes, I did." She doesn't move, doesn't open her eyes, just murmurs the three words.

"I'm proud of you for sticking up for yourself today, but God, how I wish you would have let me defend you."

"I don't need anyone to defend me, Ledger. I can take care of myself."

"I know you can. Fucking hell, I know you can, but would it hurt you to need my help every once in a while? *To need me?*" My voice breaks, and she finally opens her eyes and stares at me with a storm roiling in those gray irises of hers.

We hold each other's gazes, and I have a feeling this is going to be one of the most important conversations I've ever had in my life. I've negotiated deals worth hundreds of millions of dollars. I've yanked contracts off tables without so much as a flinch. But this is the first time I've ever had to fight for something on a personal level. Truth be told, I'm fucking terrified I'm going to mess this up.

I walk forward and lower myself to my knees so that I'm sitting in front of her. "Why didn't you tell me your plans for The Fields? About the proposal? I mean, I understand wanting it to be awarded on your own merit, but . . . you completely shut me out of something that is so much a part of you. Why didn't you tell me? Why did you lie to me?"

CHAPTER FORTY-EIGHT

Asher

H E STARES AT ME, THE MUSCLE IN HIS JAW TICKING, HIS EYES imploring.

"I didn't lie to you."

"You chose not to tell me. Same difference."

"It's not."

"To me it is. Hasn't there been enough lies that have come between us, Asher? No more lies. No more deception. No more lying by omission. *Please.*"

"Ledger. I didn't mean to—"

"You opted to say you were simply updating the farm rather than tell me you were creating a whole new business for yourself. Why? Why couldn't you tell me, Asher? What is it about me that made you think you couldn't confide in me?"

My stomach twists in a knot at the hurt etched in the lines of his handsome face. "I know you won't understand, but I just . . . I needed to do this for me."

"Do you think I would have stopped you? That I would have tried to control it? Your transformation of The Fields, your idea to make it a destination, is incredible. There's no way you could have thought I'd tell you otherwise. So, what is it, Asher? What are you not telling me?"

You're going to leave me, and I need something to soften the heartbreak.

My hands tremble as I open and close my mouth. I don't have an answer other than that.

"What are we doing here, Ledger? Fooling ourselves? Pretending that your *penance* here isn't up in a few weeks, and you're not going to go back to your life, and I'm not going to go back to mine?" His expression falls at my words. "Is it too much to have one thing in my life that you haven't touched? One thing that's completely mine so I'm not reminded of you every time I'm around it or see it or think of it?"

And that's the crux of it, isn't it? That's why this has been so important to me. I know he's leaving and when he does, everything in this town, in my house, even the goddamn lavender fields, will remind me of him. And now, even my inescapable failure to start a business will be tied to him too.

"So rather than talk about it, talk about us, you'd rather just bury your head in the sand and act like this—like we—didn't happen?"

"Bury my head in the sand? I think my actions are perfectly justifiable considering your intentions—your plans—are pretty self-explanatory." I can feel my armor slipping on. Layer upon layer. Shielding me when I fear nothing is going to be able to protect me from the hurt that's to come.

"What the hell do you mean my plans are self-explanatory?" he demands.

"It's just a fling that will be over in a few weeks. Then your penance will be done and you'll get to go back home." I blink away the tears that those words cause. "I believe those were your words, weren't they?"

"Asher. No. You don't understand." He puts his hands on my knees and squeezes. I try not to flinch at his touch because everything inside of me is telling me to run, right now. To pull away while I can, but even I'm not that strong. He chuckles disbelievingly, but I feel like I'm being mocked, and it rubs me the wrong way.

"So you didn't say that?" I damn well know he did.

"No. I did. It's just"—he scrubs a hand through his hair—"my brothers were harassing me over what we, you and I, were. They wouldn't let it go. The easiest way to get them off my back was to say something like that. To play it down so they'd back off . . ." He searches my eyes. "Why didn't you say anything to me? Why didn't you just flat-out ask me?"

"Ask you? Why? So I could look like an idiot when you see how hurt I was because I thought we were more than that? After what happened before . . . do you think I wanted to open myself up more to you to be torn back apart?"

He sighs, and I try to ignore the compassion in his eyes. The understanding. "And so you started to close down instead . . . to make it easier to walk away."

"This'll never work," I whisper the fear that has been creeping into my head for days.

"Why not? Why can't we make this work?"

"Just ask anyone. It's clear you're the more important one here. For it to work, I'd have to be the one to pick up my life and walk away."

"Why is that such a bad thing? You live in a town that doesn't treat you with the respect you deserve. That holds your mother's past against you. Today at City Hall was case in point."

"But that's not for you to decide," I shout at him, rising to my feet. Needing to move, needing to think, and needing to fight. "And the fact that you assume it is without ever asking me should be enough in and of itself to explain my hesitation. You come first. Your work comes first . . . and frankly, I deserve better than being second to those things."

"I would never put you second."

My laugh is anything but humorous. "No? What about you and your ten-year plan, huh? The one you never waver from with its bullet points and set parameters. Unfortunately for me, a relationship with me"—*loving me*—"isn't valid because it comes before its scheduled time."

"Don't be like this, Ash. The plan . . ." He shakes his head in frustration. "It's just that, *a plan*. Not set in stone. If anything, you've made me realize that life . . . it can't be planned for. Hell, both times you've come into my life have been completely out of the blue. Completely unexpected . . . and I . . . fuck. I'm saying this all wrong." Regret tinges his voice. So does hope. So does fear. "All you need to know is *I want this, I want you*."

"But on your terms," I whisper.

"I just can't up and walk away from my life, Asher." He follows me as I pace.

"I get it. I know what that's like because I left *my life, my dream*, to come back and care for my family. My gran is here, Ledger. So is The Fields. It's *my* family legacy, much like S.I.N. is *yours*. I can't leave it behind just as I'd never ask you to leave yours behind. This is how I make my mark. For me. You're wealthy and revered in business, and no doubt believe you're more important than I am because you basically own the world but—"

"That's not true—"

"But that's what it feels like to me. What you don't get is that for the first time in so goddamn long, I feel relevant. Full of possibility and . . ."

I lift my head to the sky and close my eyes. *Too much.* This is all just too much—emotion, fear, hope. I'm waiting for it to all come crashing down. And if not now, *then when?* "I just need time, Ledger. To think. To—"

"This should be the easiest decision in your life, Ash. *Choosing me* should be the easiest decision." His voice breaks, and it nearly kills me.

"But I shouldn't have to give up my life just to have you in it."

He hangs his head and sighs. "So just like that, you're not going to try? Not fight for us?"

"I didn't say that." Panic starts to claw at my throat.

"You didn't have to."

"Ledger. I don't know what to do. I don't know . . . I don't know how to feel."

Why do things I want always seem just out of reach? Acceptance, my career, my dreams for The Fields. *Ledger.*

The only thing I've been able to grasp and hold on to is my sense of self. Who I am. And it's taken me time to do that, to work through the grief from Pop's death, and find that woman again. I refuse to give her up just to keep him.

I blink back tears and force myself to meet his eyes. It's only then that he speaks. "Maybe we need to take some time to think. A week. I don't know. Maybe we just need some time for you to clear your head and me to . . . I don't know."

I lose the battle, and my tears fall over my lashes and slide down my cheeks. I nod, even though I'm still not certain it's what I truly want. "Maybe."

He takes a few steps toward me. "I once told you that only one girl has ever broken my heart before. *That was you, Asher.* And I swear to fucking God, I think you're breaking it again." He puts my face in his hands and presses the gentlest of kisses on my lips. "I love you, Asher Wells. I think I always have."

Those words should fill my heart, instead, they fracture it a little more.

Because I'm not sure if love is enough to conquer the obstacles we face.

And without another word or meeting my eyes, Ledger Sharpe walks out of the clearing and, I fear, out of my life.

CHAPTER FORTY-NINE

Ledger

"You did it, Ledge. The Retreat can officially open next month," Callahan says. "I don't know how you won that fucker Grossman over, but you did."

"Congrats, man," Ford says. "See? You were the right man for the job after all."

"If you come home in a pair of cowboy boots or Wranglers, though, be prepared for me to never stop giving you shit." Callahan's laugh bellows through the speaker.

"Me? In cowboy boots?" I snort and *then sigh*. Hearing my brothers' voices should make me happy rather than have emotion lodge in my throat. I clear my throat to try and get rid of it, but it remains.

"But why are you still there? Wasn't your plan to get in, get it done, and get the hell out of there?" Ford asks. "We were both surprised you weren't jonesing so bad to get back that you didn't fly home to tell us the good news, face-to-face."

"Nah. I've got some loose ends to tie up here." Asher's face flashes in my mind, followed by a pang in my chest. "Just a few things."

"That's code for one last hop in the sack with Asher," Callahan says.

"Funny," I mutter, the words affecting me more than they'll ever know. "Look, I have to meet with Hillary on something."

"Sure you do." Ford laughs.

"I said I have to go," I snap.

"Whoa. Down, boy," Callahan says. "You sure everything is good, Ledge?"

"Fine. Fucking perfect." And I end the call before they can say another word.

I lean back in my chair at my desk, close my eyes, and blow out a slow exhale.

She ran.

Isn't that what's eating at me? I offered to give us time when I fucking don't need it. But I offered it because she looked like a scared fucking rabbit . . . and *she ran.*

And the only reason I know is that I stopped by The Fields today to see if we could talk. To see if I could fix whatever needs fixing.

Asher doesn't need fixing, Ledger.

I replay the scene from earlier in my head.

The empty echo of the house as I knocked on the door.

The flutter of panic when it didn't open. When no one answered.

"She's not home." George's words behind me making me jump.

"Where is she?"

"She took off. Packed a bag, asked me to take care of the place, and left."

"Did she say for how long?"

"Nope."

"Did she say anything else?"

"Just that if this place can ever get up and running"—he points toward the barn area—"then she'd love to hire on my wife to help run some of the events." I must give him an odd look because he continues without my prompting. "She's afraid she's going to lose her job because of The Retreat."

"The Retreat? *Why?*"

He shrugs as he sizes me up, clearly still uncertain what to think of me. "It's a big operation. The assumption is tourists will jump ship from her hotel to yours."

"At the height of the tourist months, there will be plenty of business for both hotels."

He gives a measured nod. "It's the non-height months that put people out of jobs."

I'm used to facing people, to dealing with the repercussions of the decisions I make. This one doesn't sit well with me, and there is no quick fix. "Let's see what happens. Asher always has my number if need be."

"That's generous of you, but we don't expect any handouts or hand-ups."

Our eyes meet, and pride wars against concern in his eyes. "Understood. The offer is there."

"Noted."

I look back to the house and the porch swing that looks so empty without her curled up on it. "You helped Asher out with the changes here. It looks incredible."

"It does."

He's not going to give me a fucking inch, is he?

"I think it's a smart business decision on her part. It'll give an added income stream. Give this place a new life to people who would have never noticed it before."

"Is there a reason you're on her porch, talking about her business with me . . . *sir?*"

Definitely not an inch.

I clear my throat and level with him. "Why did she leave, George? *Run?* Why not stay and fight for this place?" *For me?*

"Who said she wasn't fighting?"

"She's not here, is she?" I ask.

"That girl has fought her whole life. The scorn and judgment she's faced in this town is enough to break most people. *It never broke her.*"

"I know, but—"

"No, you don't. With all due respect, you don't know shit about what it was like for Asher year after year. And yes, she's worked tirelessly to not live under the shadow of her mother's disgrace and abandonment." He looks out toward the fields as the lavender ripples like a wave. "She's building something here. With her grit and her tenacity and her courage. Would it make Pop proud? Damn straight. But it also made her proud of herself for the first time in a long time . . . and when something you're hoping for falls through, sometimes it takes time to accept that blow. To figure out how to live without it."

"So what are you saying? That she's coming back?" I'm more desperate for that answer than anything—so it takes me a second to hear him. It's not just the dream she's created here she's afraid of losing . . . *it's me too.*

Jesus Christ.

She can't be figuring out how to *live without it.*

Goddammit, Asher. I'm here. I'm waiting. Come back.

"Of course, she's coming back." He snorts in disdain at me. "Asher Wells isn't a quitter. My guess is she's looking for another way to make this happen. She's taking time to accept the reality she was handed and move forward."

Accept reality and move forward. Have I done that? Have I moved on from what my dad did?

And long after George has explained the reasoning to me and took off for home, I'm still sitting on the porch swing, listening to it creak. Trying to work through the question.

My father fabricated a lie that has affected me in some way or another for the past fifteen years. My fear of letting him down. My fear of not living up to the potential he gave me by "saving me" that night with his lie. I've moved goalpost after fucking goalpost to make him happy. To make him proud of me. To live up to the Maxton Sharpe standard . . . *and for what?* To put off my happiness in the hopes of achieving his approval? To almost lose the woman I love for a second time?

Dad is gone, Ledger. Isn't it time you abandon his goals and create ones that make you happy? Isn't it time to no longer be in and *under* his shadow?

"My gran is here, Ledger. So is The Fields. It's my family legacy much like S.I.N. is yours. I can't leave it behind just as I'd never ask you to leave yours behind. This is how I make my mark. For me. You're wealthy and revered in business, and no doubt believe you're more important than I am because you basically own the world . . ."

How could I ever ask her to give up her goals? How do we make this work so we can both live out the dreams we have individually and the new ones we want to create together?

Fuck.

Just . . . *fuck.*

She doesn't think it's possible. That I'm capable of it.

I told her I loved her.

And she left anyway.

CHAPTER FIFTY

Asher

"It's been over a week. You're taking this whole 'drive to clear your head and talk to no one' thing to a whole new level this time, aren't you?" Nita asks.

I smile and sink back into my chair on the balcony of my hotel room. Glacier National Park is in the distance and it's mesmerizing. And believe me, I've been staring at it *a lot* over the past week. "You know me," I tease.

"What's going on with you? He hurt you, didn't he? Am I going to have to go over and kick his ass?"

"No. It's not him."

"Then what is it?"

"It's me."

"Girl, you need to give me more than that."

"It's hard to explain. He's everything I've ever wanted, Nita. He's kind and loving and thoughtful. But maybe he's always lived as a figment of my imagination—my *what-if*—and now that he's a reality, it's messed me up."

"You know I love you, right?"

"Yes."

"So when I tell you that you're batshit crazy and you need to get the guy, you'll still love me, right?"

I laugh and then fall silent.

"Asher?"

"I still love you. I promise."

"Whew. So you're driving to clear your head. Do you have answers yet?"

"No. Yes. A few."

"Well, at least it's a start."

CHAPTER FIFTY-ONE

Ledger

I TOY WITH THE CORNERS OF THE PAPER. THE FIELDS LOGO IS emblazoned across the top of the lavender-colored paper, but it's the short note scrawled in Asher's penmanship and the second piece of paper in my other hand that I can't stop staring at.

Ledger,

You asked for no more deception. No more lying by omission. Enclosed is what I found while cleaning out Pop's things. I didn't tell you originally because I didn't want to hurt you further, and the past can't be undone . . . but you deserve to know. I'm sorry.

-Asher

I drop the stationery and focus on the check. On my father's unmistakable penmanship. In his attempt to buy off her grandfather to keep Asher away from me.

To be unscrupulous in business is one thing.

To be it when it comes to your own children is unforgivable.

Even knowing now that he apologized to me for this, for his actions, does nothing to lessen the sting seeing this causes.

My idol.

My biggest example of who not to be.

I'm not certain how long I stare at the check, but when my phone rings and Ford is on the other end of the line, everything—Asher leaving, my dad's actions, the wrongs that can never be righted—hits me harder than ever.

I almost don't answer. But I do. *"Hey."*

"What's wrong?" Two words are all Ford needs to say to have me clos-ing my eyes and taking a deep breath.

"Nothing. Why?" I lie.

"You're full of shit. Callahan's here too."

"Hey," Callahan says. "Something's wrong. We can both feel it." *Goddamn triplet voodoo.* "What are you not telling us, Ledge?"

I stare at the check and question myself and my previous decision not to tell them about Dad. About his deception. About his lies.

And even now, I stand by it. We're all finally healing. All coming out of the darkness we each fell into when he died. I still can't bring myself to ruin the image they have of him in their eyes.

If there's one thing my father taught me that I'll still choose to hold on to, it's to bear the brunt of a burden for the good of everyone else.

I just hope Asher lets me do the same for her.

Asher.

God, I fucking miss her.

"Ledge?" Callahan asks.

"She left." The dam of silence breaks and it feels so fucking good to tell someone. "She left, and I don't know what the fuck to do."

"Isn't that a good thing?" Ford asks. "It being a fling and all?" His tone mocks me.

"Do you think we believed for a goddamn second the two of you were a fling?" Callahan asks. "You made puppy-dog eyes at her all night. Not once did you take your eyes off her to look at Cindy Dempsey's cleav-age—and believe me, it was so noticeably displayed that Sutton couldn't keep her eyes off it."

I smile. And it feels fucking good to for the first time all week. Callahan and I may have had our differences in the past, but it's weird for us to have switched roles for the moment. For him to be the one trying to take care of me.

"Shit. You've got it bad, don't you?" Ford asks.

"I told her I loved her . . . and *she left anyway*," I murmur.

"Then what the fuck are you doing sitting in your office?" Callahan shouts. "Find her. Fight for her. Make her an offer she can't refuse."

I snort at the notion . . . and yet, isn't that what I want? Her? Forever? As mine?

"Fuck." I sigh the word out and both brothers laugh.

"Ding. Ding. Ding," Ford says. "I do believe the light bulb just went off. You owe me one hundred, Cal."

"What the fuck are you talking about?" I ask.

"We bet on how long it would be before you asked her to marry you. He said three months. I said one."

"Jesus," I mutter, but my smile only grows wider as hope begins to swell in my chest from an idea that's slowly forming. "You two . . ."

"Please know that it's taking everything I have to bite my tongue right now and not razz the fucking shit out of you over this," Callahan says as I chuckle. "I'm showing you mercy, brother, but it's coming. There's no way Mr. I'm-Not-Falling-in-Love falls in love and gets away with it scot-free from us."

"Thanks for the warning."

"Hey, Ledge?"

"Yeah?"

"Go get your lavender girl. You've waited fifteen years. I don't think you should waste another minute," Ford says. Or Callahan. I'm not sure which one, but it doesn't fucking matter.

I already have more important things on my mind.

CHAPTER FIFTY-TWO

Asher

"Asher?"

"Yes. Hi," I say, even though I already know from Caller ID that it's Hillary.

"Hillary here."

Dread drops into my stomach. Does she know I haven't secured the loan yet? That I can't fulfill my promises? Certainly the town rumor mill has already filled her in. "Hi. How are you?"

"Good. Great. Look, I have a prospective client coming into town in an hour. They're a huge client of S.I.N. resorts. He's extremely interested in seeing The Fields because he's looking for a spot to hold quarterly meetings and the like. Is it possible for you to show him around?"

"Um. Yeah. But I'm not in town—"

"When can you get into town? What time? I only have him here for the day, and he really wants to meet with you and see if it's a good fit."

"But not everything's done yet," I say, my thoughts scrambled as I glance at the clock. It's four in the afternoon. Tonight? What the hell?

"That's okay. I explained that to him and he's fine with it. Where are you? What time can you get here? Seven p.m.? Eight p.m.? Eight might be best so the lights can be on and the whole mood can be set."

"Eight." I make a split-second decision. "Eight is fine. I'll call George and have him get everything we have set up so it looks perfect when he gets there."

"Good. Thank you for doing this. I know it's last minute."

"No, thank you."

I'm on an adrenaline high when I hang up. Funny how I'd already packed my bags given the decision I'd made earlier today.

It's time.

It's time to go home.

CHAPTER FIFTY-THREE

Asher

TRAFFIC.

Who would have thought I'd encounter traffic on the way home? But sure enough, I did. I'm going twice the speed limit down the road leading to my house. Luckily no one is on it because it's ten minutes till eight, and the last thing I want to do is screw this up and be late.

When I turn the corner and The Fields comes into view, it takes me a second to believe it's mine. The lights illuminating the trees. The spotlights on the barn. The dark silhouette of the hill behind it.

It's mine.

Pride like I've never felt before fills me.

I'll find a way to make this work. It's the only option.

But when I go to turn down the driveway, there's asphalt. And not just a road patch onto the gravel driveway, but the entire driveway is paved.

How did George get this done?

I know we'd talked about it, but that was when I thought I was getting the loan.

Shit. I can't afford this. Not the driveway or the whole section to the left that's a mini-parking lot with a lone car parked in it. Oh my God.

Oh.

My.

God.

How am I going to pay for this?

I pull up to the house and screech to a stop. I have to find George. I have to ask him why he did this, I have to . . . *can they just un-pave it and take it all back?*

I hustle down the pathway toward the barn and pasture. There are paving stones here too. Slabs of rock cemented down on the path.

It's exactly like I wanted on the quotes I showed George, but I never told him to pull the trigger. Never.

Tears of sheer panic threaten as I move through the darkening night. I need to shove this away. I need to calm down. I can't come off like a crazy lunatic when I meet this possible repeat client.

Just when I hit the clearing, I start to hear music. And not just music, but what sounds like stringed instruments. It's soothing, and I know the tune but not the name.

It's not until I turn the corner of the barn and come face-to-face with Ledger does everything hit me.

He's standing beneath the big oak tree, a soft smile on his lips, the lights above highlighting his hair.

"Ledger?" I look around to see where Hillary is but only jump when I see the barn completely furnished with tables and chairs and— "Where's Hillary?"

"There is no Hillary," he says as he moves toward me.

"But I'm supposed to—"

"You're supposed to meet me. Here. In the setting you created. In the place we originally fell in love, *then and now*."

"What did you do, Ledger?" I start to take a step back, my head shaking. "I can't accept all of this."

"Yes, you can." He reaches out and holds my hands in his. "You told me you wanted this place because it was the only place I'd never touched. It was the only place where you could forget about me. I don't want you to forget about me. I don't want you to live another day without me. So I've touched it now, Asher. I've made it so that we're partners in this venture . . . and hopefully in life. I touched it because I don't want to spend another day where either of us doesn't feel one another's presence."

"Ledger." His name is a whisper of disbelief.

"And I figured if I was going to cash my father's check, it might as well go toward something we make together. To a new beginning for us."

I want to look everywhere and nowhere but him all at the same time. Time hasn't changed that. "I'm at a loss for words."

"We'll figure us out. Maybe you come with me to New York for part of the year while George and Angel run The Fields. Then we come and spend summers here like I used to. You always said George was family to your pop and gran, so you'd still be keeping it in the family. If that doesn't work, we'll split our time more evenly. You can go to school in New York if you want. Fulfill your dream. Make your mark. Be whoever you want to be . . . so long as you be with me while you do it."

I look all around me and am stunned.

I have never felt more loved than in this moment. Than by him. "I don't know what to say."

"Say yes, Asher. Say you'll do this with me. That you'll be with me. That you'll depend on me." He kneels and when I look down, all I can see is the love swimming in his eyes. It's then that he opens a box with a ring in it. It's gorgeous and sparkly. I don't even look at it long enough to know what it is because he's all I want to look at.

He's all I want.

Ledger. *My moonlight boy.*

I love him. I think I always have. I press a kiss to his lips.

"On one condition," I murmur.

He leans back, his eyes dancing with amusement. "What's that?"

"That you'll love me forever."

EPILOGUE

Ledger

One Year Later

THIS IS WHAT SHE WANTED.

I offered her a trip to anywhere in the world. The private jet. Adventure. Relaxation. Anything she could ever want or think of to ring in her birthday, and this is what she chose.

It's not like I should expect any less.

It is Asher, isn't it? And it's one of the main reasons I fall more in love with her each day. The number of zeros in our bank account doesn't matter.

But this does.

Her family.

Her history.

Her connection to this place that no amount of time will ever break.

And there she is, standing beneath the strings of lights, with the lavender at her back and her friends all around her.

Christ. She's gorgeous. Easygoing yet complicated. *And all fucking mine.* How in the hell did that happen? *How did I get so lucky?*

"You're her one birthday wish. All she wanted was for you to be here," I murmur into Gran's ear. She barely responds—a flicker of her fingers, a barely-there lift of one corner of her lips—but with her steep decline, it's more than any of us could hope for. "Thank you for that."

I give a gentle squeeze to her shoulders as I glance at the two private caregivers I hired to get Gran here and give a nod in appreciation.

The music on the speaker changes, followed by a cheer of approval by everyone on the dance floor. They arrange themselves in lines and start doing matching moves as they dance in unison.

Nita can't stop smiling as she tries to teach her son the moves, no doubt embarrassing the hell out of him. Hank weaves in and out of the moving rows, delivering drinks despite my insistence that he's not to work or tend the bar tonight. Carson Allen trips over his own feet but doesn't care, because he's too busy flirting with the date he brought. And then there's Tootie in her neon pink dress with crooked pigtails, unabashedly mowing down every sweet there is on the dessert table.

Asher's laugh rings out, drawing my attention back to her. I move toward the edge of the barn so I can see her better as she dances with our friends.

Happiness has never looked so good on someone. I like to think that I helped get her to this point, but then again, the woman is a force to be reckoned with. Her happiness is her own.

She looks up and searches through the small crowd of people. She pauses mid-dance move when she finds me. Our gazes lock. Her eyes dance with fire she reserves just for me. And when she smiles, I know I've never made a better decision in my life than fighting for her.

I note when both of my brothers step up on either side of me.

Callahan whistles. "Should we entertain the crowd for you?"

"What do you mean?" I take a sip of my beer.

"That look can only mean one thing when a woman gives it to you." Ford chuckles. "She wants you. Right now. Maybe even in the loft of the barn for a quickie while we're all obliviously occupied out here."

"You're so full of shit." The teasing never stops.

"Full of shit?" Callahan snorts and points to where Sutton is cradling my adorable baby niece dressed in a bright yellow romper. "It's the same look Sutton gave me that got me *that*."

"And you wouldn't have it any other way," I say as I look at Callahan. He's still staring at Sutton and his daughter with an expression I never thought I'd see on his face—absolute and complete love and adoration.

"You're right. *I wouldn't*," he murmurs.

"What about you? When do you two plan to have kids . . . or is that not on the Ledger-approved ten-year plan?" Ford asks, earning the arm I hook around his neck and the tug I give it.

"There is a ten-year plan still, right?" Callahan asks as I stand there silently and simply watch Asher.

"For some things, yes," I murmur, still mesmerized by my wife. "For other things, not so much."

"Holy shit." Ford staggers back playfully. "Did I just hear that right?"

I nod and smile.

He sure did.

Chaos has overtaken my life—and I've welcomed it. It's been in the last-minute decisions to fly back to Cedar Falls to unwind. Or the impulsive midnight run for an ice cream cone and a walk in The Battery. It's been in Asher's greeting me at the door after a long day of work for me and studying for her in nothing but heels and some lacy panties—and then making love on the outdoor terrace of our penthouse.

Spontaneity is something I never knew until Asher. Never appreciated. An intimate wedding she planned in a few weeks' time. Study groups in our family room. Playing hooky from work to steal a few more hours with her. Forgetting to move the goalposts because I'm perfectly fine with where they are.

All plans out the window.

Asher taught me that.

Is still teaching me that, and honestly, I couldn't be any fucking happier.

She helped me find joy—genuine fucking joy—for the first time in my adult life. It didn't come from sealing a multi-million-dollar deal or getting the write-up in Forbes that came out a few months back—it was in her.

Simply put . . . *it is her.*

"Uh-oh," Ford mutters, drawing me back from my thoughts and to the party.

"What?" I look up to see Asher moving toward me.

"Time to go keep the crowd busy so Ledge can get busy himself up in the loft," Callahan says.

"Whatever." But by the time I look at either of them, they're on the move, their laughter loud.

And then she's in front of me with that disarming smile of hers that presses against my lips.

"Having fun?" she asks.

"I am. You?"

"I'm fine. This is perfect." Another press of her lips to mine. "Thank you for throwing me a birthday party. For getting Gran here. For . . . being you."

Is it possible to fall more in love with someone each day?

"I'm glad. It's not lounging on the beach in Seychelles, but . . ." I tease.

"But it's exactly what I needed to refuel after finals and a busy season here at The Fields—"

"And all that incredible sex we've been having."

"Yes." She laughs. "That too."

I chuckle. "I guess this is when I tell you that my brothers just bailed because they're convinced you were coming over here so we could have a quickie in the loft."

She arches one eyebrow as a mischievous smile slides onto her lips. "Is that so?"

"It is." I nod. Her eyes challenge me, sending my hopes soaring.

"Hmm." She purses her lips and looks around. "It's only natural for the host and hostess to disappear every now and again to check on supplies and make sure we have everything our guests need."

"Is that so?" I set down my beer, shove my hands in my pockets, and take a few steps toward the open barn door.

"It most definitely is." She leans into me. "Knowing how many napkins we have is of vital importance." And then whispers against my lips, "Meet you up there in five."

When she walks away from me with an extra swing to her hips, there is only one thought in my head.

I'm glad she chose me.

So fucking glad.

Did you enjoy Asher and Ledger's journey back toward each other and their deserved happily ever after? Are you intrigued by both Callahan and Ford and want to find out more about them? There are two other books in the S.I.N. series.
The books can be read in any order). You can find them here:
www.kbromberg.com/books/sin-series

Last Resort
Final Proposal

Are you looking for another wealthy book boyfriends to warm your metaphorical bed? Why not get acquainted these other K. Bromberg's heroes:

Faking It (standalone, billionaire hero, fake dating, forced proximity): After a little white lie spirals out of control, billionaire Zane Phillips hires Harlow Nicks to play his girlfriend to promote his new dating website. The problem? She doesn't exactly like him. But a job is a job and she has bills to pay. But as the miles unfurl, so does their passion . . . and if Harlow's not careful, she might end up believing that fairytales really do come true. **Find Faking It here**: https://geni.us/FakingItWb

Wicked Ways Duet: This two book series (Resist, Reveal) will hit all your buttons. Taboo/Forbidden Romance. Enemies to Lovers. Strong Alpha. A hint of suspense. Vaughn and Ryker are a battle of wills from the start but will win each other's hearts in the end. Find out more about the Wicked Ways duet **HERE**: https://geni.us/WickedWeb

Play Hard Series: Four sisters try to save their family's sports management agency, and in the process, they find their soulmates. Tropes used are sports romance (each book deals with a different sport), military romance, enemies to lovers, forced proximity, British hero, childhood crush . . . and on and on. Each book focuses on a different set of tropes. Find out which ones by clicking **HERE**: https://geni.us/PlayHardWeb

ABOUT THE AUTHOR

New York Times Bestselling author K. Bromberg writes contemporary romance novels that contain a mixture of sweet, emotional, a whole lot of sexy, and a little bit of real. She likes to write strong heroines and damaged heroes, who we love to hate but can't help to love.

A mom of three, she plots her novels in between school runs, sports practices, and figuring out how to navigate parenting teenagers (*send more wine*!). More often than not, she does all of this with her laptop in tow, and her mind daydreaming of the current hero she is writing.

Since publishing her first book on a whim in 2013, Kristy has sold over two million copies of her books across twenty different countries and has landed on the New York Times, USA Today, and Wall Street Journal Bestsellers lists over thirty times. Her Driven trilogy (Driven, Fueled, and Crashed) has been adapted for film and is available on the streaming platform Passionflix, Amazon, and other streaming platforms.

You can find out more about Kristy, her books, or just chat with her on any of her social media accounts. The easiest way to stay up to date on new releases and upcoming novels is to sign up for her newsletter or follow her on Bookbub.